ECHOES
OF GRACE

Guadalupe García McCall

TU BOOKS

An Imprint of LEE & LOW BOOKS, Inc.

New York

TU BOOKS, an imprint of LEE & LOW BOOKS Inc.,
95 Madison Avenue, New York, NY 10016
leeandlow.com

Manufactured in the United States of America
Printed on paper from responsible sources

Edited by Stacy Whitman
Book design by Sheila Smallwood
Typesetting by ElfElm Publishing
Book production by The Kids at Our House
The text is set in Dante MT Pro

10 9 8 7 6 5 4 3 2 1
First Edition

Cataloging-in-Publication Data is on file with the Library of Congress

FSC
www.fsc.org
MIX
From responsible
sources
FSC® C103098

To our dearly departed—
nuestros angelitos en el cielo—
the ones who passed before us
and especially those who passed too young.
Your memory is a blessing.
You are beloved.

CHAPTER ONE
Eagle Pass, Texas
June 2011

THERE IS A FUZZY BLACK CATERPILLAR sitting on the wooden railing of the porch. It's quite unusual to find them in the light of day, especially here in the scorching-hot South Texas sun, because the caterpillar of *Hypercompe scribonia*, the giant leopard moth, is a nocturnal creature. It prefers to stay out of sight and only comes out to feed at night.

I know that because we have thousands of them in our yard. Most of them live off the old mulberry tree in the front yard. Some of them hide behind large patches of perforated leaves or under heavy rocks, in between the planks of the creaking floorboards, or under the rickety porch steps. Others cling to the underside of the dating bench, the only piece of furniture in the yard, handmade by my father at my grandmother's request. My father's mother, Guelita Rosa, is very old-fashioned and demanded a space out here where she could keep an eye on us from the kitchen window when we got old enough to have boys over.

"Hurry up!" I yell as I pound on our front door again.

There are a million things I'd rather be doing than standing around waiting for my older sister, Mercedes—or Mercy as she prefers to be called these days—to come out of the house.

She's late again, which means that I can't get my day started, not until she's left the driveway and I am alone with my daily ritual: wake up Guelita Rosa, feed her and Alexander, wash the dishes, and sort and put away the laundry. Once that is done, I can sit down and sketch and think and create.

There's a giant moth I have been itching to work on. I don't quite have the shading yet. Somehow, I can't get the 3D effect right on that curled-up belly. Maybe it's the angle of the thorax. Although it might be in the abdomen. I'm not quite sure yet, but Mercy's lateness is keeping me from it, and I bang on the door again.

"Come on!" I yell, hanging my head in resignation.

Mercy pulls the curtain aside on the living room window. "Stop it! You're scaring Alexander," she says, which is code for *I'm taking my sweet time putting my fake eyelashes on and you can just wait until I'm done.*

I look across the yard, where the sun filters through the dark green leaves of the mulberry. A ray of light pierces the moldy branches, and I think about that bench. Nothing my grandmother did would have kept Mercy from doing what came naturally with boys. Nothing would have stopped her from getting pregnant at seventeen and ruining our plans.

I wince at the thought of what Mercy did, how she made it impossible for us to go off to college the way we'd always intended. *You could leave her behind,* the tortured little voice inside me whispers, but I could never leave Mercy behind. We promised to take care of each other. We made a pact when we were six and seven years old. The day our mother died, we swore we'd never leave each other's side, no matter what.

Tears threaten to form in my eyes and I look away, back to the black caterpillar in front of me. The pretty *scribonia* with its thick coat of black bristles is sitting completely still on the wooden rail, and I wonder if it is alive.

A bus drives down the street, chugging along the road with all the grace and agility of a yellow long-horned beetle. The sun shifts in the sky, shedding light on the rotting wooden slats at the corner of our porch, and still Mercy doesn't come out.

Frustrated, I walk over to the window and slam my open palm against the glass several times. "Mercedes Aurora Torres!" I yell loud enough for the neighbors to hear. "Get your scrawny butt going! Now!"

Mercy walks out of the house then. She is hoisting my two-year-old nephew, Alexander, on her hip. He's clinging to her neck with both arms. "Don't nag," she says as she hands him over to me. "Alexander couldn't find his teddy bear, so he wouldn't let me get dressed until we found it. Can you please take him?"

"Don't I always?" I ask.

Mercy doesn't answer me. She grimaces, pulls her beloved Gucci sunglasses out of her handbag, and shoves them on her face. Her light mauve lipstick glistens in the sun. She looks like a grown, professional woman with her long black hair flowing silkily off her temples and down her back. She always takes her time getting ready, because she wants to give the illusion of having a good head on her shoulders.

Only I know different. She is a nineteen-year-old high school dropout. But she sells the sophisticated look very well, which means older guys really like her. She likes them too. Their wallets are always full of cash, and she loves pulling those wallets out of their hands and taking what she needs from them. I don't approve, but she won't listen to me about it.

"Looks like it's going to be a hot one again today," I say, when Mercy steps off the porch and flips her beautiful hair back.

"Do me a favor," she says, pushing her *new* Coach bag high up on her left shoulder. "Try to keep Alexander inside until I get home, okay? I don't want him running around outside in the heat of the day and getting a sunburn."

"Okay," I say.

"I mean it, Grace," she warns. "Don't zone out the way you always do or get all caught up scribbling and just ignore him. Be present. Watch him carefully. Are you listening to me, Graciela Inés Torres? You know how he likes to get into things."

"Yes." I roll my eyes.

Mercy doesn't respect anything I do. To her, my drawings and the poetry I create when I look at nature are just *scribbling*. She doesn't know the difference between a metaphor and a simile, but she knows how to get a guy to fill her tank at the gas station with one little smile. "What's it good for, all that scratching on paper?" she asks. "It won't get you anywhere, Grace."

It isn't just our differences of opinion about devotion to school and intimacy with boys that's created a gap between me and Mercy. The last four years, we've grown into complete opposites of each other. I love nature and art and books. She loves eyeliners, lipstick, and discount racks. I stay as far away from guys as I can. She can't stay out of their cars. I don't believe in love at first sight; she capitalizes on it.

But it wasn't always that way.

When we were young, especially after our mother's untimely death, Mercy and I were inseparable. We used to really take care of each other. We were like those tiny brown caracoles you find sitting side by side, clinging to each other on the underside of a wet leaf after a great rainstorm. Nothing could tear us apart back then. But then puberty struck, and she became a whole other person. When she turned sixteen, she went completely off the rails and straight into Jose Valdez's arms.

On the porch, Alexander stands on his tippy-toes and picks up the bristly black caterpillar from its place on the railing. It rolls itself into a semicircle in the palm of his tiny hand and remains there. Each segment is open, separating the black spine and exposing the tender crimson skin between, one bright layer after another.

I try to stay present, like Mercy warned, but something has changed, and I know it's happening again, that weird thing Guelita Rosa calls *echoes*—the don, a kind of woman's intuition with sights and sounds and smells shared by most of the women in my family, starts to manifest something before me. I stand very still, trying not to be overwhelmed, waiting for the premonition to pass through me as it does most times.

The morning light pulses and wavers, making each bristle of dark hair on the caterpillar glint and bounce back light. Suddenly, I am somewhere else. The echo is clear as raindrops shimmering on freshly polished black patent-leather shoes, and I am suspended in another time, another space. A light breeze filters through the dead leaves of the mulberry tree, and the caterpillar's fuzzy hairs tremble. Its soft red belly starts to quiver and palpitate, as if something inside it is trying to push itself out.

Spotted wings, like white oleander blossoms, burst through the caterpillar's back and almost as quickly desiccate and drop off. Delicate yellow sprouts begin to break through the tender segments of red flesh. They spiral upward and outward, spiky horns that grow and grow. But then the flesh darkens and dulls, and one after another, the black bristles fall off and lie glistening on Alexander's hand like dark poisoned pine needles, and hundreds of tiny white starving maggots, thin and spindly as grass roots, crawl out. They devour the moist innards so fast, so swiftly, it frightens me, and I slap the dead thing out of Alexander's hand.

The caterpillar goes flying and lands on the corner

of the rotting porch. Alexander shrieks and shrinks away from me.

"Grace!" Mercy shouts, reaching for Alexander. "What the hell!"

I look at the caterpillar, but it isn't decomposing anymore. It writhes and squirms on the far corner of the porch, lifting its head and lolling it side to side. Mercy pushes me aside. She isn't trying to be mean to me. She just doesn't understand. She doesn't have the don, like me and my mother.

"I'm sorry," I whisper. "I thought it was dead."

"See? This is what I'm talking about, Grace." Mercy picks Alexander up and holds him against her shoulder. "You can't do this. You can't zone out and then lose it because he gets into something. You've got to pay attention!"

Alexander wails and squirms, and Mercy glares at me.

Then you take care of him! I want to scream at her. *You make sure he wipes his bottom before he pulls up his pants. You take crickets out of his mouth and chase after him when he's running after lizards in the yard.*

I want to yell, to fight, to make Mercy responsible for the care of her own son. I want to be responsible only for myself—but that would be selfish. It wouldn't be right. And it definitely wouldn't be sisterly. We have come so far in mending that broken fence—I just can't jump to the other side again, so I don't say anything.

Mercy snaps her fingers in front of my face. "See?" she asks when I look into her big brown eyes. "This is what I'm talking about, Grace. Where did you go? Just now? Where were you?"

Where did you go?

Where?

Where were you?

Where?

The questions roll around in my head, like roiling clouds in my mind. Over and over again. In a strange man's voice. In my father's voice. In Abuelita Rosa's voice. In Mercy's voice. Again and again and again.

Where did you go?

Where were you?

Where?

Where?

In the darkness. With a merciless light glaring in my eyes. In Mercy's car. In a police station. In our living room. In my room. Over and over and over again.

Where?

Where?

"I don't know!" I yell, pressing my palms against my ears to stop the thunderous echo rolling around in my head. Somewhere, far away, a baby cries. Realizing it is Alexander, I open my eyes.

On the sunlit porch before me, Alexander is screaming in Mercy's arms. Mercy is trying to hush him even as she glowers at me.

"Stop it, Grace!" Mercy hisses. "You're such a child!"

"I'm sorry," I whisper, quietly, because even the sound of my own voice hurts my ears when I've just had an echo.

But then I see the tiny tears glistening in Alexander's eyelashes and guilt slices through me, a hot-cold knife that cuts me to the core. I love taking care of Alexander. He is the love of my life. We do everything together. When Mercy isn't around, we hide under furniture, sing songs, climb trees, and catch chicharras. The fat little tears rolling down my nephew's cheeks make me miserable, and I am undone.

No matter how much Guelita Rosa claims they are a gift, and even when I am able to help others, like the time I told my father Guelita Rosa needed us because she'd fallen in the vegetable garden behind her house, I still hate these stupid echoes. Especially when they come like this morning, one right after the other, without warning. They're even worse when they are distorted or disconnected and I can't make sense of them, like these two were, repeating words or phrases that I can't decipher—questions I can't answer.

Because, believe me, nobody wants to know where

I was three years ago, the summer before Alexander was born, more than I do. But having those stupid questions roll around in my head doesn't help. I can't remember where I was, and that troubles me more than it troubles anyone else.

It's my mind that's locked—my memories that are lost. This doesn't have anything to do with my echoes. I'm almost sure of it. It's an entirely different thing. I *want* to remember. I do. I just *can't* for some reason. Sometimes I wonder, *Is this how Cassandra felt when no one would believe her premonitions?*

When the police first found me, sitting quietly on a pew in front of our Virgencita inside the Santuario de Nuestra Señora de Guadalupe, looking filthy and lost as a vagrant, the doctor in the tiny clinic in Piedras Negras had pressed down on my tongue with a huge stick that almost gagged me. He'd pulled and peeked into my ears, listened to my passive heart, checked my pulse, pressed and prodded at my abdomen. But when nothing seemed to bother me, he told my father I was fine and sent me home with a clean bill of health.

"Esta chiflada," my father told my grandmother that first evening after I arrived, when he couldn't get anything out of me. "Says she doesn't remember where she was. A whole week, and she doesn't remember? I don't know what to do with her."

"¿Bueno, y un psiquiatra?" my grandmother had proposed.

"¡Ay, n'ombre!" my father had exclaimed. "I don't have that kind of money. No. She's just going to have to live with whatever she was doing out there. God knows, I can barely keep the bills paid these days!"

Somewhere in the midst of that foggy memory, I hear my sister yelling again.

"Guelita!" Mercy hollers, leaning over to look into the house. "Guelita? Can you hear me? I need you to help Grace with Alexander today!"

"I don't need her help!" I say, shaking myself back to the present. "Stop acting like I'm a moron or something."

"That's the problem," Mercy says, looking at me like I am evidence of everything broken in her world. "You're smart, but you refuse to step up to the plate. You'd rather live in that little notebook of yours. Writing and drawing all day. When the real work is out here, waiting for you. Guelita!" she yells over me again. "Are you up? I need you. I can't take the day off again."

"Please don't fuss at her," I say, patting my nephew's chubby arm. "She's an old woman. We should be taking care of her. Not the other way around."

Mercy's perfectly arched eyebrows furrow over her eyes and she presses her lips, sighs, and then whispers, "Finally. Some common sense."

"Let me have him," I say, reaching for Alexander, hovering over him like a bumble bee over the tiny honeycomb cell in her charge. "Please. It's not like I've never done this before. I've taken care of him most of his life."

Mercy hesitates. "Sure?" she asks, fawning over Alexander's hair and clothes, dusting dirt off the kneepads of his tiny pants.

"Yes. Yes." I nod and force myself to smile brightly. Because I don't want her to think that I am anything but ready to take responsibility.

Mercy shakes her head. "Grace. Grace. You've got to pay attention," she says. But then her eyes soften, and she isn't so angry anymore. "I'm not mad at you. I'm not. You understand that, don't you? I just need you to watch every move he makes. Okay?"

"I will," I assure her. Relieved. "You don't have to worry about it. I love him. I wouldn't let anything—"

"Here," Mercy interrupts, releasing her hold on Alexander and handing him over quickly. "I don't have time to wait for Guelita to wake up. I'm already late. Carmen's going to kill me!"

"Come on, baby," I coo at Alexander, who comes willingly into my arms.

Mercy caresses his curly, dark hair and places a kiss on his forehead. "Play with him," she pleads. "And for God's sake, stay inside. It's already hot as hell out here."

"You hear that, Alexander?" I say, hoisting my nephew onto my hip. "No 'side-'side today. Okay? We're staying indoors, like Mami says."

Alexander turns and twists his little body in my arms, squirming and pointing at something on the ground. I turn away from Mercy and see that he's watching intently as the caterpillar inches itself across the porch, away from the railing.

"Okay, I'm off. Give Mami a kiss," Mercy says, pushing her red Coach purse high up on her shoulder again so she can lean over and kiss Alexander. "Thanks for watching him this summer. You're a good sister," she says. "I trust you—you know that—but if anything happens to him, I'll gut you like one of those frogs in science lab."

"Thanks," I say. "Thank you for that lovely image. Now go. You don't want to get fired, remember?"

I watch Mercy step off the porch and sprint across the lawn toward her car in her red high-heeled shoes, the ones she bought at seventy percent off. *Who runs in high heels?* I ask myself, shaking my head. *A fashion victim, that's who.* Because that is the best way I can describe my sister. She is a victim of our social climate, dancing on the edge of a precipice while I try coaxing her to safer ground.

Although I can't understand her, I love my sister. It

took us a long time, almost two years, to get back to this place of understanding, this place where differences of opinion are not worth fighting over. Things are still not perfect, no sisterhood ever is, but our contentious relationship has reached an eddy, a gentle push and pull of emotions that we are both willing to wade in from time to time.

Our words are kinder when we criticize each other. We are more aware of the things we say. It is hard to live with her in this house, where broken dreams share space with reality, and grief and suffering linger in the darkness and come out at night to lose themselves in decay, like leopard moths mating in the summer heat.

My mother's unsolved murder caused us all a great deal of pain. It baffled the police and wounded everyone in my family when it happened, but my mother's senseless killing more than hurts me.

It haunts me.

Mercy looks worriedly up at the sky, then turns back to me. She points to a group of white clouds drifting inconspicuously to the east of us and I shake my head and roll my eyes. There is no chance of rain. She is worrying about nothing, like always.

I hold Alexander tightly in my arms, but he kicks and fusses until I relent. He likes standing on his own two feet.

"Here, hold my hand," I say, putting him down. Alexander stands still beside me and watches Mercy getting into the Beast, a baby-blue 1991 Oldsmobile Cutlass Calais with a gray interior that smells of Mercy's expensive perfume and flavored-coffee stains. The rusted monster is left over from Mercy's abusive relationship with Jose Valdez, the ex-husband from Hades who used to get drunk and beat her often, para sosiégarla, to remind her that he was the boss in the house—*our house*!

Thank God my father finally put an end to that!

"Wave—Mami?" Alexander asks when he sees Mercy buckling her seat belt inside the car. I nod, watching him lift his chubby little arm for the big goodbye that has become part of his morning ritual this summer.

Things are going to be different in the fall. Once Mercy and I start community college, we'll have to take turns watching him while the other one attends class. Then, once Alexander is older, we'll go off to a university. Mercy can study textiles and apparel, and I'll finally get to work on a degree in graphic design from the University of Texas.

So far, we are all set. Mercy finally helped me fill out her application for financial aid at the annex at Southwest Texas Junior College, so we are ready to sign up for classes in August. It's nice how everything is coming together for us. How, even though she's taken a major detour, Mercy and I are finally going to start making our dreams come true.

When Mercy sits too long in the car with the rearview visor flipped down, I know that she's redoing her mascara. I squat beside Alexander and shoo him away from the caterpillar, giving the tiny creature room to make its way off the porch. "Don't touch him, Papis." I say. "He needs to go home."

"Go-go?" Alexander asks, his eyes bright. Intelligent.

"Yes," I say. "Go-go. Like Mami."

Alexander stands beside me as the caterpillar moves away, its back arching up and then coming back down, making ground inch by inch, like a miniature locomotive. There is a whole world of purpose in that caterpillar's life, I am sure of it. He is determined to get off this dusty porch and onto the dark rich loam under the mulberry tree. "See there," I tell Alexander. "He wants to get through that hole, past the rocks to climb up to that tree and find a juicy green leaf to eat before he starts to weave a coat around himself and begins growing wings."

"Go-go," Alexander repeats.

I hear rustling behind me.

Guelita Rosa is coming out of the house. She is struggling with her walker, trying to get it past the rickety screen door.

"Graciela!" Guelita Rosa hollers, as she pushes at the screen. I turn around to help, taking hold of the door and then prying the front leg of her walker loose.

"¡Ay, no!" Guelita Rosa cries, waving her hand in my face, trying to get me to stop. "¡El niño! Graciela, look! ¡El nene! ¡El nene!"

I turn sideways, scanning the porch, looking for Alexander, but he isn't beside me anymore. Guelita puts her hand on my shoulder and shoves me away from her. "Go," she screams. I straighten up and look past the stairs, past the driveway, but I can't see Alexander anywhere.

"Alexander?" I call, my voice high-pitched. "Alexander!"

I call out again and again, but he is gone. My mind reels and swims in circles as I scan the yard and walk around frantically, looking for him, but he isn't hiding behind the dating bench or under the picnic table.

Suddenly, he is out there, traipsing past the fence, rushing off, running out into the street, out into traffic.

Tires screech, a loud squeal that does nothing to disguise the screams leaving my lips. The impact is harder than anything I could have imagined. I run. Like a madwoman, I run out into the street. Screaming, "Alexander! Alexander!"

But I am too late. There is nothing I can do to help Alexander. There is nothing.

Nothing.

I can do nothing.

I freeze and stare at the brake lights of an old Impala burning bright, like red-hot pokers in an old chimenea. On the street before me, I see Alexander's left shoe, and I lean down and pick it up. Mercy is behind me now. I look back at her. Her wild eyes are luminous, beautiful, because she doesn't know yet.

She doesn't understand.

She looks from me to the young girl who is hauling herself on trembling legs out of the car with the blinking lights.

"What is it? Was it Doña Lety's dog? Did she hit him? Where is he? Chucho!" she calls out to our neighbor's tired old dog, who is probably asleep on her porch.

I want to say something, but I can't.

Clutching the little red shoe against my heart, I can only cry. Looking first at the shoe, then into my eyes again, Mercy's face twists, contorts. She is still confused for a moment, but then she begins whimpering.

"No—no—no!" She keeps blubbering, even as she runs around the car with the blinking lights, looking for Alexander. The driver, a young teenage girl with stringy long brown hair and a loose-fitting summer dress, steps back, crying and shaking her head, looking more confused than any of us.

When she can't find Alexander anywhere around the car, Mercy drops to the ground and starts screaming for him. "Alexander! Alexander!" she keeps crying, reaching under the car and coming up empty-handed every time.

"Don't!" a voice yells, and I see our new neighbor, the güerito who just moved in next door last week, running toward us. "Stop!" he says as he reaches Mercy's side. "You shouldn't move him."

"Help me," Mercy begs. Our new neighbor takes Mercy's elbow and tries to help her up, but Mercy pulls her arm out of his grasp and stays on the ground, leaning forward, looking under the car.

Then she stops flailing around and lies very still. Her eyes are fixed on something under the shadow of the idling car. "I see him," she finally whispers. "He's right there. I can't reach him. He's too far. But I can see him."

"We need to wait for the ambulance," our next-door neighbor says, his voice soft but firm. "My mother's calling them. They'll know what to do."

But Mercy doesn't listen. Somehow she finds a way to reach Alexander and she pulls him out. I stand in the middle of the street, listening to Mercy cry as she lies with Alexander cuddled in her arms. His little body shudders as he gasps for air, and he gurgles and coughs tiny crimson bubbles that burst and run out of his mouth and down the side of his cheek.

Mercy rubs and rubs. "It's okay, baby. It's okay," she keeps saying. "I'm here. Mami's here."

At the sight of that sickly trickle of blood, I cry out too—an emaciated, breathless sobbing that ricochets off Mercy's loud, pulsating wails. Clutching Alexander's tennis shoe until the hard rubber of the sole threatens to break the skin of my palms, I stare at the road. Waiting for the ambulance that is taking its sweet time coming, I listen to the eternal questions rolling around in my head again.

Where did you go?

Where were you?

Where?

I was present, I keep reminding myself. *I was. I was present.* Guelita Rosa called for me. There was danger in not helping her. She could have fallen and broken her hip again. She could die—disintegrate, like the caterpillar in Alexander's hand. I couldn't risk having her go through another surgery. She's fragile. She might not survive another fall, another break. No. *I was present. I was. This wasn't because of my echoes.*

But then my mean mind whispers the accusatory questions again and again.

Where were you?

Where did you go?

Where?

I try to tell myself *This was something else. Something horrible. An accident. Yes. It was an accident.* But no matter how much I try to tell myself that this terrible thing wasn't my fault, a wounded guilt crawls inside my head. It stirs up the questions, making them roil and boil, again and again.

Where were you—

Where—

Where—

*Where—were—you—*until the brightness of the white-hot sun consumes the atmosphere, bleaching everything around me, blasting the trees, blanching the road, bleaching everything in its path.

Then it happens.

The white sky parts.

A sliver of memory creeps out of the whiteness, clawing its way through the fog, and I remember the morning I found out Alexander's father, Jose, was moving in with us.

Around and around the blurred world goes, until the only things left are the malnourished, wafer-thin rays of sunlight coming in through the wide-open gape of the mouth of our kitchen window three years ago.

CHAPTER TWO

Three Years Earlier

"**H**E CAN'T MOVE INTO OUR HOUSE!" I told my father. "He's volatile. I've seen him go off on people."

"It'll be all right, Graciela," my father said. He was in the dining room, scraping dried mud off his work boots over a page from an old newspaper splayed out on the floor before him.

"What if he goes off on us?" I asked, pacing up and down in front of him.

My father stopped scraping. He dropped the boot in his hands. It clanked hard against the linoleum and landed on its side. He shoved it aside with his right foot and picked up the other one. Then he took a deep breath and stared at the floor. "I'd take care of it," he said, inspecting the leather sole.

"What about his gang friends?" I asked. "What are you going to do when they come over? Who's going to protect us if they get out of control? What if they attack one of us? Have you thought about that?"

"He's not in a gang," my father said, scraping a big chunk of mud off his boot onto the newspaper. "He's a wannabe, Graciela, a punk. I said I'd take care of it, and I will. Now quit fussing at me."

"No!" I stood in front of him, so close to the news-paper with its clumps of mud piled high on it, I had to fight the urge to kick the dirt up at him to get him to listen to me. "How? When? You're never here," I con-tinued. "How are you going to take care of anything if you're never around, huh?"

"Shut up! Just shut up!" my father screamed, slam-ming the boot against the table and raising his voice. "That's the problem with you. You think everything's black and white, but life is messy, Graciela."

"I'm not stupid," I whispered, more to myself than to him. "I know life is hard. But this is beyond—"

"Life is more than hard," my father interrupted me. "Life is rotten, putrid. Here today, gone tomorrow." He snapped his fingers to punctuate what he was saying.

I stared at my father. "Are you talking about Mom?" I asked quietly.

"People change," he said. "Dreams have to be

moved, reworked, or they die, Graciela. Dreams die if you don't shift with them." He hung his head and let out a long, shaky breath, the kind that says *I am trying hard to check my temper,* which he used to do a lot when my mother would lose her mind and run around the house crying, saying things that didn't make sense to anyone except her. "People make mistakes, Graciela. They ruin things for themselves and others. You'd know that if you weren't always in your own little world, locked up in that notebook of yours. Lost in thought. Daydreaming about God knows what."

"I'm not . . ." I started to defend myself, but I had a hard time validating my actions. I liked drawing and writing. There was nothing wrong with it. It centered me, kept me focused, despite the echoes that no one except Guelita Rosa had the courage to talk about. If it wasn't for her explaining that there was nothing wrong with me—that, like my mother, I had a special ability—I don't know how I would have dealt with this don.

"Wake up, Graciela! It's time to grow up!"

A tiny speck of my father's spit landed on my cheek, and I wiped it away without saying anything because I knew, deep down inside, I knew he was making a mistake by letting Mercy and her new husband, that loser Jose, move in with us.

What was happening? Dad never screamed. He

never slammed things either. He was never in the house long enough to do such things. In fact, ever since my mother's funeral, he left the house early in the mornings and stayed out until late at night, when he could slip into his room without ever having to interact with any of us.

The fact that he was there in our dining room, doing something personal, something conventional, in the same house where we lived our lives day in and day out without him—well, that was even more unusual.

"What are you doing here anyway?" I asked, fighting the heat of tears threatening to form and spill over the rims of my eyes.

"What do you mean?" he asked as he dusted his boot absently. "I live here."

"No you don't!" I crossed my arms in front of me and stared at him as he continued to polish the tired leather. "You pay bills here, and you come in and sleep at night. But you don't really *live* here. Not the way a normal father does. So why are you here today?"

Dad put the boots under the dinner table and picked up the newspaper, folding it inward at the corners as he talked. "I thought you might need some help moving the big things, like your girlie bed and your chest of drawers."

"What?" I asked. "Why?"

"Well, you don't expect Jose to move in there with you and your sister, do you?"

"No," I said, horrified by the thought.

I'd been so angry about the idea of Jose moving into the house that I hadn't even thought about the fact that we didn't have the room to accommodate a married couple. We only had three bedrooms and, with Guelita Rosa having to move in with us, they were all occupied. The house just wasn't big enough for all of us. "So, what am I supposed to do? I'm not sleeping on the couch."

"Of course not." My father wadded up the newspaper into a big, crumpled mud-filled ball and tossed it into the trash as he headed into the kitchen. "You'll have to bunk with your grandmother for a little while, until Mercy and Jose get on their feet and can afford a place of their own. After the baby comes, you understand?"

I turned around and followed him. "That's almost five months from now! You can't be serious," I said.

My father washed his hands in the sink absently. "I hate to say it, but I am."

"I can't do that," I cried. Then, because I love Guelita Rosa and I didn't want to hurt her feelings if she was listening to us from her room on the other side of the wall, I lowered my voice. "Dad. She wets the bed. The whole room smells like pee. It's not her fault.

It's a medical thing. I get it. But you can't make me bunk with her."

"Well, it's either that or the couch," my father said, shrugging and heading out of the kitchen.

"That's it?" I asked, rushing ahead of him as he walked into the living room. "That's your solution? What about them? Why can't you just tell them to go live with *his* mother? There are other options, you know. They don't have to live here."

My father reached his room and opened the door. "It's your guelita or the couch. Take your pick, Graciela."

"Neither," I said.

My father took a deep breath and let it out. "Let me know if you need my help with the bed."

"I won't do it," I said, putting my hands on my hips. "I won't move one single thing out of my room."

Then I walked off, going into the room I shared with Mercy and slamming the door as hard as I could. Then, because I was so furious, I opened it and slammed it again—harder this time, so he'd get the message.

My father did more than get my message. He opened the door and, without saying a word, started stripping the covers off my bed and throwing them at me.

"What are you doing?" I asked, pulling my blanket off my shoulders and holding it against my belly because he was scaring me.

"What does it look like I'm doing?" he asked. "I'm moving you out."

He tossed my pillows on the floor in the corner, like he was in a rush to get it over with, to make me change my entire way of living to make room for Mercy.

"That's what you always do, you know," I said. "You always fix things for her. You never correct her. You never punish her. You just fix whatever she messes up."

"You have to do this, Graciela." My father stopped long enough to take a breath. He ran his fingers roughly through his hair. "You have to move out. There's no other way."

"You want me to move out?" I asked, throwing my blanket at him and picking my denim mochila off the desk. "Fine. I'll move out. You don't have to tell me twice."

I was so mad, I pushed past him. Without looking at him, I opened my dresser drawers and shoved as many of my clothes as I could fit into my mochila. I had a suitcase somewhere, an old tired thing, but it was too big and clunky for my situation, so I didn't even look for it.

I didn't know exactly where I was going, but I knew I couldn't stay in a house where I was in the way.

"Graciela?" Dad asked. "Where are you going?"

"Out," I said. "Away. Somewhere where I'm not a burden on people."

"Will you please stop?" Dad said. "You're exhausting me. I don't have time for this, Graciela."

"That's the problem. You don't have time for us. That's why she did this. That's why she does everything, to get your attention," I said, moving from the dresser to the nightstand, where I kept my socks and intimates. Shoving a few more articles of clothing into my bag, I walked out the door.

My father followed me. I could hear his feet coming close behind me, even as the tears started rolling down my cheeks. I didn't want him to see that he'd gotten to me, that his decision to push me aside for Mercy's sake was hurting me. So, I dashed through the living room and out the door before he had a chance to stop me.

As I trotted down the driveway, I shoved my arms through the loops of the denim backpack. It was old and ratty, but I loved that mochila. My dad had bought it for me when I graduated from elementary into middle school. It meant that once, a long time ago, my father had loved me. I'd been important to him.

At the corner of Williams and Brazos Streets, I caught the city bus. It was pulling up to the stop sign just as I was heading up the hill toward Mall de las Aguilas, which was the only place I could get lost for a while, at least until I figured things out. But catching the bus, getting away from my neighborhood, appealed to me, and

I jumped in and sat in the back, where I could sit alone and think, consider my choices.

As the bus started pulling away from San Luis Elementary, I felt my life slip away from me. I sat silently holding my feelings in and swallowing my tears, while people got on and off the bus oblivious of my pain— my rage.

It wasn't until the driver, who'd parked in front of the downtown bus terminal, turned to look at me sitting there all alone in the back that it occurred to me I needed to do something. I couldn't just sit there until the bus filled up again. Going round and round in circles all over Eagle Pass until I calmed down didn't make sense, so I got off and headed toward the International Bridge.

Chapter Three
Eagle Pass, Texas
June 2011

SOMEONE OR SOMETHING WAILS IN THE distance.

A burst of brightness flashes, pierces my eyes, shatters the memory.

I blink.

Everything fades to white, and I stare into the starkness of sunlight—firmly planted in the present, standing in the gray gravel driveway with the pale, hot sun beating down on us as the ambulance pulls up in front of our house.

When my father finds out about Alexander's accident, he leaves work in a hurry and joins us at the hospital. He stands beside me and Mercy in the waiting room by the soda machine, shifting his weight from one foot to the other with his hands in his pockets, swiveling around on his boot heel every time someone new enters the room. By the time Dr. Hernandez, the emergency room doctor, comes looking for us, the silence between us has grown so stale it stifles our thoughts.

We are suffocating.

I can barely breathe, much less speak, when we stand up to talk to him.

"I'm so sorry, Don Fernando," Dr. Hernandez whispers as he puts his hand on my father's shoulder. "We did everything we could, but I'm afraid there was just too much internal damage."

At his words, Mercy drops her purse and starts running.

Halfway down the hall, she pulls off her red high-heeled shoes, throws them aside, and darts toward the emergency room doors. "No. No," Mercy cries out. Her voice sounds hollow, like it's coming from inside a dark, cold well as she slaps her open hands against the double doors and screams, "My son! My son! Let me see my son!"

We run after her.

"Mercedes, m'ija—por favor, controlate," Dad begs, wrapping his arms around her waist and pulling her toward him.

Mercy collapses in his arms. Her lashes flutter, her eyes roll back, and she faints. Dad puts one arm around her torso and the other under her knees and lifts her up like a child, holding her against his chest, as the metal doors open for us. Mercy isn't heavy, so it's easy for him to carry her into the ER, where she's given the nearest bed. But when she wakes up, things get worse. She howls and tears at our clothes, trying to get out of bed. She cries out for Alexander over and over again; the doctor has no other choice than to sedate her.

After a quiet conversation, my father follows the doctor down the hall, leaving me alone with Mercy. I sit there looking at my sister, waiting for her to wake up, telling myself not to listen to the things whispering around in my head, not to give in to my don, not to let the aggrieved voices swirling around in that place of trauma overwhelm me.

My sister needs me.

So, I fight to stay present.

In the evening, when we bring a disheveled Mercy home, give her a sedative, and settle her in, I go to my room and fall into my bed and cry until I think I might die.

When I don't die and I wake up bright and early the next morning, I get up and go to the bathroom como sonambula. I rinse my face and press a cold, wet cloth over my puffy eyes and resolve to go back to my room to start cleaning.

But then I do something I don't know quite how to explain, something I've never done before. Something beyond the realm of my ability to see things before they happen. I walk back into my room and pretend Alexander is walking behind me, following me around the house, the way he's done every day this summer, and suddenly, he *is* there, following me.

I don't talk to him.

I just watch him.

Without looking at me, Alexander wanders over to the closet and starts to go through his toy box. He doesn't acknowledge me or give me any sign that he is really there in my space, and I sit on the edge of my bed and watch him crawl onto my rocking chair like he did every morning before the accident.

I swear I can see him sitting there, his hair tousled, his cheeks flushed, as he rubs the sleep out of his eyes with his little fists. Like me, Alexander is a morning spirit. He likes to tinker about the house when everyone else is still asleep. Most of his toys are strewn all over the house, but his morning toys, the ones he likes to snuggle with, are in my room.

He likes to pick up his teddy bear, Red, by an arm or a leg and drag him across my room to the rocking chair by the window which he climbs onto so that he can look at the sunrise.

Because I don't want this peculiar echo to dissipate, I get up and go about my daily routine. I put my clothes in the laundry bin and stack my books neatly on my desk, pretending everything is exactly as it has always been, and Alexander is still alive.

Then, when my room is clean and I have nothing else to do, I sit on the edge of my bed again and watch Alexander sort through his books, which we store on the bottom shelf of my bookcase. Finally, because I can't stand the pain inside my chest any longer, I walk over and sit on the rocking chair and call to him.

Quietly.

Carefully.

The way you speak to a wild creature, afraid to get too close, hoping that it won't bite.

"Come here, baby," I whisper, shaking Red in my hand, making his teddy dance in the air. "You want to play?"

Alexander turns to look at me for the first time since I manifested him. He shakes his head and frowns. "No!"

"Come on," I say, smiling at him. "Red's waiting."

Alexander comes over, grabs Red, and throws him across the room. The stuffed animal lands in the middle of the floor with a muffled thud. Alexander turns back to me. He takes my hand, pulls at me, and says, "Run, Grace, run! Jump!"

"Run?" I ask. "We don't run in the house."

Alexander pulls harder on my hand, his little body almost perpendicular to the floor as he tries to get me out of the rocking chair. "Yes!" he insists. "Come on. Up, up! Jump! Jump! Like this!"

Alexander runs toward Red and jumps over the teddy. "Now you!" he demands.

"No," I say. "I'm tired. Let's read a book."

Alexander grins, shows me his white baby teeth, and then he scuttles over to me on his hands and feet, like a giant black beetle. I giggle and reach for him, but he gets up before I can touch him and runs and jumps over Red again. "Jump, Grace," he says. "Come on!"

I hear noises outside my door and listen. I'm not sure if it's Mercy or my father, but someone is in the hallway.

Alexander runs across my room, picks up Red, and brings him to me. Then he drops down on his hands and knees and crawls under my queen-size bed.

"What are you doing?" I ask him.

Alexander puts his chubby index finger in front of his lips and says, "Shh! Mami's mad."

"No," I whisper, smiling. "She's not up yet."

Suddenly my door flies open.

Mercy is standing on the threshold, her hand on the doorknob, scanning every corner of my room. Her eyes are red. Her long hair is lose, untamed, and she looks like she's ready to attack someone.

I grip the armrest as she enters the room and walks toward me.

From under the bed, Alexander reaches out and pulls the blanket down slowly, quietly, so that he is soon well hidden from sight.

Mercy circles the rocking chair. Her eyes are wild and vicious. She looks like a rabid dog about to pounce.

"Hey. How are you feeling?" I ask.

"Shut up. Don't talk to me," Mercy commands. Then she starts picking up all of Alexander's belongings. When she is done collecting everything that belongs to her son, Mercy rips Red from my hands and picks an errant yellow Lego off the floor and shoves it in her pocket.

"Mercy—" I start.

"I want his things," she says. "All of them."

I look at the pile in her arms. "I think that's everything."

She leaves the room for a moment, but then comes right back, empty-handed.

Still ignoring me, she rummages through my laundry basket. She throws my clothes all over the floor before she finally finds what she's looking for—a stray blue sock with white nonslip dots on its sole.

"You can't keep his things here anymore," she says as she scans the open closet shelves. "I don't want his things in this room. Ever again. Understand? From now on, everything that belongs to him stays in my room. Not here, not in the living room, not in the kitchen. Just my room! Mine! Understand?"

"Can I just keep one thing? Red? Can I keep Red?" I ask, but my voice is a wisp of air, barely audible, and she is too mad to listen.

"Shut up!" She turns around and leaves my room, slamming the door behind her.

I sit still, silent, telling myself that it is important to give Mercy space. Then I remember Alexander and I rush over to the bed, but when I lift the blanket and look under it, he isn't there anymore.

I sit on the floor, the bedsheet still in my hand, and call out, "Alexander? Baby? Where are you, chiquito?" When he doesn't come, I close my eyes and concentrate as I call his name, over and over again. But no matter how hard I try manifesting my sweet nephew, I can't do it again. I can't make him come back. He's gone. I can't conjure him at will. I have to face it. Alexander is not with us anymore.

He's gone. Forever.

I am looking for a ghost in broad daylight.

As I sit there, mourning for Alexander, hot angry

tears start rolling down my face and I close my eyes. "Where did you go, baby?" I ask him.

Run, Grace, run!

Alexander's last request lingers inside my head.

Jump! Jump!

I listen to Alexander's request. Over and over again.

Run, Grace, run! Jump! Jump!

And I do jump. I jump all the way back to that foggy, dizzying day, the day I left—the day I ran away to Mexico.

CHAPTER FOUR
Three Years Earlier

THE CUSTOMS AGENT IN THE CASETA took my money and waved me through so quickly that I didn't have time to consider the consequences of my actions. I walked down the length of the International Bridge in a trance, letting the hot wind whip my long hair across my face, while I pondered and debated, wondering what I could do to keep Jose Valdez from moving in with us.

Once I got to the other side, when I was in Piedras Negras, I sat on a wrought-iron bench at the plazita, frustrated, with the angry sun beating down on me for almost an hour before deciding to visit the Santuario de Nuestra Señora de Guadalupe. Not that I thought going to church would do anything to solve my problem. I wasn't a devout churchgoer, but I was a believer, and prayer always made me feel better. It was therapeutic, in a meditative kind of way, especially when my soul was unsettled the way it was that day.

The chapel was quiet, with only a few souls sitting in the pews at the front or kneeling at the smaller altars dedicated to saints and virgins located in the far corners of the church. I scooted into the last bench, knelt, and closed my eyes. The scent of burning candles mingled with the ghost of spent incense and dead flowers brought tears to my eyes, and I called out to my mother.

"Why?" I asked her. "Why did you have to leave? Where were you going? How can a mother do that, Madre Santa? How can a mother abandon her children? How can she walk out in the middle of the night?"

Immediately after asking the Virgencita these questions, guilt struck me, gripping my heart in my chest, and I clasped my hands together in vehement prayer. Feeling repentant, I begged the Virgencita to forgive me for all my sins. "I'm sorry," I whispered. "I know I shouldn't be angry. It's not her fault. It's not."

On my knees, I continued praying, asking forgiveness for letting anger get the best of me and speaking meanly to my father. I also begged forgiveness for resenting my sister so much. And because I couldn't let myself off the hook too easily, I said ten Our Fathers and ten Hail Marys. I cried the whole time I prayed. And when I was done, my eyes were swollen, and I had a dull, pulsating headache in my frontal lobe. Exhausted, I wiped my face with my sleeve and crossed myself before leaving the church.

Outside, morning had turned to noon, and street vendors were selling their delicacies up and down the sidewalks. Not ready to go home and face my family, I purchased an ear of corn. It glistened, steaming and slathered with butter and cream.

I didn't want to eat it there, in the heat of the day, so I jumped on a city bus and looked out the window. I peeked down every nook and cranny of the dusty, quiet neighborhoods and took in the sights and sounds of the noisy avenidas in Piedras Negras as I feasted on my elote slowly, one tiny bite at a time, because I didn't want to make a mess of things.

When I was done, I wrapped the remains of it in the piece of paper the vendor had given me and got up to toss it in the trash can at the front of the bus. That's when I realized we had reached the outskirts of town. Hunched over to get a better look, I recognized the neighborhood. We were in Colonia Las Cenizas. The country road on the other side of this neighborhood cut through the woods, right to the house where my maternal grandmother, Abuela Estela, had lived way before I was born, when my mother was a child herself.

Although Abuela Estela died a long time ago, we'd seen her house more than a few times. Before my mother passed away, she used to drive out to her mother's old, abandoned house and look around at the place, although she would never let us get close to it.

She would make me and Mercy sit in the car and wait while she crossed the narrow dirt road, opened the gate, and walked around the uninhabited house, looking in all the empty, naked windows, remembering things she never shared with us—things that made her cry silently as she walked back to us and sat weeping before she drove away, looking more like an apparition than a real live woman.

As if in a dream, I got off the bus and walked down the dirt streets of Las Cenizas. The houses in that neighborhood were torn and tired. Their rusty metal roofs with their corroded lips hung limply over the edge of gray cinder-block houses with gaping holes for naked windows and crooked doors. Broken fences, dusty tires, and abandoned building projects with exposed iron rods—everywhere I looked I saw forgotten dreams, deserted homes.

I went past an old postecito, a nook of a corner store, where a blonde girl peeked out the window and stared at me as I walked past. I crossed the neighborhood and left it behind, taking the narrow dirt one-car lane that led into the woods to Abuela Estela's house. This part was familiar. This part had not changed since our childhood. I moved past huisaches and mesquites, careful to avoid the chancaquillas with their green bristly burrs that are so painful to pull out once they burrow into your skin.

Finally, after walking beyond the neighborhood for about fifteen minutes, I stood at the bottom of a hill, looking up the street at my grandmother's house. From a distance, it looked smaller than I remembered. The front yard itself was nothing more than a wide, expansive patch of dirt located at the edge of the narrow road, but then as I got closer and closer and things came into focus, my perception of it changed.

The property came to life for me.

As I walked up to the gate, I saw flowers peering out from behind the fence. The yellow petals of quiet sunflowers sprang up and turned to look at me from the low, inconspicuous, pebbled flower beds that lined the wooden fence—a fence that was not rotten like I expected when I first got off the bus, but that was actually painted a soft brown, the color of a newborn doe.

I opened the gate and stepped into the yard, marveling at the little bits of life—violet trumpet vines, sweet petunias, and fresh-faced daisies—that welcomed me as I walked along the path to the porch. I could see the minute details of everything that bloomed in that low garden: every thorn on the miniature rosebushes, every purple heart on the Mexican heather, every wrinkle on the pink primroses.

When I looked at the windows, I saw that they were not naked and agape as I had thought, but that there were actually transparent, frilly curtains hanging inside them. I could see the intricate detail on those thin sheets of fabric. From where I stood, halfway up a mottled blue-gray flagstone path leading to the front door, I could see every single thread of the embroidered eyelet of the border of the lacy curtains. It was the most peculiar thing, how everything in that house was amplified the closer I got to it.

I stood mesmerized by the whispering wind under the shade of a tall willow tree beside the iron gate and let the breeze caress my face and feed me the intoxicating scent of white, pink, and purple flowers. The willow's sweeping skirt of limbs grazed the ground, raising dust as pale and light as spirits and sending it flying in tiny clouds that lifted, lingered, then rolled out into the street like floating souls.

I had an overwhelming desire to walk around the grounds and look in all the windows, the way my mother had done every time she'd come here, but I knew that wouldn't be right. It was obvious I was at the wrong house. Either that, or someone had bought my grandmother's house and was living there now.

Resolved to leave, I picked up my stuffed backpack. I was almost at the front gate when a young woman wearing a small white apron came out of my grandmother's house. She held the screen door open with one hand as she looked at me standing there, staring at her. "Hello?" she asked. "Can I help you?"

"I'm sorry," I said. "I must be lost. I think I'm at the wrong house."

The girl cocked her head and smiled. "Who are you looking for?" she asked.

"Nobody," I said. "It's just . . . Well, this looks like my grandmother's house. She used to live around here."

"What's her name?" the girl asked. "Maybe I know her."

I pressed my lips together and took a deep breath, sure that she would not be able to give me any information. "Estela," I said. "Estela Ramirez. I thought this was her house."

"Yes, this is her house," the girl said, putting her hand down and looking at me like she knew me.

"Oh," I said, wondering what she was doing at my grandmother's house. "I am Graciela Torres, the daughter of her only child, Isabel Torres, from the United States."

The girl grinned. "How wonderful to meet you. My name is Lucia," she said, extending her hand. Her smile was warm, welcoming, and she took my hand firmly in hers. "Come in. Come in. Your grandmother's in bed, but maybe this will make her get up and come to the table for some coffee."

"My grandmother?" I blinked, confused. "No. My grandmother is dead. She died before I was born."

"Dead?" Lucia crinkled her nose. "Doña Estela? Oh no. Doña Estela's not dead. She hasn't left the house in years, unless it's to play with her cats out back, but she's not dead."

"You mean *my* grandmother? Estela Ramirez?" I asked. "Is alive?"

"Yes," Lucia said, smiling. "You want to come in? See for yourself?"

I looked around the yard and up the empty dirt road that had brought me here. A chilly breeze was blowing from the north. It caught my hair and swept it forward. I reached up and pulled the hair away from my face.

I remembered my mother leaving me in the car while she peeked in through the windows of this house and shivered. *Had I imagined our visits here? Had my mother been lying to us all those years? Why didn't she let us see our grandmother?* "Yes," I finally said. "Yes. I would. Thank you."

I stood waiting for Lucia to close the door behind us and then followed her into the small living room. She picked up a ball of yarn and a half-finished scarf with a pair of knitting needles sticking out of it and placed them in a basket on the coffee table, then lifted an old book off the floor and placed it beside the basket. "You must excuse the mess," she said. "Except for the doctor, we don't ever have company."

We turned right and went through an archway into a small kitchen, where Lucia cleared a few knickknacks from the table and dusted the invisible grungies off the tablecloth, snapping a dishcloth over the surface again and again until she was satisfied that it was clean. Then she said, "Just a moment. I will be right back," and disappeared behind a curtained-off doorway at the other end of the kitchen. The fabric of the heavy dark navy drapes rustled and sighed as they settled back into place, warily guarding whatever was behind them.

Lucia returned with another chair from somewhere behind those secretive drapes and redid the seating arrangement around the kitchen table so that we could have a view out the window. "There," she said. "Is this okay? A place to sit and talk to her."

Still a bit confounded, I nodded. "Yes," I said.

I couldn't do much else. My grandmother was alive,

and I was about to meet her for the first time in my life. *Could she—would she—talk about my mother?* Somewhere inside me, something stirred and shook itself awake. My nerves bristled and I shivered again.

"Good," she said. "Should we go get her?"

I took a deep breath and released it.

"Okay." I smiled, a panicked little smile, because it was all too surreal.

"Are you staying long?" Lucia asked.

"Staying?" I asked.

Lucia pointed to my backpack, slung behind me, hanging off my right arm. "You came to stay. Yes?"

"Oh." I laughed, rolling the backpack off my arm and holding it in front of me like a lost little child. "Well, no, I hadn't considered it."

"You *should* stay." Lucia's eyes crinkled at the corners as she smiled at me, a sweet, genuine smile—a smile full of compassion and grace. "To get to know her. That would be so good for her. It might bring her back."

"Bring her back?" I asked.

Lucia nodded. "Yes. From the places she goes in her mind—from the past. You'll see. Come. She's in bed right now. But it's time she woke up anyway. Don't be alarmed if she seems confused or calls you by another name. She's very old, and a bit out there, in another world—has invisible friends and everything.

It's part of her condition, so it's best to just go along with whatever she says."

"Invisible friends?" I asked, thinking about my own tendency to conjure things up during those moments of suspension, my echoes. It made sense. Guelita Rosa had explained it to me a long time ago. I inherited my don, my ability to see and feel things coming, from my mother's side of the family. "You mean echoes?"

"What?" Lucia pulled the heavy curtains back.

"Nothing," I said. "Never mind."

We walked down a narrow hall and into a darkened bedroom.

"Señora? Doña Esteli-ta!" Her voice was a song, the words a lingering lullaby. "Wake up. You have a *vi-si-tor*."

As the form under the covers stirred, I looked around the room. To the right, there was an old dresser with a rusty metal tray where a pale-bristled brush and a huge array of toiletries sat, a dusty collection of bottles in every color and shape imaginable. In the corner, there was a cloudy full-length mirror with a strand of thin, colorful scarves layered one on top of the other on its stubby arms. To the left of the dresser sat a bulky chest of drawers and a tiny drawing table with a pencil sitting on an open spiral notebook.

"I take notes for her," Lucia said. "When she requests it."

I touched the spiral. The paper was onion-skin thin, cheap.

"Notes?" I asked.

"Yes. Letters. I keep most of them there, inside the drawer," she said. "Because I don't know where to send them."

I opened the drawer and took out a wad of tightly bundled pieces of paper. "How sad," I whispered, more to myself than to Lucia, as I read the names of the people the letters addressed. Lupe, Marianita, Don Luis, Sarai, Magdalena, ghosts from a distant past, people who slipped in and out of my hands with the quiet rustle of the delicate papers that I pulled from the drawer with reverence.

"Not really. Most of those people are probably dead," Lucia said, watching me sort through the notes before putting them back in the drawer respectfully.

"They're not dead," a hoarse voice said, and I turned around.

My grandmother was attempting to emerge from within a cocoon of bedclothes slowly, like an ancient moth. Finally, one hand had come forth. It broke itself free of the gauzy fabric like a naked, leathery wing. Then her other arm pushed past the linens. Gradually, deliberately, my maternal grandmother pushed at the blankets until she uncovered her pale, balding head.

Frowning, she shoved her left elbow into the lumpy mattress, and, waving Lucia away, she sat up.

"Is this your child?" she asked Lucia, who turned around and smiled at me.

"No," Lucia said. "This is not my child. I'm too young to be her mother."

"I'm your granddaughter, Graciela," I said when Abuela Estela didn't say anything. "Isabel's daughter."

My grandmother didn't look at me but stared instead at something behind me. I turned around and noticed the dark navy curtain covering the doorway was moving, as if a strong wind had suddenly passed through it. "Yes. Of course, of course," my grandmother said, looking up and down at me and then past me again. "She looks like you."

I looked behind me, but there was nobody there.

Lucia stopped fussing with my grandmother's bed-clothes long enough to giggle. "See?" she asked, looking up at my face. "I told you."

Lucia lifted the translucent window curtains and folded them over the iron bedpost. "Did my mother ever tell you about me?" I asked my grandmother, stepping forward into the dull, waning light of dusk that came through the window.

My grandmother Estela shifted in her bed, cocked her head, and waved for me to give her my hand. When

I placed my left hand in hers, she tugged on it and shook it side to side, like she was testing it. She flipped it over and looked at my palm, examining the lines. Then she reached up and took a strand of my hair. She tested it too, feeling its texture between her fingertips. "Florencia . . . mi flor silvestre," she whispered. Then she reached up and touched my cheek. "You have such silky skin, fine and soft as satin."

"Who's Florencia?" I asked Lucia.

She shrugged and lifted her eyebrows high. "Could be anybody. From the past. She hasn't made sense in years," Lucia said.

"Where have you been, florecita linda?" my grandmother asked when I smiled at her.

"My name's Graciela. Graciela Torres. I'm your granddaughter." I introduced myself again. "Isabel's daughter."

My grandmother frowned. She gripped my hand, lifted it to her lips, kissed it, and then pressed it against her cheek. "No. No. You are my little wildflower," she said. "My first moon. My first star. My first love."

Her words brought to the surface a vague memory— *bright moonlight illuminating the darkness of the night outside my window, the heady scent of purple lavender blossoms, and my mother's voice, whispering, "You are my first moon! You are my shining star! I love you!"*

Startled, I stepped back, away from my grandmother's bed. No. I didn't want to remember. I didn't want to return to the darkness of that terrible last night. I'd gone to Mexico to escape, to get away from the painful realities of my life. So, I pushed the memory into the darkest, deepest recesses of my mind and turned to Lucia.

"Does she know about me at all?" I asked, quietly, so that only she could hear me. "Did anyone ever tell her she has two granddaughters?"

"I don't know," Lucia whispered. "I just take care of her. I don't ask questions. It is the only thing I know how to do. The only thing I'm allowed to do for her."

"Allowed?" I asked. Lucia's words were so strange, so cryptic. I thought about questioning her, but it felt wrong somehow to interrogate her. I was an interloper, and it wasn't quite my business to question Lucia about my grandmother.

"Doña Estela, this is your granddaughter. She came to visit you, from the other side," Lucia explained, putting her hand on my grandmother's shoulder and leaning in to talk to her. "Will you get up and come to the table? Will you sit and have breakfast with us?"

"Do we have goat cheese?" my grandmother asked Lucia. "She looks hungry. We need to feed her something hearty, to nourish her soul. She's real, you know."

"I know she's real." Lucia laughed and winked at me. "I saw her coming down the street."

"Good." My grandmother let go of my hand and pushed the covers off her legs. "Give me a minute. I have to make myself presentable."

"You can go look at the guest room if you like, while I help her get dressed," Lucia instructed, pointing to the door. "It's to the left, at the end of the hallway. It's not much, but you can stay there if you like."

"Thank you," I said, and I walked back into hallway. As I wound my way through the house, I could tell that the guest room was an attachment to the house. By the look of the dull azure paint, it was easy to see this part of the house was older. Maybe this long suite-like building, with a bathroom at one end and a six-inch concrete trough with the waterspout coming out of the wall beside it, had once been the main house and my grandmother's bedroom and kitchen were the additions.

There was no use speculating because it didn't matter. I was just glad to see a cot at the far end of the room, under the wide windows, next to the back door. The room was lovely, but by the looks of it, it was not vacant. There were some clothes folded neatly on top of the armoire to the left of the cot. One of its doors was slightly ajar. I walked over, opened it, and touched

the fabric of a set of summer dresses draped over thick wooden hangers.

"Try the yellow one. It's my favorite." Lucia was standing just inside the door to the hallway.

I shook my head. "Oh, no. I brought enough clothes. You don't have to lend me anything."

"They're not mine," she said. "You should wear them. They would look lovely on you."

"They're beautiful," I said, examining the delicate detail of the scoop neckline on the yellow dress. "Whose are they? I'm not putting anyone out, am I?"

Lucia waved the idea away. "No. You're not. Come. Let's go have some goat cheese. It is divine, fresh and light. Just beautiful. It's your grandmother's favorite thing to eat. When you taste it, it will make you want to stay longer, maybe even the rest of your life."

"Oh, I wouldn't say that," I said, laughing as I followed Lucia out of the room and into the hall, where the portraits on the wall hung one right after the other, faces I didn't recognize, spirits from a past I did not understand.

CHAPTER FIVE

Eagle Pass, Texas

June 2011

BECAUSE WE HAD TO MAKE SURE Mercy was all right, we waited five days after the accident before holding Alexander's velorio in our living room. When our sandy-haired next-door neighbor and his mother come around the fence to pay their respects, the guy is soaking wet. He stands on our porch that soggy morning looking a bit uncomfortable.

He is younger than I thought. When I first saw him last week, I'd guessed he was in his late twenties, but as he stands there holding an umbrella over his mother, I can see that he is closer to my age, maybe eighteen or nineteen. He is wearing a white dress shirt and tie and is in charge of the dark umbrella because his mother's hands are full, carrying a covered red casserole dish.

"Hello," the mother says. "I'm Connie Perez. This is Daniel, my son. We just moved in next door. I—uhm . . . we—made you some chicken alfredo."

"Oh—thank you. Come in. Please," I say, once I come out of my fog long enough to realize I am supposed to take the casserole and let them in. Our sala looks smaller than usual with the older couple who lives across the street, two of Mercy's co-workers, my father, and Guelita Rosa sitting around together. My father has pulled out several mismatched chairs from the garage because our couch is too small to accommodate everyone.

"Thank you for coming," my father says, shaking their hands. "I am Fernando Torres, and this is my younger daughter, Graciela. My other daughter, Mercedes, Alexander's mother, is . . . indisposed."

Mercy was in her room, the room my father gave up after he moved himself up to the attic to accommodate her and Jose. Mercy had lain down for a nap because she took a couple of Guelita Rosa's baby-blue pills. Finding something to help ease Mercy's anxiety is easy around here.

Thanks to her many medicos across the border in Piedras Negras, my grandmother has a wide variety of medications at her disposal. She has three rows of medicine bottles lined up along her dresser in her room.

Many of them are prescribed, but a whole lot of them are not. She calls those "herbal remedies," but I suspect there's more to them than that. Let's just say I don't think the FDA would approve them.

Connie sits down beside Guelita Rosa on the sofa. "I am sorry for your loss," she whispers. My grandmother nods, her gray eyes unblinking as she stares at the coffee table in front of her. She's been on the phone with her comadres all morning and is apparently all talked out.

"Me too. I'm sorry," Daniel says, shaking my father's hand and then nodding to me before stepping back and standing directly behind his mother with his hands on the back of her chair, as if to hold himself up.

It is customary, I know, to sit around eating and reminiscing about the deceased—in a sense, celebrating his life. But Alexander was so small, his life had been so brief, that there is not much we can talk about without bringing up things nobody else in the room knows anything about. So instead of talking we sit around silently drinking coffee, taking turns going over to the window to watch the rain pound against the glass panes and pour out of the gutters at the corners of our house.

When it is my turn to stand at the window, I catch sight of a dark figure, a woman dressed in black. Her long wet hair is hanging over her face so that her features are hidden, and she is no more than a shadow. She

is standing on the other side of the fence by the flower bed at the edge of the yard. I push the curtains back so that I can get a better look at her, but the woman bends her head, turns around, and walks away.

A shiver runs down my spine, and before I can shake it off, I catch a glimpse of Alexander. He is standing in the shadows of the hallway that leads to my room, waving for me to come over.

I looked around the room to see if anyone else can see him, but everyone seems to be deep in their own thoughts. When I turn to the hall again, Alexander is gone. He has slipped away unnoticed by anyone but me.

"Can I go to my room?" I ask my father, who is sitting silently on the love seat across the room.

My father frowns and shakes his head.

I sigh and sit down between my father and my grandmother. My dad moves aside to make room for me, but then he reaches over and puts his arm around me. I lay my head on his shoulder and he kisses my temple. I sigh and close my eyes for what I think is a moment, but when I open them again the light overhead is on, and everywhere around me people are clutching rosaries as they pray together.

One phrase echoes another, perfectly cadenced invocations that swirl and spin softly around the room, rising together to the ceiling light on enormous white speckled wings—so beautiful, so delicate, they take my breath away.

I look down at my hands and see that someone slipped a fragile-looking rose-beaded rosary into my hands while I napped. I turn to my grandmother to see where we are in the sequence of prayers, and she reaches over and touches the bead corresponding to the prayer. Instinctively, my lips move and my voice joins the echoes of grace swirling around the room, and I pray and pray.

"Receive our beloved Alexander," Guelita Rosa says after the prayer of Eternal Rest, and we all echo her words. But then, because she is moved by the moment, Guelita Rosa adds her own bits of prayer, "May he join our antepasados in heaven. May you receive him in your kingdom. May you hold him in your glory and grace."

Beyond the flowing living room curtains, on the other side of the closed window, the sky turns dark purple and a wounded, tortured night replaces the light of day. I stare at the darkness, entranced. The prayers emanating from the deepest, most reverent part of my consciousness spill out of me, but I'm not listening to anyone around me anymore. I am somewhere else now, in another time, recalling and reliving another night. A night that had slipped away from my memory. A night that comes back to me in that moment—as I pray.

Chapter Six

Three Years Earlier

THE EVENING AFTER I ARRIVED AT my maternal grand-mother's house, Lucia announced she was leaving.

"Leaving?" I asked. "Why?"

"I have to go before the sun comes up." Lucia placed a small plate with a glistening ball of goat cheese in the center of the small round table between us. "I want to get a good seat on the bus. I haven't been home in almost two years, and since you are here for a few days, I can go visit my family in Nava now. You understand, don't you? Family comes first, right? That's why you're here."

"Yes," I said. "But I don't know anything about her medical care."

Lucia pulled out a chair and sat down next to me. She took my plate and put a corn tortilla on it. "Have some of this cheese. The gardener makes it fresh and hangs it up there, in that corner." She pointed at the corner of the kitchen with her knife. "For us to eat when it's ready."

I took the knife she offered me and dug into the little mound of soft cheese, scooping a bit of the white creamy substance and spreading it over the tortilla before rolling it and taking a bite. It was delicious, delicate but firm, like nothing we had in the States. "It's good," I said, after I swallowed it down. "Does my grandmother take any medicines?"

"No." Lucia watched me take another bite of the cheese taco. "She stopped taking her pills years ago. Says she doesn't need them anymore. Something about her age. She says she's not of this world anymore. That she can go at any time. So, there's no use fighting it."

I looked toward the bedroom and thought about my grandmother's condition, the way she had lain there all wrapped up in her blankets, sleeping the day away and talking to people who weren't there. "I'm not sure I can take care of her. I mean, I help my Guelita Rosa, my father's mother, at home, but she's pretty self-sufficient. I don't know what this grandmother likes or doesn't like to eat. And honestly, I don't know how long I'll be here."

"She's not a lot of work," Lucia assured me. "She gets around by herself. Takes a shower by herself. Does her own toileting. All you have to do is make sure she gets something to eat when she finally gets up. It would just be for a few days, three or four. I'll be back by Friday evening at the latest."

I looked around the kitchen. It was rustic, but it had all the necessities—a narrow white refrigerator, a small gas stove with slim worn buttons, baskets of fresh fruits hanging from the ceiling beside the deep aluminum farmer's sink, and a tiny herb garden growing in a wooden box on the windowsill. "Where's the nearest store?"

"Ah, yes. There's a postecito in Las Cenizas, on the second street to the left, but that can get expensive. But don't worry. I'll leave you some money. Three blocks past that, on the right, there's a small warehouse, Pajarillos. You can get almost everything you need there for a more reasonable price. Even things like socks and brooms. The floors get cold at night in this house, so you'll want to wear socks when you to go bed. If the store owner, Don Maldonado, doesn't have what you need, he can get it for you from Piedras in one or two days."

"When does she eat?" I asked. "I mean, what does she like to do at mealtime? Does she eat in bed or does she come in here?"

Lucia smiled and patted my hand before standing up. "She's got a weird schedule. She eats breakfast in here, at dusk, and dinner outside at dawn because her days and nights are switched around. Anyway, she takes breakfast at around eight or nine in the evening, sometimes earlier, depending on her mood."

"What do you mean, switched around?" I asked. "Like she's up all night?"

Lucia laughed. The sound was low and light, like a tiny bell ringing somewhere deep in her throat. "She's nocturnal," she explained. "Like a kid on summer vacation. Come. Let's go see if she's ready to eat."

I followed Lucia into my grandmother's darkened bedroom. Abuela was sitting up, looking out the window at the setting sun through the sheer curtains. Her cloudy gray eyes focused on us when she heard Lucia calling her. "Doña Estela, it's time to eat. Are you hungry?"

"Hmm, yes." Abuela Estela pushed at the covers, shoving at the thick woolen blankets until she freed herself of them.

I watched her move her legs, slowly throwing them over the side of the bed, until she was facing us. Then she reached up, like a child would signal a mother that she needed help. Lucia offered her a hand so she could steady herself as she stood up. The whole process was simple. She didn't need much assistance, and she didn't have a walker like Guelita Rosa at home, but she looked fragile, rail thin and bony, her face angular and sharp.

I followed as Abuela Estela walked slowly beside Lucia into the kitchen. She sat at the chair I pulled out for her and put a napkin on her lap while Lucia reached into a basket on the counter and brought out a brown egg. "These are fresh," she said, holding the egg up in the air for me to see. "The gardener puts them on the windowsill at dawn. There's a chicken coop out back with a handful of chickens. They don't lay more than six or seven eggs a day altogether. But she only eats two a day. I eat two myself, so I give the gardener the rest."

Lucia turned on the stove and put a small frying pan on the burner. She fried the egg and served it on a saucer, placing it in front of my grandmother.

"Does the gardener live here too?" I asked. "Will I meet him in the morning?"

Lucia shook her head and reached into the basket for another egg. "He lives up the street, but he hardly ever goes home. Most days he sleeps out back. He has a little shed back there. But you won't see much of him. He keeps to himself," she said. "You want some eggs?"

"No." I shook my head and looked down at my half-eaten cheese taco. "This is plenty. I'm not very hungry."

"Me either." Lucia put the egg back in the basket and sat next to my grandmother. Abuela Estela hadn't started eating, and Lucia scooted the cheese plate closer to her. "You want some cheese?" she asked, and Abuela Estela reached over. She carved off a sliver of goat cheese with her dinner knife and placed it beside the fried egg on her plate.

"Eat your egg." Lucia patted my grandmother's delicate, pale hand gently and then put a fork in it. "Sometimes she needs reminding," Lucia said. "Of what we are doing."

"Oh." I took a bite of my taco and nodded. "This cheese is very good. I wish I knew how to make it."

My grandmother stared at the cyclops egg on her plate. Her cloudy eyes were huge, bulging, and looked even more so in the context of her small, bald head with its sparse strands of long gray hair curled up against her shoulders and neck.

"You should eat your egg," I said. "Before it gets cold."

"I can't see anything. Where are my glasses?" Abuela Estela looked around, patting the tablecloth and lifting the napkin off her lap. "I need my shawl. I want to go outside to see the kittens."

Lucia reached up and touched my grandmother's shoulder. "You should eat first," she said. "Before you go outside." Then, looking at me, she said, "She likes to go outside to drink her coffee on the patio, after she's had her first meal of the evening."

At that first strange night's breakfast, I found out everything there was to know about Abuela Estela's habits. She always got up sometime in the evening, at about seven or eight when the sun was setting, because she said the sun hurt her aging eyes. She had become nocturnal first out of habit and then out of necessity, Lucia explained.

After her first meal, she always had a shower and took coffee on the porch out back. She liked to walk around and talk to her plants, a series of wild-looking perennials pouring out of a set of red clay pots lined up along the porch against the side of the house, before she went back inside.

"The plants here take a daily watering, nothing major, a light splash of rainwater from that container there. The gardener takes care of the rest." Lucia pointed at a lidless five-gallon paint bucket sitting on the edge of the porch. "She only eats one egg and one piece of toast every evening. She doesn't care for anything else for her breakfast. She'll reject anything else you offer her."

"Okay," I said, watching my grandmother try to entice a gray kitten to step onto the porch by bending over, rubbing her fingertips together, and cooing to it.

"Sometimes she stays out here a long while," Lucia continued. "But most of the time, she'll go back inside by midnight and sit down to watch soap operas on the television. Unless she wants me to write a letter, that's pretty much the scope of our days. Pretty easy—uncomplicated."

But there were other things Lucia hadn't mentioned, things I noticed as I sat observing their interaction before Lucia left. Abuela Estela enjoyed listening to the night creatures. While Lucia swept the porch, my grandmother became entranced by a white owl that hooted on the rooftop of the gardener's shed beyond the expansive yard, past the shrubbery of overgrown flowers and plants. There was a new litter of calico kittens living out back, and my grandmother spent hours watching them tumble around and chase one another in the backyard.

At dawn, my grandmother took the kitten she'd brought inside off her lap, let it walk on wobbly legs across the living room floor, and turned off her television set. "I'm hungry," she finally said, and she stood up and walked into the kitchen. She took dinner inside right around five in the morning and afterward, she lay sideways on her bed watching the television again before she finally drifted off to sleep at around six. I had to make sure to turn off the television and close the curtains because she liked to keep her room dark while she slept during the day.

By the time Lucia left before sunrise the next morning, taking a small suitcase with her and disappearing down the dark, foggy street, I knew everything I needed to know to take care of my Abuela Estela for a few days. I wasn't worried about the cooking, and it helped that she wasn't on any medication. It was the idea of turning my nights and days completely around that worried me most. I didn't want to get into a bad sleeping pattern like she obviously had because I would need to adjust to my life as a high school student when I returned to the States.

I stood watching the street from behind the metal gate in front of my grandmother's house after Lucia disappeared into the morning mist, not knowing if she was ever coming back but not too worried either. I was glad to be alone with my grandmother Estela. She seemed to be very quiet, and quiet was what I needed, what I craved at that time, while I sorted out what I wanted to say, what I wanted to do, about my situation at home. One thing was for sure, I had no plans of giving up my room until my father figured out a way of letting me keep my personal space.

The way I saw it, either Mercy and Jose moved out or I wasn't going home. They had all summer to figure it out, and I intended to stick my talons into the dirt of my ancestral homeland until my father met my terms.

CHAPTER SEVEN
Eagle Pass, Texas
June 2011

IT RAINS THE REST OF THE week after Alexander died, so that by the time we bury him the ground is so soaked the three-inch heels of Mercy's black patent-leather shoes keep piercing the grass, sinking deep into the dark earth as she walks across the cemetery to Alexander's grave site. I watch the thin, taut tendons at the backs of her ankles tighten and stretch under her skin as she struggles to pull the heels completely out of the ground with every slippery step she takes.

Again and again she unearths those heels as she walks ahead of me, clinging to Jose's arm. I follow them, with my father walking solemnly beside me, a quiet shadow of a man. I can sense Dad's sadness weighing him down at having to be here again—so I put my arm through his and pull him close. He looks over at me grimly and pats my arm. His hand is cold and clammy against my skin, and I place my hand over it.

With the heavy rain pouring over us and the wind whipping our black umbrellas and clothes about, the graveside service has to be cut short. The whole thing lasts less than twenty minutes, but I am relieved, because the truth is we need to go home. We need to mourn and heal. Together. As a family. But also alone. Away from everyone else for a while.

After the service, I wait for Mercy beside the black sedan that transported the immediate family to the cemetery. However, somewhere along the way, and unbeknownst to any of us, Jose must have convinced Mercy to ride with him because she doesn't come back to the car. I watch her cut across the cemetery with Jose and get in a black Camaro that looks too new to belong to him. They speed away before I can call out to her, ask her what's going on.

I turn around and look for my father, thinking that maybe he can do something, but he isn't getting in the family car either. Because he is nowhere to be found.

"Are you ready?" the driver of the family car asks me, holding the door open.

I shake my head. "No," I admit. "Can you wait?"

The driver nods and turns away, holding his hands low in front of himself respectfully. The rain has turned into a light drizzle, so I collapse my umbrella and put it on the car's floorboard before following the pebbled driveway that meanders around the cemetery.

That's when I see him—Alexander is standing on a hill on the other side of the graveyard.

I consider calling out to him, but that feels weird. Instead, I walk silently toward him. When I get over the brow of the hill, I see that Alexander is watching my father, who is standing in front of another grave.

My mother's grave.

I stand paralyzed, breathless, because after Mom's funeral, I never saw him at my mother's grave site. As far as I know, he's never visited her. But seeing him there, staring at her headstone with his hands in his pockets, I can see I'd been wrong to assume that. Why wouldn't he come here to see her? He loved her, protected her during all those episodes. The nightmares, the wailing, the wandering—he was always there for her, hugging her, soothing her, putting her to bed afterward.

He still loves her, which I suspect is the reason he's never told us why she left that night or even who killed her. He wants us to remember her as the good mother she always was to us. He is most certainly devoted to her memory. That's why he's never remarried. Of course he would visit her. She is his true love.

I consider joining him at her grave site, and even start walking that way, when something catches my eye and makes me freeze in place. A woman's figure steps out from beside my father's silhouette. It startles me, because I hadn't seen her there, standing beside him. Her black dress and dark, slim figure had been camouflaged by my father's larger frame. I try to find out who she is, but her dark hair is covering half her face. As she turns to look at me, I step back because she looks a lot like the woman I saw out the window during the velorio.

"Let's go," Alexander whispers from behind me.

"Just a minute," I say, unable to look away from the dark woman.

Alexander raises his arm and says, "C'mon." Then he turns around and starts running up the hill, away from my father and the strange woman at my mother's grave. "Run, Grace! Run!" Alexander screams back at me as he runs away.

The dark figure of the woman turns to look at me again. I still can't see her face, but I am sure of it now. It is the same woman who was standing on the other side of our fence in the rain. As I stare, the woman starts walking toward me purposely, like she wants to get to me before I walk away.

I smell rain, and flowers, and something else, a musky, cloying-sweet scent, like lavender blossoms. Yes, lavender. The fragrance overwhelms me, and I am there again, six years old and cowering in my bed with Mercy while our parents argue.

"You don't understand," my mother cries. "He's out. They let him out. I have to warn Mamá. She's in danger. I have to get her out of that house. Now. Today."

"We'll go tomorrow," my father says. "It's late, Isabel. Please, think of the children. We can't leave them alone."

"It can't wait!" my mother cries. "It can't! It can't!"

"We've called the police," my father whispers. "Please, Isabel. Control yourself. You're scaring the girls."

"Run, Grace!" Alexander's cry pulls me out of the memory, and I shake myself out of my trance.

The woman in black is still walking toward me. For a moment, I consider the possibility that this might be my mother coming toward me. But then her silhouette starts changing. Her whole body shimmers and wavers, getting lighter and lighter, and she begins to glitter, the way a moth sparkles in the sunlight in the palm of your hand. The closer she comes, the more surreal she becomes, and the sadder I feel, until the sorrow takes my breath away and I am overcome with emotions. Emotions I do not understand. Dolorous and distressing. Deeper than grief. Darker than loss.

I stumble and catch myself as I step backward. The lack of oxygen to my lungs is overwhelming, and I begin to fear that I might collapse.

"Stop! You're hurting her!" Alexander screams, and suddenly, he doesn't sound like a baby anymore. I turn to look at him, but he is still the same two-year-old I love so much it hurts.

Alexander's words spark something inside me, and I shake myself loose from the disturbing wave of emotions and bolt. I run over the hill as fast as my legs can take me. When I reach the car, I yank the handle and open the door. Alexander is inside, though I never saw him crawl in. He waves, urging me in. "Jump, Grace! Jump!" he says, so I hop into the back seat.

"Go! Go!" I tell the driver, who is already putting the key in the ignition and starting the car. "Go!"

As the car speeds away, I turn around in my seat and look back at the cemetery, but there is no one there. The dark woman is gone. The cemetery is empty, because everyone who attended the funeral has left. Even my father is nowhere in sight. I sit forward again, panting, releasing the pent-up emotions in my chest, fear, sadness, despair.

The seat beside me is empty. Alexander has disappeared, so I recline, rest my head back, close my eyes, and tell myself to breathe. *You're safe,* I keep telling myself. *It wasn't real. Just one of your episodes, an echo—a really bad one. But you're safe now. Safe.*

I stay like that, breathing in and out in the back seat of the car without talking to the driver the whole way back to the funeral home. As I concentrate on the sound of the tire treads on asphalt, the roar of my heart beating against my eardrums gets softer and softer until it fades and the only thing left is the soft sound of rain against the windshield and the rhythmic back-and-forth of the wipers.

I wait in the lobby of the funeral home until my father arrives in a separate car. "You ready?" he asks, without saying one word to me about where he's been all this time. So I nod and follow him.

We walk to the parking lot together, in silence, and get in his truck. I think about asking him how often he visits my mother, but then the image of the woman who chased me over the hill comes to mind and I push it all away.

When I get home, I hand Guelita Rosa Alexander's memorial prayer card. She didn't attend the funeral because the rain was making her hip ache more than usual, and she didn't want anyone leaving early on her account. Guelita Rosa takes the card between her trembling hands and kisses the naked angelito on the front of it before she flips it over to read the back.

"Qué lástima," she says. Then she closes her teary

eyes and murmurs a small prayer in Alexander's name.

I can't bear another moment of pain between us, so I hug her and excuse myself. I go to my room and wait for Jose to bring Mercy home. She hasn't talked to me since the night she took Alexander's things out of my room. She locked herself away from everyone while she waited to bury Alexander, so I sit in my room and wait anxiously for an opportunity to speak to her, to ask why she left with Jose.

When Mercy finally comes home in the middle of the night, I peek out the window and watch Jose get out of his car to hug her before she comes inside. He holds her for a long time, and then, as in the old days when they were dating, he leans in to kiss her.

Only, this time, my sister steps away from him before he can touch his lips to hers. After seeing that, I know Mercy is going to be okay. So, I close the curtains, quickly turn off the lights, and slip under my quilt. From the silence of my room, I hear Mercy getting ready for bed.

I hear her turn on the light, open the creaking top drawer of her dresser, and move around, back and forth, to and from the bathroom. Without knowing what I am going to say to her, I get up, open my door, and sort of stand there, clinging to the left side of the doorframe of my room, waiting for her.

Mercy slips out of the bathroom and walks by me. She doesn't make eye contact, so I push myself off the doorframe and follow her down the hall.

Suddenly she stops and whirls around.

"What do you want?" she asks, her eyebrows raised as she looks at a spot on the wall beside me.

"I just—thought . . . that maybe . . . we could . . ." I stumble to put words together.

"What?" she asks, piercing me with her swollen, angry eyes. "Spit it out, Grace."

"I wanted to . . ." I shift from one foot to the other and clear my throat. "I mean—I thought we could—you know . . . talk?"

"No."

"Mercy, 'manita—" I reach out to her, but she slaps my hand away.

"Don't call me that." Mercy steps into her room and stands staring at the doorframe with her arms wrapped around herself. "I can't do this yet."

"But I need to talk to you," I whisper. I know I am begging. I hear myself doing it, but I don't care. Maybe begging is what I should be doing. I want to reach out and wrap my arms around her the way I did every time I crawled into her bed at night after our mother died. "I wanted . . . to say that I'm sorry . . . for—"

"Stop!" The word is a cold, hard slap to the face.

I cringe. "I'm so sorry," I whisper, reaching out to her, trying to hug her.

"Stop torturing me!" Mercy screams, pushing me out the doorway.

"Please, Mercy."

Tears start rolling down my face and I wipe them away with the end of my shirtsleeve. "Please understand. I didn't mean to let him go."

"Leave me alone!" Mercy cries, her eyes reddening with unshed tears. "Don't you see? Sorry won't bring him back, Grace! Nothing will bring him back!"

"Please. Don't shut me out," I beg as she closes the door.

I stand still in the hallway, my forehead pressed against the door of Mercy's room, letting the hot tears roll down my cheeks, wondering what I can ever do to make things right between us.

My father comes down the stairs and walks toward me. He is holding his Bible in his hands. He caresses my hair and kisses my forehead before gently pushing me aside. Standing in front of Mercy's room, he raps gently on the door with his knuckles.

When Mercy doesn't answer, he bows his head, leans forward, places his right hand on the handle, and wiggles it. "Mercedes?" he calls softly to her. "Open the door, m'ija."

A few moments later, my sister opens her door and looks at him. I press myself flat against the wall, wanting to make myself invisible. Mercy stands there, the door barely cracked open, staring at the floor in front of my father.

A long, dead silence extends between them, and then, lifting the Bible up so she can see it, Dad says, "I earmarked some passages I thought you might . . . want to read."

"I have a Bible," she says. Her voice is flat, distant.

When Dad doesn't say anything else, Mercy slowly closes the door between them and locks it again. He stands there for a few more seconds, tracing a hairline crack on the top panel of the bedroom door, a remnant of a long-ago fight between Jose and my sister. My father doesn't say anything. He just presses his Bible against his chest and walks past me. He goes up the stairs and into his room, leaving me standing in the empty hallway with no one to talk to.

I consider going to Guelita Rosa's room to talk to her, but she's already taken one of her blue pills and gone to bed. So instead of waking Guelita up, I go back to my room and lie down. But I can't stop thinking about Mercy and the terrible pain I have brought her.

In the silence of the night, I listen to her every move, her every tear, her every sigh, wishing I could go to her, sit next to her, and hold her tight. I turn away from the wall between us and stare at my closet door. I must have fallen asleep, because suddenly I wake and shoot straight up in bed. My lungs hurt, and I take in a deep, painful breath.

In my dream, a giant leopard moth sits on my chest, pressing me into my bed. Its giant antennae moves in slow motion and its dark, shiny eyes stare into my eyes, searching my soul. The insect is so big, so heavy, it breaks my sternum. I can hear the dull cracking of bones and tearing of ligaments, the slow snapping of tendons, as it presses down on me.

In my dream, my chest collapses and my ribs splinter and pierce my innards.

In my dream, my lungs stop working and I know I am dying.

In my dream, I stop breathing.

CHAPTER EIGHT

Eagle Pass, Texas
Twelve years earlier

THE FIRST TIME I EVER EXPERIENCED an echo, I was six years old. It was a warm summer day and our parents had decided to teach us how to fly a kite in the backyard.

My mother was having an especially good recovery day. She'd had one of her spells, a particularly bad echo, the night before, and the dark circles were still prominent under her eyes. She'd been very vocal during the incident, wielding a kitchen knife and wailing, "Socorro! Socorro!" as she'd run out of the kitchen, down the hall, and out the front door.

Guelita Rosa didn't live with us back then, so there was no one else to take care of me besides my sister. I'd clung to the doorframe of her bedroom, scared to death and crying inconsolably when Mercy reached me and held me close. "It's okay, 'manita," she'd whispered. "Mami had a nightmare. She'll be okay soon. You'll see."

Although my mother's episodes, the secretive premonitions she didn't reveal to anyone but my father, had been disturbing the neighborhood for months, nobody had called the police that night. They had let my father catch up to her, disarm her, and escort her back up to our house with his arm around her shoulders, while she walked with her head down, hair covering her face, and her arms wrapped around her middle, wailing, "Something bad is coming," all the way to her room.

The next morning, Mom's laughter as she watched Mercy's kite get higher and higher was carefree. Although I couldn't get the memory of the night before out of my head, Mercy seemed to have forgotten all about it. She chased our mother around the yard until the kite was flying freely, and she was given full control of its cord.

Unlike me, Mercy was a natural at everything physical. She ran around the yard with her red kite soaring high up in the air. My mother laughed and laughed and tried to keep up with Mercy, while I struggled to get my yellow kite up the air. It would start soaring for a second, then, like a tired moth, it would lose momentum, tilt sideways, and start diving downward, hitting the ground hard as it landed on its nose.

"Wrap the cord around your hand," my mother yelled from across the yard after my several failed attempts to keep the kite up in the air for more than a few seconds. I didn't know exactly how to do it, so I took the thick kite string and wadded it together. Then I wrapped it over my knuckles once and shoved the rest into the cupped palm of my hand. The kite above me lost momentum and took a nosedive again, landing directly in front of my mother.

"No! Not like that. Help her, Fernando, help your daughter!" my mother yelled, her voice high-pitched and out of control, more of a cry or a howl, the way she'd screamed when she'd wandered through the house the night before holding the knife in front of her and crying out, "¡Por favor, ayudenme!"

I'd turned around to look at her, and that's when it happened.

My mother wasn't herself anymore.

The wind whipped her long black hair wildly around her head so that her face was hidden from me, but there was no mistaking the fact that the thick rope in her hands was not a kite string anymore, but something else—a smashed, crumbled mass of purple flowers smeared with crimson. My head had spun with the image of those violent, bloodstained flowers. So vivid. So real. I'd smelled them too. A heady, floral scent that overwhelmed me, and I'd felt woozy and sick to my stomach.

Then the wind changed direction and I finally saw her face again.

Only it wasn't her face anymore.

Instead of her bright brown eyes, her crinkled nose, her pretty smile, I saw a human skull, hollow-eyed and devoid of flesh. I froze and stared at the ugly thing, and the skeleton face grinned back at me.

A sob, low and mournful, rose up from deep inside me, and I started to wail. Slobber fell out of my mouth because I couldn't move my hand up to my face to wipe it away. I was paralyzed by the frightful sight.

"Papá!" I cried out.

The skeleton opened its mouth and said something I couldn't hear because I was screaming so loud by then. As sobs racked my body, I released my grip on the red spool of string and tossed it away from me.

"Graciela? What are you doing?" My father came up from behind me and put his hands on my shoulders. "Why are you crying, m'ija? Don't you want to fly your kite anymore?"

"No!" I cried when he tried to put the yellow kite back into my hands.

"What do you mean, no?" he asked. "What's wrong?"

"I'm scared," I said, closing my eyes tightly and

trying to put my mother's skeletal face out of my mind.

"What?" my father asked, picking up the red spool and holding it between his hands. "Why?"

"What's the matter?" my mother asked, from somewhere behind my father.

I didn't dare look up at her.

My father wrapped the string over the spool to put it away. My mother came over. She put her hands on her hips and was looking down at us. "What is it, Gracie?" she asked. "What's wrong, baby?"

"It's nothing, Isabel. She's just tired, that's all." My father's hand tightened around the crossbars of my kite.

Mercy's kite had lost its momentum and started taking a dive, and my father put my kite in my mother's hands and ran off to help my sister. My mother put a hand over her brow and looked at Mercy's kite struggling against the wind.

Her face was back to normal.

She wasn't a skeleton anymore.

She was beautiful and young and full of life.

The following week, while my father slept, she'd snuck into our room and kissed Mercy and me before getting in her car and driving away. She promised to be back soon, but she never made it home.

We've never been told exactly what happened. Only that she was murdered. My father and Guelita Rosa refuse to speak of it. They say we have to respect her memory. But my memory of her is tainted by these echoes. My mind is like her mind, and I am just as haunted by this don.

CHAPTER NINE

Three Years Earlier

I WENT TO SLEEP THAT FIRST MORNING at Abuela Estela's house in Mexico, telling myself I would only take a nap and then I would get up and do something during the day to keep my own schedule as best I could. But when I woke up, I was disoriented. I looked at the azure ceiling in the dark, foreign room and tried to focus. The naked light bulb hanging from a wire in the ceiling swayed softly, as if someone had opened a door and let a ghostly breeze into the room. I watched it for a second, and then something moved in the room behind me. I sat up in bed quickly, like a mouse caught in a wooden trap.

It was a false scare—a big, beautiful cat with enormous green eyes was scratching at the window, trying to get inside. I pushed the bedclothes out of my way and went to open the window for it. "Well, hello," I said, caressing the calico momma cat's back while she danced back and forth on the windowsill.

I closed the window and went to the door. Standing on the threshold, I put my hands on the doorframe, threw back my head, stretched, yawned, and hung like one of those lazy, transparent house geckos, letting the sun warm my face and neck for a long time. It was going to be another warm day, but not so hot that I couldn't enjoy it. The coolness of the glazed concrete floor felt nice against my bare feet, and I stood there enjoying it.

A thud caught my attention and I looked up. The sun was high in the sky. I squinted and found the source of the noise. Two men were tearing down the roof on what I believed to be the gardener's shed out back. They were working quickly, pulling the dull old shingles off the roof and tossing them on the ground to the side of the small building.

I continued to hang from the doorframe, watching the men working—tearing, plucking, and discarding without regard for anything but their work. One of them whistled as he worked, and the musicality of his tune was pleasant, inconspicuous. I closed my eyes and abandoned my thoughts, telling myself to just enjoy the fresh air as it entered my lungs, awakened my muscles, and chased the sleep out of my body.

When I finally opened my eyes again, the two men had stopped working. The older of the two was drinking water out of a small yellow gourd, but the younger one was crouched, holding a hammer in one hand. He turned and looked at me intently, and suddenly I felt ashamed for standing there in my nightgown. It wasn't a particularly attractive nightgown, nothing sexy or revealing. As far as nightgowns were concerned, it was rather boring and matronly. Light and breezy but long, it covered me from neck to foot. Even my arms were hidden by the loose sleeves that buttoned at my wrists.

The stranger's dark eyes centered on me. I felt pinned down, pierced through, as unable to move as one of those giant leopard moths sitting behind the glass of the shadowbox I created for Mr. Mata's science class last year. I wanted to look away, but I couldn't. Something about the young man's eyes held me motionless.

I felt . . . exposed.

I smiled nervously, apologetically, but he didn't smile back. In fact, he frowned, and then he looked down at the shingles in front of him and spoke softly to his companion. The older man turned to look at me as he capped the gourd and strapped it back on his tool belt. Then he turned back to the young man, said something, and punched his shoulder with his fist, laughing. This made the young man lift his head and sneak another look at me before turning away, giving me his back as he returned to work.

I went into the house and took a shower. The water was ice cold, but I suffered through it, washing up as fast as I could. Once I was dressed, I stood in front of the antiquated mirror dressed in jean shorts and a T-shirt, ruminating, trying to figure out what had made me feel so embarrassed.

Why did he frown at me? I asked myself as I dried my hair with a tattered towel. I wasn't being rude. I knew I wasn't. I was watching them work. How could that possibly be offensive? And the other one, why had he laughed? He didn't think . . . ?

No, I told myself.

Oh my god! my mind screamed. *Why can't we just look, set eyes in their direction, without men getting the wrong impression! Disgusting! All of them!*

I ran a brush through my hair then, forcefully, kicking myself for having smiled. *You're so naive!* I kept reprimanding myself. *Think before you act! You're in a strange town, in a different country, a whole other world. Remember what Guelita Rosa always says, don't put yourself in these kinds of situations!*

Refusing to let the incident with the workers unsettle me, I walked around the side of the house until I found the utility closet and checked the water heater. But I wasn't able to figure out if it was broken.

Cold showers, however, were the least of my problems. There was a whole lot of cleaning to be done around the house. There were dust bunnies and cobwebs everywhere.

I spent most of the afternoon giving my room a good cleaning, and was glad to see that the men were no longer on the roof when I went out to shake the dust out of the carpets. I threw both floor rugs over the fence at the far end of the backyard and gave them a thorough beating with the broom.

I took out an old box of caked powder soap I found under the lavatory in the bathroom and dusted the carpets with them. Then I wrestled the garden hose out of the overgrown ivy in the garden and hosed the rugs down.

I was in the process of giving the soapy carpets another beating, trying to whack the excess dirt and grime out of them, when I heard a long, low, disturbing whistle coming from behind me.

"Hello, beautiful," someone called from behind me.

I turned around, broom held high up in the air over my shoulder, to find the young roofer standing on the other side of the fence. His whistle had startled me, but the crooked smile resting on his lips unsettled me even more. Then, because I just stood there saying nothing, he jumped over the fence. "Can I help you with something? Anything?"

I was so stunned, I didn't say anything—just watched him stroll across the backyard toward me. He moved lithely, like a jaguar. Tiny little bumps formed on my arms as the little hairs stood on end.

Sunlight glistened off the young man's brown hair. His generous lips formed a smile and showcased his bright teeth. *Slick and sleezy,* I thought, *like something out of a telenovela,* and I cringed. The blood rushed inside my ears as my mind raced for how to react, what to do. This was not the way boys came on to girls at my high school in Eagle Pass. They weren't so . . . solicitous.

Don't smile!

Be nice, but not too nice.

Be friendly, but not too friendly!

"Here, let me have that," he said, reaching for the broom.

"No. I'm done with it for now." I pulled the broom out of his reach and put it down, leaning it against a tree, and stepped away from him. "I'll give it another scrub later today."

"I'm Manuel," the young man said, extending his hand out. "At your service, chulita."

I touched my fingertips to his hand and gave him

a weak little shake—the kind I hate when others do it to me. But I couldn't help it. Even though I wanted to give him a hearty, strong handshake, the sound of his low whistle and his sleazy remarks were still ringing in my ears like an alarm. My body vibrated with anxiety, urging me to get away from him.

"Excuse me." I stepped back, keeping my eyes averted. After a few awkward seconds, Manuel moved out of my way. I started back to the house, looking down at my feet as I walked, because that was the best way to assess how close his shadow was to mine, and I wanted to make sure I kept a good distance between us.

The pink phlox that carpeted the length of the garden was almost purple in the shimmering light of the setting sun. I had a passing thought that the gardener must be very good because he was keeping things beautiful for my grandmother. Except for the stone pathway, everywhere I'd set my eyes that early evening, plants bloomed: crepe myrtles, bougainvillea, roses, vinca, and pansies blossomed among a multitude of other flowering shrubs I didn't recognize. And in the center of it all stood a huge jacaranda tree, lush and gorgeous, with its lavender blooms dancing in the warm breeze.

As I wound my way toward the house with Manuel's soft footsteps behind me, I thought about my mother, growing up with all this beauty, and I wondered why she never brought us here to spend time with my grandmother.

That's when it happened. An echo began to take over me. My vision blurred. The phlox underfoot wobbled and blurred. It seemed to move but didn't move, shifting sharply, swaying side to side under my feet.

My heart raced, almost as if I'd been running, only I wasn't running. In that moment, I became aware of myself standing very still. Then I had a sense of falling, of the ground coming at me and my face hitting the pink phlox, of smelling it—of tasting the pink perfume, sharp and bitter on my tongue, powerful and strong, overpowering my senses.

"Hey, are you okay?" Manuel asked, stepping closer to me.

Nauseated, I closed my eyes and held my breath for a moment, until the dizziness passed. When I opened them again, Manuel was standing in front of me. The scent of pink phlox that had attacked my senses clung to the air around us, and I shook my head. "No. I mean, yes," I said. "Please, excuse me. I have to go inside."

I rushed toward the porch.

"Hey, what's your name?" Manuel called out to me.

I ignored his question. I had no interest in making new friends. So, when I reached the back porch, I stood with my hand pressed against the cool wall of the house beside the blackened, mildewed screen door, silent as a statue, shaking the echo out of my mind.

I grabbed the screen door handle, but Manuel took a long leap and jumped onto the edge of the porch. His dirty, worn work boots thudded loudly behind me. "You're seriously not going to tell me your name?"

"Please go away," I said, holding the door ajar.

"You're very pretty, you know that?" he asked. "That other girl? Lucia. Is she your sister?"

"No," I said, and I opened the screen door, fully intent on going in and slamming the door behind me.

But I was too late, because Manuel was suddenly there, standing between me and the threshold. An alarm went off in my head, but I decided to give him space, so I let go of the door and stepped back.

"Are you scared of me?" he asked, shutting the screen door gently. "Don't be scared. I'm a nice guy."

"If you're a nice guy, you'll get out of the way," I said. The orange glow of the setting sun was in my face, and I put my hand over my eyes to shade them.

"I knew it. You're scared. Listen, I saw you looking at me," he said. Then, because I didn't say anything, he added, "Don't get me wrong. I just thought you might be lonely. Want some company."

"No," I said. "I'm not lonely. And I have enough company. Anything else?"

Manuel smiled again, an easy, suave smile that lit his eyes and made them glisten mischievously. "Okay," he said, and he pushed his thumbs into the belt loops of his work pants and stepped backward, away from the door. "Can I at least have your name?"

"No," I said, and then I stepped away from him and opened the screen door again.

"Okay then," he said. "I'll just have to make up a name for you. How about Chata? Cha-ti-ta bo-ni-ta!" He tried the nickname out. His voice dragging the syllables out in long, thin musical notes that made me cringe.

Infuriated by the taunting nickname that made fun of my flat little nose, I stepped into the house. When the door snapped shut behind me, I turned around and looked out into the backyard through the freshly scrubbed glass of the window. Manuel was standing on the edge of the long porch, staring at me.

"See you later, Chatita linda," he called.

I pulled the curtains closed and stepped out of his line of vision. Afterward, I sat shaken on the edge of the cot, clasping my hands together in front of me.

Still trembling from both Manuel and the echo in the garden, I closed my eyes and took a deep breath, holding it. *Four days*, I told myself. *You can keep it together for four days. He's just a stupid boy. No need to panic.*

CHAPTER TEN
Eagle Pass, Texas
June 2011

Ever since Guelita Rosa came home from rehab after falling down and breaking a hip in our kitchen, I made sure we had a system in place to help her call on us. Whenever she needs something, she pulls on a wide satin ribbon resting beside the headboard of her bed. The ribbon makes a bell move on the wall in the living room. When that bell rings, we jump up, abandon whatever we're doing, and go check on her.

When Guelita Rosa's bell rings this morning, I open my eyes. The sun filters through the threadbare curtains, bright and beautiful, without regard to the heaviness in my heart. I am glad to see that Alexander is back in my room, standing by the door, waiting.

I smile at him as I get up, push my feet into my slippers, and open the door. Alexander trails behind me but then disappears as I make my way past the living room to Guelita's room.

"Oh, good. You're awake. I can't reach my chancla." Guelita Rosa is sitting up in bed, already bathed and dressed. Her thin hair is skillfully slicked back against her scalp like a silvery-white helmet. "It's under the bed, I'm sure. It couldn't have gone anywhere else. Is it down there? Can you see it?"

"Yes," I say after dropping to my knees and reaching far under the bed for it. "There you go."

"Thank you. What am I going to do without you, Graciela?" she asks as I wrap the little black slipper over her thin elevated foot with its crooked pinkie toe. It isn't a real chancla, but one of those soft sock slippers they give you at the hospital with worn-out rubber pads for soles. She insists on wearing them every day, in or out of the house, even in the garden or front yard when she looks in on the daylilies in the rock flower beds.

"Call Doña Paula, I guess," I say, referring to her usual caregiver, who came over and stayed with her before I graduated last spring.

Guelita Rosa babysat us a lot right after my mother passed away, but that wasn't necessarily the best situation for us because she isn't very motherly. In fact, she is anything but maternal.

She's always been brutally honest, with a knack for lacing the truth with just the right amount of meanness and spite to make things interesting. But she cooked and cleaned and washed our clothes and made sure we didn't go astray in the summers, so she served my father's purposes while he wandered around the great state of Texas, looking for some chambitas to support us.

We are indebted to Guelita Rosa. So, we take care of her now that she's the one who needs us.

"Ay, si, but Paula is getting old," Guelita whispers. "Soon she'll be in a walker too, and then we'll both sit around waiting for the other one to get up and cook for her. What will become of us then, I wonder, dos ancianas just staring at each other como tontas?"

I shrug my shoulder. "Starve, I guess."

Guelita Rosa slaps the back of my head playfully and calls me, "¡Grosera!"

Then she pulls over her walker and uses it to stand up. I help her get through the door of her bedroom and then walk ahead of her, making my way toward the kitchen. "She's not that old," I say. "Come on. I'll get your coffee started."

I rush ahead with the intention of starting her toast first, but when I enter the kitchen, Mercy is standing at the sink looking out the window with a cup of coffee in her hands. Alexander is sitting there. His chin and arms are resting on the table, and he is playing with the blue doily under the salt and pepper shakers, flicking it with his fingertips and watching it fall down again. I wrinkle my nose, and he smiles up at me.

"Mami's mad," he says, then he goes back to playing his doily game.

I look at the stove and see that Mercy has already started Guelita Rosa's usual breakfast. A pot of water is simmering, and a pack of flavored oatmeal sits next to it, waiting to be poured in and cooked for exactly three minutes because she likes the texture of it to be soft and silky without being watery.

Guelita Rosa's walker clanks against the floor as she makes her way into the small kitchen. The space is suddenly smaller, confining, with the four of us in it.

"Mercedes! You're up," Guelita Rosa says, her eyes softening as she looks at my sister. "Pero, mira nada mas. You look like one of those half-dead birds the cat drags onto the porch, all plucked and no spunk. What are you doing up? You should be in bed, resting."

Alexander sighs loudly and rests his cheek on his arms, bored.

Mercy mumbles something that sounds like "thanks" against the lip of her cup and takes another sip of her coffee. She holds the mug with both hands in front of her, keeping it close to her face, while she continues to stare out the kitchen window.

"Thank you for setting up Guelita's breakfast," I say, crossing the kitchen and standing in front of the stove. "Can I get you something? English muffin, a bowl of fruit?" I remember Mercy's penchant for having something light in the mornings. "Are you going to the . . . to see . . ."

"Work!" Mercy says, interrupting me pointedly.

"Work?" Guelita Rosa asks, shocked at the sight of Mercy dumping the rest of her coffee down the drain and setting the cup in the sink to rinse it.

"Yes, work." Mercy walks past Guelita Rosa. Alexander scuttles out of his chair and follows his mother into the living room, where he watches her pick up her black patent-leather bag from the coffee table and rush out the front door. He stands facing the door for a second, then he turns around and runs down the hall, making a beeline into my room.

I consider following him, but I know exactly what he is doing. Even as a figment of my imagination, a manifestation born out of my grief, he always goes to my window in the mornings to watch Mercy get into her car.

"She shouldn't be going back to work so soon," I tell Guelita Rosa.

Guelita Rosa sits at the table. Quiet and slow as an old tortuga, she takes her morning pills out of her pocket and sets them on her saucer. There must be at least twenty colorful pills dancing on the saucer when I sit down beside her.

"We can't tell her what to do," Guelita Rosa says, watching the pills tremble and then settle until they're just sitting there, nestled up against one another on the saucer. "It's up to her and what she thinks she can handle."

I get up, walk over to the breakfast nook, and draw back the dull lace curtains to peek out the window. My stomach tightens at the sight of Mercy driving nose first out of our driveway. She doesn't have to reverse the car because she's been parking it far away from the house, backed up against a cluster of scraggly huisaches at the edge of the property.

I go back into the kitchen, tear open the packet of oatmeal, and dump it into the pot. The water boils over, making a mess in the process. I clean it up while Guelita Rosa scoots sideways along the window seat, to her usual spot by the bay window in the breakfast nook. She leans over and slides the saucer and the trembling pills toward her. I serve her coffee and then sit down beside her, resting my head in my hands and staring at the empty driveway in our front yard.

"¿Y porque lloras?" she asks, reaching out to swipe at my face. Her gnarled hand rubbing roughly against my cheek makes me realize I *am* crying, and I wipe the hot tears away.

Guelita Rosa grabs my hand and slaps it gently. "Come on," she says. "It'll be all right. Your sister's up and running again; things could be worse, you know."

"How?" I ask, watching as Guelita Rosa takes a sip of her coffee.

"Oh, please." Guelita Rosa guffaws, toying with the pills, taking a red one in her hand and weighing it as she thinks about what to say. "Are you sad because your sister's gone, or are you sad because you're still here?"

"What?" My stomach knots itself tighter and tighter inside me, like those balls of overextended rubber bands wrapped one over the other, threatening to break and hurt someone. "I'm sad because . . . because . . . well, you saw it, didn't you? She hates me, Guelita!"

"Oh, hush!" Guelita pops a transparent red gel pill into her mouth and uses her saliva to swallow it. "She does not. She's your sister. She's not allowed to hate you."

I think about it for a moment.

No. She hates me.

My big sister hates me.

"Better check on my breakfast," Guelita Rosa says.

"It's possible to burn the kitchen down with one small pot of boiling water. I know, I've almost done it."

I get up, turn the fire off, and pull the pot off the stove. Taking it over to the sink, I scoop the oatmeal into a bowl and set it aside while I wash out the pot. Guelita Rosa taught us to clean as we cook. That way the dishes don't have a chance to pile up on us. After a few seconds, I put the bowl of oatmeal on a small plate, walk it over to the table, and place it in front of my grandmother, sighing.

"Oh, stop that. She'll be back tonight," Guelita Rosa says, placing her fingertips on either side of the plate and turning it counterclockwise several times, until she's made it go full circle twice, an act that never fails to mesmerize me, even though she's been doing it every day since she came back from the hospital after her fall. My father said the doctors told him she had a mild stroke, and she'd be doing odd things like that for the rest of her life.

"Tonight?" I ask.

"Of course," Guelita Rosa says. "Where else is she gonna go?"

I think about that near kiss I witnessed between her and Jose the night of Alexander's funeral, and my body shudders. The idea that she might meet up with Jose after work and stay out all night with him the way she used to when they were dating turns my stomach again, and I decide I can't have any breakfast.

Guelita Rosa picks up her spoon. She fills it with oatmeal, hits the rim of the plate with it, shifts it, and hits the rim again, before lifting it up to her lips and blowing on it. "This is her home," she says after swallowing a mouthful of oatmeal. "It's not like she's left for good."

My mind is still back there, caught up in the days when Mercy was with Jose. I remember how happy she was the day she found out she was going to have a boy. She didn't care about anything else except giving Jose a son. A dull ache starts to form in my temples. "No. But she could," I whisper, speaking more to myself than to my grandmother. "She's emotionally fragile. If Jose were to—"

"Jose?" Guelita Rosa asks. "What does he have to do with anything?"

I pull my feet up onto the chair and fold my knees in front of me. "He was at the funeral," I say. "Mercy left with him. Afterward. I got the feeling, when he dropped her off, that he—was interested again."

"Interested? Interested in what?" Guelita Rosa puts down her spoon. She leans over and stares at me head-on. "Grace?"

I shrug. "You know," I whisper. "In getting back together."

"Nonsense." Guelita Rosa reaches over to toy with her collection of pills. She picks a huge yellow oval capsule and pops it in her mouth. "Your sister's got more sense than that."

"You don't understand." I reach for a napkin and wipe my eyes with it. I don't want her to know I'm on the verge of tears again. Too many tears is something my grandmother can't understand. She's a tough old crow and proud of it. Before Alexander's death, I don't think I'd ever seen her cry a single tear. Not once. "They have a bond. He could try to use this to get back with her. And then she would never forgive me or be close to me again. Not if she has him to lean on."

"You mean grief?" Guelita Rosa asks. "No. That's not how that works."

Tears start rolling down my cheeks and I pull my shirt up and swipe my face with the inside of the collar. "Ay, Guelita . . . how—am I—how am I ever going to make it up to her?"

"Make it up to her?" Guelita Rosa asks. "What are you talking about?"

"It's my fault Alexander died," I cry. "He was my responsibility—"

"Oh, no, no, no!" Guelita Rosa shakes her head and pops another pill into her mouth. She takes a swig of water to make it go down before saying, "It is most definitely not your fault. It was a tragedy. That's all. A terrible, terrible tragedy."

"But I put him down," I continue. "I let his hand go."

"It was unfortunate, I know," Guelita Rosa says, putting a hand under my chin and turning my face to look at her. "Listen to me. People die every day, Graciela. It was just Alexander's time."

"That's a horrible thing to say!" My body trembles as I hurl the words at her. "You don't honestly believe that, do you? That Alexander's death was pre-destined, that God intended it that way?"

My grandmother stares at me. Her dark eyes settle on my face for a moment, unwavering, as still as the pills on her saucer. My words don't faze her. It isn't the first time I have raised my voice at her. I used to do it all the time when I was a child, but I've grown out of it. She made sure of that.

Guelita Rosa drops her eyes and sips her coffee, then bites into a piece of toast. "Mercy had no business having a baby that young," she finally says. "That's all I'm saying. No business."

"Agh!" I push myself away from the table, stand up, and go back to my room. As I lie in bed, I wonder where Alexander has gone. Did he hear what Guelita Rosa said? The thought gnaws at me. "I'm sorry, baby," I whisper into the emptiness of my room.

But Alexander doesn't answer me. He doesn't answer me that day or the day after that either. On the third day, I go looking for him all through the house. I wander around from room to room, lifting curtains where they look bulky, shifting tables and chairs to see if he is hiding under them. I even open the old wardrobe in Guelita's room when she is sleeping, because I can't very well call out to him.

What would my grandmother think if she heard me calling out Alexander's name? She understands my don, but I don't think she'll understand that I've been in touch with her great-grandson now that he's gone.

"What in the world are you looking for?" Guelita Rosa asks, shifting to sit up in bed.

"Oh, nothing," I say. "I'm just . . . I'm bored."

"Well, help me up," she says, waving her hand in the air. "I'm hungry and there's a concha with my name on it in the kitchen."

After a quick trip to the bathroom, I help Guelita Rosa to the breakfast nook and pull the white bag of pan dulce off the refrigerator. There are still two pieces of bread in it. I give her the pink concha and take the marranito for myself. It isn't my favorite kind of pan dulce. I prefer cuernos, but I bite into it anyway.

"What's up with you?" Abuela asks, swiping concha crumbs off the tablecloth into the cup of her hand and putting them on her plate. "What are you mooning about?"

I look out the window, wondering if I will ever see Alexander again. The sunlight bounces off the crystal tassels on our hummingbird feeder, sending sparks of light into the house every few seconds. "Guelita, do you believe in ghosts?"

"Of course not," she says. "They're figments of our imagination. Longings. Unfinished business with our dearly departed ones. We're the ghosts, Graciela. We're the spirits left behind, the ones roaming the earth, chained to our emotions, our memories."

I look at her then. "Really?" I ask. "Then why do so many people claim to see them?"

"It's our fears that haunt us," Guelita Rosa says. "Our sins. Guilt. Shame. All of it. We make things up to hide what's really bothering us."

Guilt. Shame. Yes. Yes.

It makes sense.

CHAPTER ELEVEN

Three Years Earlier

AT ABUELA ESTELA'S HOUSE THAT SECOND evening, I climbed off the porch and sat on the cool concrete, careful to fold the hem of my dress so that it was tucked under my knees to protect my thighs from the dirt and grime. Because no matter how much I had swept and scrubbed it with the scraggly broom and soapy water that afternoon, after Manuel left, the porch never quite got clean enough.

Manuel was a puzzle to me.

Even though he wanted me to believe he was a nice guy, he gave me a bad vibe with his whistling and his little pet names. I couldn't explain it, but something about him unnerved me. Something about the way he looked at me from that roof, averting his eyes when his friend was around, and then showing up later when I was alone in the yard, well, it was all too creepy.

What was this strange feeling I'd gotten in the pit of my stomach when he came back late in the afternoon, long after he and his co-worker had packed up and left for the day? Trepidation? Fear? Repugnance?

Certainly not all men were bad. *But how does one know who is good and who is bad?* I wondered. I was only fifteen years old. I had no experience with dating. Mercy had been sneaking off with Jose behind everybody's back, and she knew I didn't approve of her wicked ways, so she wasn't telling me anything about how she knew the difference between good and bad men. Not that she had much credibility in that department. Jose was a loser. So, I couldn't very well trust her advice.

One of the worst things about not having a mother was not having anyone to help me figure things out. I sighed and looked over at Abuela Estela, who was sitting quietly beside me. She had picked up a kitten and was kissing it and whispering lovingly to it in the crook of her arms. I watched her for a moment and drank my lemonade while I looked out at the garden and then at the gardener's roofless shed at the edge of the property. I wondered where the gardener was, because I'd been there two days and still hadn't seen or heard a word from him.

"Guelita?"

It was the first time I referred to Abuela Estela using the same diminutive, the affectionate title I used for my paternal grandmother, Guelita Rosa, at home. I didn't know how she would react, since we hadn't been acquainted very long, but the new title didn't seem to faze her. Abuela Estela just kept her unfocused eyes averted, looking out at the garden absently, as she mumbled, "Hmm?"

"What was my grandfather like?" I asked, reaching up and putting my hand gently on her thin, bony knee. The act startled her. The kitten in her lap was startled too, and it hissed at me for disturbing them. Then it jumped off Abuelita's lap and ran off into the grass to join the rest of the litter languishing under the light of the moon.

"What?" Abuela Estela asked, focusing her gaze on me and looking straight into my eyes for the first time since I'd come outside with her.

I blinked.

It was unnerving, that gaze, darkly bright and astute. An ancient wisdom seemed to emanate from her dark pupils and fixate itself on me, centering me, and I cleared my throat. "My grandfather," I whispered. "Your husband. What was he like?"

"My husband." Abuela Estela took a deep, ragged breath and held it. Her head shook with the effort it took to pull it into her lungs. I could hear the heartbreak in her silence, even before she said, "My husband was a thief!"

"A thief?" I asked, shocked. *Why hadn't anybody told me that? Did Mercy know?* "What do you mean? He just went around stealing? Is that what he did for a living?"

"No. No," Abuela Estela blustered. The air left her lips in quick little spurts of exasperated breath, and she pulled at her long, wrinkled earlobe and flicked it as if something were burrowing itself behind it. "Your grandfather was a rancher. He had cows and goats and horses. Lots of horses. His father and grandfather used to bring them down from the hills, where they roamed free. They cultivated them. Tamed them. Bred them. Made good money from them. Those wild beasts were the only thing he loved."

"I don't understand," I said, softly, trying not to break the spell of coherence she had fallen under. This was the longest she had stayed focused and spoken to me in the two days we had spent together since Lucia's departure. "I thought you said he was a thief? What did you mean, he was a thief? What did he steal?"

Abuela Estela didn't answer me. She just looked at me with those sharp, dark eyes. Then she reached over and picked up a strand of my hair and examined it. She tested its fine, thin texture between her fingertips. "You have beautiful hair," she whispered.

I didn't want to talk about my hair. It was long and straight and wouldn't hold a curl for more than ten seconds without falling flat again. I hated its complacency. "Guelita," I pressed on. "What about my grandfather? What did he steal?"

Abuela Estella fixated on the strand of hair in her hand. She twirled it around her index and middle finger, once, twice, three times, until she had secured it tightly between her fingers and thumb. Then, without warning, she yanked at it, bringing my face so close to hers I could see every eyelash on her eyelids.

"My life!" she cried. Then she yanked on my hair again, until I was closer to her face than I've ever been to anyone outside the circle of my immediate family. "That man stole my life!"

"Guelita!" I cried, trying to pry my hair out of her fist with both my hands. "You're hurting me!"

Abuela Estela opened her hand and my long, thin hair slipped out of her grip. I gathered it at the nape of my neck and twisted it gently into a loose knot to keep it out of my grandmother's reach should she decide to go after it again.

"I had beautiful hair too," Abuela Estela continued as she went back to looking out at the garden. "He liked it. And my teeth. He said I had nice, even teeth. He told my father that when he came to trade for me."

Her words sent a little chill over me and I shuddered, a tiny little shake that lasted a millisecond, her words echoing in my mind. "Trade?" I asked. "What do you mean trade?"

"I didn't even know him," Abuela Estela said. She dusted her skirt at the knees and picked off cat hairs with her thin, crooked fingers. "I'd never seen him before, not until that day, not until he came to our house that morning, pulling those two cows behind him."

"Cows?" I asked. "I thought you said he raised horses."

"Well, he wasn't going to trade in his horses!" Abuela Estela explained, still picking at her skirt. "They were too valuable. Besides, we needed the cows more. There were fourteen of us kids, three unweaned little ones. My family needed the milk more than we needed horses. Horacio knew that. He knew my father wouldn't say no to that trade. Two cows for one less mouth to feed. I was doomed from the moment that man knocked on our door."

"Wait?" I asked. "Are you saying your parents sold you for two cows?"

"The way you talk!" Abuela Estela whispered. "Look at you, all made up like a harlot! You think men are going to respect you? Go wipe that off!"

"But I'm not wearing any makeup," I said.

Abuela Estela frowned. Her sharp eyes scanned my face and lingered on my lips. "Ay, Isabel. What am I going to do with you now?" she cried. Tears glistened in her eyes, the soft glimmer of them contrasting with their sharpness. "You're ruined, child. Ruined."

CHAPTER TWELVE

Eagle Pass, Texas
June 2011

Now that Mercy is acting like her normal self again, I try not to let Guelita's theory about Alexander's death enter my thoughts. I am happy to just sit in my room and manifest my precious nephew. He is at home here, returning every evening to chatter as he plays on the floor in the center of the room, and then disappearing when I am ready to fall asleep.

Every day I wake up hoping that Mercy will begin talking to me again. But Mercy is busy now. She is immersing herself in her life again. She's even taken on double shifts at work and is hardly ever home anymore. I keep tending to Guelita Rosa by day and playing with Alexander at night. But I am aware that the days are moving on, and I can't let time slip by without making

an effort to get Mercy back on track with the plan—
our plan.

Unfortunately, we are teetering on a precarious
ledge, Mercy and I. Communication is important, yet
she's ignoring me all the time, acting like I don't even
exist. So, I do the only thing I can do. I leave the house
early to catch the bus. In my purse, I have our birth
certificates, our social security cards, and our state IDs
tucked into my old backpack. It wasn't hard getting
these things out of Mercy's purse. She leaves it on the
little table by the front door every evening before she
goes to bed. I just hope she doesn't notice they're gone
before I have an opportunity to put them back.

She'll be mad, of course, but how can she blame me?
After everything that's happened, I am not really expecting her to be thinking about the future. Nevertheless,
the idea of letting go of that shared dream, that con-
nection, is inconceivable to me. But I don't have time to
think about what I'll do if she changes her mind.

I have to act in her best interest.

I can't move on without her.

I can't leave her behind.

That's what I'm thinking as the admissions clerk at
the community college riffles through the paperwork
I filled out on my own at home, pretending to be my
sister, forging her signature with a flourish at the end,

the way she does when she signs the backs of her checks from the movie theater where she works as a hostess, which my father says is a fancy word for *flunky*.

"Is everything in order?" I ask before she has a chance to zero in on my forgery. Not that she has anything to compare it to, but what if she sees that some letters in both our papers look the same because I wasn't quite as careful as I thought I was being and our *t*'s and *h*'s look too much like each other's?

"Yes, yes," Mrs. Martinez says, pulling the papers together and tapping them lightly against the counter before securing them with a paper clip. "This looks great." Then, because I don't say anything, she sets the papers aside and leans in to speak to me quietly. "How is she?" she asks.

"What?" I ask, my mind running furiously through every excuse I rehearsed for why Mercy is not here turning in her own paperwork, looking through the semester's course schedule, considering changes, asking questions.

"Your sister," Mrs. Martinez asks. "How is she doing? I heard about the tragedy in your family. She's very brave. But she's doing the right thing. Maybe going to school will help get her mind off the loss."

My heart is beating wildly in my chest. My head is starting to throb. And I am afraid an echo is coming, so I slide my thumbs behind the straps of my backpack and roll back on my heels, ready to bolt if I have to. Where I'll go, I don't know, but anything's better than this place. I'm not ready to discuss Alexander with anyone.

"She's . . ." I start to say something, but my voice trails off. I feel out of breath. Like there's no air left in my lungs.

I am suffocating.

I can't breathe.

"I gotta go," I mumble as I turn around and head for the door.

Behind me, I hear Mrs. Martinez take in a shocked little breath. "I'm so sorry," she says. "I didn't mean . . . I'm sorry for your loss."

I bolt. Out the door. Into the bright white parking lot. Like a deer into traffic. And then, because I don't know what else to do, I take off running. I run down Bibb Avenue, past a lane of cars, over another parking lot, toward El Indio Highway.

My thighs are burning, and I am sweating like a beast. But I can't stop running. I trot through the intersection until I am at the corner of Brazos and Williams. Then, because I am in pain, I stop and grab at the stitch in my side, breathless.

I don't remember ever being so sick as I am at that

very moment. I lean over and retch into the brush beside the sidewalk. The heat of the passing cars lifts the scent of vomit and sends it up into the air around me. When I am done, I kick hard at the packed dirt until it covers most of the vomit. Then I wipe my lips with the edge of my T-shirt and head home, walking back the same way I came.

Nobody notices me when I get home.

I am invisible, so I go on with my life, happy in the knowledge that Mercy and I are about to start the next phase of our lives. Because, like it or not, she is going to school with me in the fall.

∾

As the weeks go by, Alexander becomes my constant companion. He is always there, playing with his toys on the floor or sitting at the rocking chair, minding his own business. Most of the time, he acknowledges me with a smile but then goes back to looking out the window for birds and planes. Other times he prattles on and on, in that mature voice he's found in the afterlife, asking me questions about his environment.

"When is the moon coming?"

"Can the sun sneeze?"

"Who puts the leaves on the trees?"

"Where's Mami?" he asks when Mercy doesn't come home immediately after work. "I see her, yes?"

"Yes," I say. "You'll see her. When she gets home tonight."

But no matter what is going on in the house, who comes and goes, how long they stay gone, how lonely the house feels, Alexander is always there for me. "I love you, Grace," he says from across the room when I become disheartened.

When he says that, I want to reach out and grab him and hold him tight and ask him to make ojitos at me the way he used to when he was alive, but I know he isn't able to do things like that. I think he knows it too, because he never reaches out for me, never asks me to pick him up or carry him to bed the way he used to before the accident.

I am bemoaning this fact when the doorbell rings. Our neighbor Daniel is standing just outside the door, smiling widely, holding a wide basket covered with a checkered tablecloth. He looks as sheepish as the wolf in *Caperucita Roja*, if the wolf were the one carrying the basket to the grandmother's house.

When I don't answer, Daniel lifts the basket upward a bit and gives it a little shake. "I brought you some corn bread."

"Corn bread?" I ask. My left eye twitches, a nervous

twitch, I believe. I put my index finger on it, trying to make it stop, but even under the pressure of my fingertip, I can feel it convulsing.

"Yeah, well, I didn't make it. My mother did. She bakes when she's trying to figure out a new painting. She's got a new project that's not quite ready for the canvas, so she baked all day yesterday. Anyway, I thought you might like some."

"Graciela, m'ija, where are your manners?" Guelita Rosa asks from her seat on the couch. "Let the poor boy in before he keels over from heat exhaustion."

"Come in," I say, pulling the door open and stepping aside to let Daniel through.

"Did you say you have corn bread?" Guelita Rosa asks, and when Daniel nods his shaggy head, she grins. "Well, come into the kitchen and let's take a look at it. We'll need some milk to go with it, Grace."

"Way ahead of you," I say, as I turn around and start for the kitchen.

"I like to dunk mine, but Graciela likes to cut hers up into little squares and just drop them in one at a time, watches them float, and then just before they sink, she spoons them up," Guelita Rosa prattled on. "Do you float or dunk?"

I have to stop myself from groaning and rolling my eyes as Daniel follows Guelita Rosa through the living room, into the archway that leads to the kitchen, all the while listening to her jabbering on and on. I am more than a little embarrassed to have my corn-bread-eating habits disclosed to what feels like a perfect stranger, but my mortification doesn't faze Guelita Rosa. She even tells Daniel about the time when I was seven years old and I surprised her by trying to make corn bread muffins from scratch.

"With corn from a can!" she hollers as she recounts my epic fail. "Can you imagine?"

"I didn't know about cornmeal," I admit, taking the container from Daniel and transferring the corn bread squares to a red serving platter that we use to set out the pan dulce from the panaderia down the street. "Here, let me put these away so you can take the basket home."

"Oh, you don't have to give it to me just yet. I can get it later, when I come back," Daniel says, taking the basket out of my hands and placing it on the counter next to the oversized platter.

I look at the slices of corn bread, each adorned with a tiny little painted sprig of summer light in bright yellow and orange swirls. It is obvious his mother has taken great care in preparing the display, filling the large basket with perfectly cut corn bread squares. *Or did Daniel do that?*

"No. You should take it now," I say, putting the rest

of the corn bread hastily on the platter. "That way, you don't have to come back for it."

Daniel takes the basket from me. I smile as I rest my left hand on the counter for support. Then, because Guelita Rosa is staring at me with that knowing lift of her left eyebrow, my hand slips off the counter and I almost lose my balance as I fall forward. Daniel reaches for me. The basket gets between us, but I recover before he puts his hands on me.

"I'm all right. Counter's slippery. Must be time to clean it," I say as I right myself.

"Good," he says, smiling as he looks into my eyes.

He is so close, I can see the freckles on his nose. I've never met anyone with freckles before. Realizing that I am staring, I move toward the wide archway that separates the kitchen from the living room area, hoping he gets the hint and follows me to the door. "Well. Thank you for bringing these," I say. "I'm sure they're delicious."

Taking his cue, Daniel says goodbye to Guelita Rosa and begins making his way to the front door with me. Alexander comes out of my room and stands in the living room. He looks silently up at Daniel and follows us sedately as we walk to the door.

"Are you okay?" Daniel asks, oblivious to the ghost trailing behind him.

"Yes," I say, opening the door and standing there, waiting.

"Well, I'll see you then. Enjoy the corn bread. Let me know what you think of it," he says, tossing the basket side to side as he backs down the porch steps like someone not really ready to leave.

"Thank you." I close the door and sigh as I lean against it, relieved to be rid of him finally.

"That boy's smitten," Guelita Rosa says when I get back to the kitchen. "Quiere noviar. He'll make a good boyfriend."

"Smitten kitten!'" Alexander rolls out the words and giggles as he runs off to my room.

"Don't be silly. Are you done here?" I ask, picking up a plate full of corn bread crumbs.

"Nothing silly about that. He's a healthy young man, with a young man's hopes and dreams," Guelita Rosa says, setting her coffee cup down. "You're the pretty girl next door. It's natural."

"Well, I'm not the pretty girl next door," I say. "Mercy is. Anyway, he's not interested in me. Not like that, anyway."

"And what makes you think he isn't?" Guelita Rosa frowns. She seems shocked to hear me say that.

"I don't know. Guys are just so . . ." My voice trails off as I try to figure out what I'm feeling. *How* I'm feeling.

"What?" Guelita Rosa asks, cocking her head as she waits for an answer. "Spit it out, Grace."

"They're like . . . lice. They serve no purpose, no purpose at all," I say, pushing the recently regained memory of that boy in Mexico—Manuel and his icky way of approaching me—out of my mind, and thinking instead about that sleazebag Jose.

"What do you mean, no purpose?" Guelita asks. "Men have their purpose. I don't have to remind you of what that is, and I'm sure, pests that they are, there's a purpose for lice too."

"Well, I don't have time for parasites," I say, trying to get the image of Jose leaning over to kiss Mercy out of my head.

I stare out the window at the porch steps and wonder if Mercy and I will ever get back to that place where we are more than friends, that place where we are still sisters, when we can talk about anything—even men, and their strange way of being.

CHAPTER THIRTEEN

Three Years Earlier

"LUCIA!" ABUELA ESTELA CALLED FROM HER room across the house. I rushed out of the shower, pulled a fresh change of clothes from my bag, and got dressed in record time.

"Lucia!" she called again as I zipped up my jeans and shoved my bare feet into my sandals.

"I'm here," I said. "Do you need to go to the bathroom?"

Abuela Estela nodded and waited for me to approach. I crouched in front of her, reached under the bed, and grabbed her shoes. The whole routine was vaguely familiar. It wasn't much different from taking care of Guelita Rosa at home.

Maybe that's why I'm here, I thought. *Destiny, not Mercy and Jose and that whole mess at home, has brought me to this place at this time. I was meant to reconnect with my maternal grandmother. Maybe, despite her disability, she can tell me more about my mother. Things about her childhood, things I missed out on discovering because I never got to know her.*

"What are you doing here?" Abuela Estela looked up at me from within the folds of her bedsheets and quilt. Then, without waiting for an answer, she looked away, past the rocking chair in her room. "Did you bring her? Is she yours?"

"Who?" I asked, looking at the rocking chair, which faced away from us in front of her small television, a square wooden console set from the 1950s.

Abuela Estela sat up and pushed her way through her web of sheets. I tried to help her, but she swatted my hands and shoved me away. She might look frail, with her veiny, thin limbs, but she was actually quite strong. Those swats stung.

"Well?" she asked, pointing sideways with her thumb at the rocking chair again. "She's been rustling about all day. Woke me up more than a few times with her racket, but I was too tired to do anything about it."

I heard a strange little noise coming from behind me, and I turned around.

The rocking chair was moving back and forth, as if someone was sitting in it, keeping a rhythmic pace that was much more than a breeze from the door making it sway. I put my grandmother's shoes on the floor and stood up carefully, quietly. The chair continued to rock back and forth as I walked toward it.

This isn't an echo.

It isn't a ghost or an apparition, either.

She's just imagining things, I told myself.

But despite what my mind told me, I started shaking; my legs felt a little wobbly as I got closer to the rocking chair. There was a big floral back cushion on it, so from behind I wasn't able to see if there was anyone in it, but I wanted to—no—I needed to know who Abuela Estela was talking to.

At home, nobody else was like me. Nobody else could see, feel, even smell otherworldly things. Nobody else had the echoes. But if my maternal grandmother could see someone who had the power to sit in a rocking chair and move it without being seen by others— well, it would make sense.

She was my mother's mother. And my mother had had the echoes. I would say she'd had them worse than I ever had. *Was my grandmother worse off than my mother? Did the don get harder to deal with, with age? Was this my fate?*

"Hello?" My voice trembled as I stepped closer to the rocker.

I put my hand on the back of the chair, but when I leaned in to look over the cushions, there was no one there. I turned around and scanned the shadows in the room. Nothing. No one else was in the room except Abuela Estela and me—*stupid, deluded me.*

"She definitely looks like you," my grandmother said, talking to someone across the room by the door. "Same hair, same hands, but there is something else, something in the golden rays of her irises, there's moonlight in her pupils. Oh, yes, she has the ojitos too."

"What?" I asked, glancing back at the door. "Who are you talking to?"

Abuela Estela smiled at the shadows across the room before she turned back to me. "But she's not that innocent. She's not. She knew what she was doing."

"Knew what?" I asked.

"Yes, she knew," Abuela Estela continued. "She knew."

My body shook, and the tiny fine hairs on my forearms stood up and bristled. "Who are you talking to, Abuela?"

Abuela Estela's eyes sparkled under the wrinkled folds of her eyelids. Then she raised her sparse eyebrows and whispered, "Isabel!"

The revelation unmoored me.

I stepped backward, head spinning.

Breathless.

Derailed.

My stomach lurched, and I felt myself being tossed about, unable to find my way through the fog of confusion. "What?" I asked. "Do you mean—my mother?"

When she didn't answer, I asked again, "What did you say about my mother, Abuela?"

My grandmother turned back to the chair and grinned. She looked almost sinister in the shadows of her darkened bedroom. Her thin, dry lips curled up over her gnarled gray teeth, and her long incisors glistened as she smiled. I thought about the wolf in fairy tales, and a startled little laugh escaped my lips as I shook myself out of the strange delusion.

"Such a disgrace!" my grandmother whispered. "Disgrace. Disgrace. Never mind. What's done is done. Help me up."

My grandmother waved for me to help her. I reached out and she took my hand. I walked her to the bathroom, where she did her business in private, and when she came out, I followed close behind as she made her way to the kitchen and helped her sit down at the table.

I made her a cup of coffee and put it in front of her. Then, because I just couldn't let it go, I leaned in and asked, "Abuela Estela, did something happen to my mother? When she was young?"

"That's when things happen, isn't it? When we're

young." Abuela Estela took a sip of her coffee and frowned. "This is bitter."

"What happened?" I took the sugar bowl and put a teaspoon in, stirring absently. "Tell me. Please."

Abuela Estela looked at me, examined every line of my face, my eyes, my cheeks, my lips. Then she let her gaze linger on my hair and sighed.

"I had beautiful hair," she said. "He liked my hair. And my teeth. Not my smile. Just my teeth. Wouldn't let me smile in public. That's why he wanted me. He was ready to have children. And I had strong features. Good stock—that was important."

"Abuela—did you have other children?" I asked, shocked, because it hadn't occurred to me that my mother might have siblings I knew nothing about. I wondered why we had been told this part of the family was gone. "Do I have aunts? Uncles? Oh my god, Guelita! Do I have cousins?"

"No." The word coming out of Abuela Estela's lips was a long, negating whisper, disputing what must be, to her, a blasphemous thought. "I didn't want children. I was glad when the Lord didn't give them to us. No matter how much he tried. Day and night. Beating me. Suffocating me. Pulling my hair out by its roots. I wouldn't give him a child. I made myself tough— sterile. Some women are soft, they cry and plead and relent, lean into that abuse. Not me. I was a stone, a statue, refusing to be moved. And when he repented, when he said he was sorry for the bruises, for breaking my wrist—I spit in his face."

"He beat you. My grandfather beat you," I said, understanding why my grandmother chose to live in another world, inside her echoes, which explained why my mother might have wanted to keep us away from her. She wouldn't have wanted us, me, especially, to think this was normal. Maybe she didn't want us asking questions about our grandfather. Maybe she was protecting my grandmother as much as she was protecting me and Mercy.

"I hated that man! Hated him!" Abuela Estela screamed. Fat, angry tears sprouted out of my grandmother's eyes. They rolled down her cheeks slowly, like thick sap weaving its way past the cracks of ancient tree bark. "He stole my life! I tried to warn you, Isabel! You knew! You knew what could happen!"

My grandmother hung her head and sobbed. I reached over and put my hand on her back, rubbing small circles on it, to comfort her. After a while, my grandmother touched her cheek and looked at the tears glistening on her fingertips. She felt the glistening wetness of them and frowned, like she didn't understand where they were coming from.

"Guelita?" I questioned again, after she wiped her fingers dry against the fabric of her nightgown. "Do you know who I am? I'm Graciela, Isabel's daughter."

"Isabel?" Abuela Estela took a deep breath and sighed. "I don't know where she is. She never came back."

My grandmother stood up, steadied herself, and started shuffling slowly into the living room. "Let's go outside," she said. "I want to see the kittens."

It was dark by the time we went outside. Abuela Estela sat on the patio and talked to the kittens, pursing her lips and clicking her tongue as she called to them. "¡Gatitos! ¡Chiquitos!" she called in a soft purring voice until all five kittens crawled out from under the house and crept around the yard, sniffing the ground and licking the dew off the thin blades of grass as they made their way toward us.

"They're hungry," I said. "Should I feed them?"

"No," Abuela Estela said, reaching down and letting a yellow-striped kitten rub itself against the back of her hand. "They eat field mice. Birds and lizards and whatever else their momma brings for them. They don't need us. They have their mother for that."

I crouched down to pet the kittens as they came over, one after another, to sniff my hand. Two of them wrapped themselves around my leg, meowing and rubbing their faces and coats against my jeans. I looked up and saw that the work on the gardener's shed looked abandoned, like the roofers were not working on it anymore.

I brought out Abuela Estela's coffee and set it in front of her. "Abuela?" I asked, sitting on the chair beside her. "Who lives there? The gardener, what's his name?"

My grandmother didn't answer me right away. She petted another kitten and purred at it. "I forgive you," she said, sitting back on her chair and reaching up to smooth her hair with both hands. She wasn't looking at anything in particular. Her eyes became blank slates, although she seemed to be listening. "Is that what you want to hear, that I forgive you? Okay. Fine. I do. I forgive you. There, I said it. Now will you go away?"

A quiet breeze lifted my hair and tossed it over my eyes. I pushed it aside and glanced over at the dark, abandoned shed across the yard again. My grandmother's house wasn't much better, dark and gloomy in its own way. No telephone. No neighbors. No family. No wonder she talked to the shadows. No wonder she was lost to her hallucinations.

"Have you ever thought about crossing the border?" I asked in the early hours of that dawn. "To live with us?"

"I've crossed my borders," she said. "I'm done with that business."

"What do you mean?" I shifted, trying to make eye contact with my grandmother.

Abuela Estela picked up her spoon and stirred her coffee absently. "Some dinner would be nice," she finally said.

I sighed. "Come on. It's time to go inside."

CHAPTER FOURTEEN
Eagle Pass, Texas
July 2011

I AM FIXING DINNER WHEN MERCY COMES rushing in through the front door after work. From the open archway of the kitchen, Guelita Rosa and I watch as she dumps her purse on the coffee table and starts tearing through our old couch, lifting the seat cushions, pulling out the sofa bed, peering under the thin mattress, then shoving it all back together.

When she's finished giving the couch a thorough body inspection, Mercy goes through and checks the rest of the furniture in the living room. Then she goes into the kitchen and gets on her hands and knees to look under Guelita Rosa's old china cabinet in the breakfast nook. When she is done going through every piece of furniture in that area of the house, she stands with her hands on her hips in the middle of the living room, breathing heavily.

"What are you looking for?" I ask, mustering up the courage to talk to her. Instead of ignoring me like she's been doing for weeks, Mercy turns around and looks straight at me. Her eyebrows are deeply furrowed, and her mouth is pinched like a tiny red rosebud.

"Where are the shoes?" she asks.

"What shoes?" I ask, thinking of the piled-up boxes of shoes Mercy keeps in her closet, a ridiculously tall pile, thanks to the clearance racks at Macy's and her friend's employee discount. As far as I know, the boxes of shoes are still sitting in her room, undisturbed.

"No te hagas tonta." My sister's eyes glisten and she blinks, like she is trying hard not to get emotional. "His favorite shoes! You know, the ones he wore everywhere! Which other shoes would I be talking about, Grace?"

I think about it for a second, and then suddenly I understand. It isn't a surprise to me why she wouldn't want to go into specifics when referring to Alexander's red tennis shoes. "I haven't seen them. Not since—"

"Shut up! Just—shut up. You're useless, Grace—useless!" Mercy throws her arms up in the air and lets them fall against her sides like she gives up on me.

"I'm so sorry. Do you want to talk about it?" I ask, watching as she puts her left hand up to her eyes, placing her index finger and thumb against the bridge of her nose, pinching her tears away. Then, without saying another word to me, she rushes out of the living room.

"What did you expect? You're crowding her," Guelita Rosa says when I plop myself into a chair in the kitchen. I didn't see her standing there in the doorway until she speaks to me. "She needs her space."

After that incident, I become even more worried about Mercy. She's started working extra hours at the mall and is spending less and less time at home. She often comes home so late, I'm afraid she might be overdoing it. I tell myself not to worry because she's stopped crying herself to sleep after work in her room and seems to be sleeping more soundly at night.

Because there is nothing I can do for Mercy, not until August rolls around and I hand over her class schedule, I decide to keep myself busy too. Determined to do more than watch Guelita Rosa sit around swallowing pill after pill, I help her declutter her closets and sew and hang new curtains in the kitchen and dining room. And because he isn't around to stop me, I go into my father's room up in the attic and listen to his old records on his turntable and translate the lyrics of old Spanish songs into English, trying but not always succeeding to keep the musicality of the verses.

When I go through the clutter in my grandmother's

china cabinet, sorting old papers, stacking everything into piles, and tracing the faces of my grandparents in faded pictures, I come across a picture of Mercy as a baby. She is small and plump, and her eyes are big and shiny as pinacates, those round black beetles I used to pull out of Alexander's hands because he liked eating them. The fact that their pee stinks didn't stop him either. He just spit them out when they started tasting bitter.

In the picture, Mercy's hair is as curly as Alexander's. I consider taking it to my room, but with the way Mercy's been acting I know that wouldn't be a good idea, so I hold the picture against my chest and close my eyes instead.

When I open them, Alexander is there again, standing on his tippy-toes, clinging to the bay window in the kitchen with his tiny hands, his chin propped against the windowsill. His bright eyes are focused on the cardinals flittering in spurts of blurred reds and grays between the pink crepe myrtles in the backyard.

He turns around and smiles. "Under the bed," he says.

"What?" I ask, speaking out loud to him. "What's under the bed?"

"A present," Alexander says, letting go of the windowsill and running out of the kitchen in his bare feet. I sit there motionless for a moment. Then I jump up and run after Alexander. Of course he isn't in my room when I get there. But his shoes *are* under my bed. I can't figure out how they got there. Mercy keeps them in a sturdy white box along with his umbilical cord and his baptismal outfit. I have no idea how the shoes came to be there.

However, the shoes aren't the only things under my bad. Back, behind the shoes, against the farthest corner, I see a shoebox I do not recognize. I lie on my side and reach for it. My fingertips touch the rim of it and pull it toward me. I sit on the floor with my back resting against the frame of my bed. The box feels light as I shake it, but I can't tell what's rolling around in there, so I open it.

Dried flowers. The box is full of beautiful, perfectly preserved spring flowers: pink phlox, purple striped pansies, and stalks of lavender.

"What in the world . . ."

"For you," Alexander says. He is half-hidden behind the curtains of my window. "You like them?"

"I do," I say, looking up from the box to my sweet nephew.

I touch the delicate petals of a small purple flower and the scent rushes up my nose like a spring breeze, a floral scent so strong, so beautiful, I am overwhelmed with emotion.

Love.

For the first time in a long while, I felt utterly and completely loved.

"Thank you," I say, grateful to have Alexander in my life. "I love them very much."

Alexander plays with the curtains, flapping them side to side, wrapping them around himself, like a superhero cape. "She gave them to me."

"What?" I ask, but Alexander is busy making the curtains swoosh back and forth over and over again. "Who? Who gave them to you."

Alexander laughs. "The lady."

"What lady?" I ask.

"The nice lady," Alexander says, abandoning the curtain and looking out the window. "Out there."

He points into the yard.

I set the box down, haul myself up, and walk over to the window. Pulling the curtains aside, I look to where Alexander is pointing. There, sitting on the dating bench, I see a woman in a simple white dress. Her brown hair is loose, swirling around in the air before her, and her facial features are hidden behind its shadow. Her silhouette wavers and fades until it is as transparent as a silk curtain, and I realize it's a spirit—a visitation from the other side.

"Mom?" I whisper.

Suddenly, the wind picks up and the woman's hair billows away from her face, revealing the terrible thing

I had seen all those years ago—the skeletal face of my dead mother! My heart quickens, beats madly inside my chest, and I jerk aside, yanking the curtain away from Alexander and closing it as I press my back against the wall.

"Don't be afraid," Alexander says.

A strong wind comes through the open window. The curtains flutter upward, and I smell flowers again. "Graciela," a woman's voice calls to me softly, and my heartbeat roars in my ears. I close my eyes and pray, un Ave Maria, asking the Virgen de Guadalupe to stand by me. I haven't prayed to her since Alexander's velorio, but I can't think of anything better to do than to ask for protection.

The scent of flowers soothes me as I pray, and when I smell lavender, my eyes pop open and I look out the window again. "Mom?" I call, because I can't see the lady anymore.

Beside me, Alexander crinkles his nose. "You have a mom?" he asks.

"I do," I whisper.

My heart beats less frantically in my chest, and I pull the curtains back and scan the rest of the yard, because my visitor is no longer at the dating bench. The woman in the white dress is gone.

Vanished.

My hands tremble as I pick up Alexander's shoes. Because my sister's not home, I go into her room. I hear the doorbell ring as I place Alexander's shoes on the top shelf and shove the derailed door in front of Mercy's closet back into place so she doesn't think I was messing around in her room.

When I walk back out, Guelita Rosa is sitting in the dining room, looking out the window. "Well, don't just stand there," she says. "Answer the door."

I hesitate.

"Come on. That boy's coming around again," Guelita Rosa says, keeping her eyes on the porch.

"What?" I ask, looking out the window, into our front porch where Daniel is standing, holding a pile of packages against his chest. "What does he want now?"

"Only one way to find out," Guelita Rosa says, pointing at the door. "He's not going away, you know."

When I open the front door, Daniel is smiling so broadly, so expectantly, it makes me cringe, and I almost close the door on his face.

"Can I help you?" I ask, stepping outside and closing the door behind myself to talk to him privately.

"Hi," he says. His sunniness is disarming, and I sigh, letting the stress of the last few minutes slip from my mind and slide down my body like molasses. "I was just wondering if you wanted to go to the post office with me. I have to mail these prints for my mother. She usually mails them off herself, but she's got to finish a big project, and well . . ."

"The post office?" I ask, sounding a bit too annoyed for comfort. I can't help it. The guy is just not getting it.

Daniel clears his throat. "Wanna tag along? It's a nice day for a walk."

"No. I've got stuff to do," I say, crossing my arms and standing my ground.

Daniel blinks. His brown eyes roam over my face, as if he's trying to figure out what I'm thinking. Guelita is pretending to be busy. I can see her head bent over, acting like she's engrossed in her work, crocheting a white doily in the dining room, but I know she is more than watching. She's eavesdropping.

"Okay. Got it. Maybe next time," Daniel says, stepping away, taking each step carefully as he goes down the porch with the load of packages in his arms. I feel bad, but I can't help it. I don't want him to think I'm interested.

When I walk inside, Guelita Rosa puts down her crochet project and teases me. "Pobre muchacho, you're breaking his heart."

She points at Daniel, who is glancing back at our house as he leaves our yard. "Mira, he's a hard worker. *And* he loves his mami. Why don't you go help him?"

"You *were* listening!" I say, putting my hands on my waist.

"I may be old, but I'm not stupid," Guelita Rosa says. "You don't have to have good hearing to know what he wants."

"Argh! I can't listen to this right now!" I turn around and walk to my room.

I ignore Guelita Rosa's teasing the rest of the week as often as I ignore Daniel, but I spend a lot of time talking to Alexander in my room. He pops in when I least expect him. Usually, he just sits on my rocking chair and tells me all about the birds he sees flying about in the front yard outside the window. But mostly, he just comes to play with his toys.

Tonight, though, I'm a bit freaked out, because Alexander does something I hadn't thought possible. I am almost asleep when I feel the bed move. And when I open my eyes, he is lying curled up next to me—with our bodies touching!

"Night night?" he asks, like it is the most natural thing in the world that he should be sleeping beside me, stroking my hair, touching my face.

"Yes," I whisper. "Night night."

I smell flowers again. And again, I feel immense love. So, I close my eyes and pretend Alexander is really there—that he isn't dead. Although I don't dare to reach over and touch him, I swear he feels real to me as he strokes my cheek.

He is alive.

Alexander is alive and well and living in my room, but I can't tell anyone about it. Even Guelita Rosa, who is the only one who understands my don, would have a hard time believing that Alexander is alive.

CHAPTER FIFTEEN
Eagle Pass, Texas
August 2011

BEFORE I KNOW IT, JULY IS gone, taking with it the oppressive heat that suffocates everything. But my father is back from his three-week stint in Dallas. He is happy as he stands shirtless, shaving his beard over the sink in the restroom he shares with me and my sister.

I sit on the lid of the toilet, holding his foamy brush while he shaves the side of his neck carefully. I want to talk to him, to tell him that I'm *remembering things*, but he looks busy, like he's getting ready for something more than eating breakfast with his family. I get the impression that a long, honest talk with his youngest daughter is not in his plans right now.

When he first brought me home from Mexico, he asked me where I'd been on a daily basis. Then, after his frustration waned, he asked less and less frequently, until he stopped asking altogether. My memory loss became a thing of the past, and we all went on with our lives. But now, with my memory coming back to me bit by bit, I need to speak to someone, to process what I'm remembering. I can't talk to Guelita Rosa, she's not always kind, and Mercy won't even look at me.

"Dad?" I ask, when he leans over and rinses the soapy glob off his razor.

"Yes, Chatita?" he asks absently.

The nickname startles me.

"Don't call me that!" I say a bit too harshly.

My father turns off the faucet and looks at me sideways, frowning. "I'm sorry. I wasn't trying to be unkind. I meant it with cariño. You know that, don't you?"

"I do," I say. "It's just that you've never called me that before."

My father reaches over and pinches my nose. Then he takes the foamy brush out of my hand and starts toward me with it. I pull back, but I'm too late, he plops a glob of it on my nose and even smears some of it on my cheek.

"There's nothing wrong with being Chatita," he says. "You have your mother's button nose. It's cute."

My father goes back to shaving, the razor scratching at his foam-covered neck, and I know this is not a good time to tell him that I remember being at my grandmother's house and meeting a young man who used that name for me, but that it had felt wrong somehow, that he'd made me feel nervous and anxious. But then my father would want to know more, and I don't know more, because the memory of my time in Mexico is still foggy, patchy, like it's somehow not all there yet. Like there's more still trapped back there, in the recesses of my mind.

"I do look like her, don't I?" I say, thinking about it for the first time in a long time. Mercy looks like her too. She has those gorgeous cat eyes and those long, sweeping lashes, but she doesn't have her small flat nose or her dark skin. She's more of a cross between our parents. But me, I look a lot like our mother.

"You do," my father says. "Eres la imagen de tu madre, God rest her soul."

I think of Abuela Estela, and how she called me Isabel a couple of times when I was with her in Mexico. "Dad?" I start. "Do you have time to talk?"

"Sure," my father says, rinsing the foamy brush in the sink before setting it on the little shelf he put up above the toilet for his personal items. It is packed with everything male, from razors to nose-hair trimmers to cologne, because he doesn't want them getting all jumbled together with our *feminine stuff*. As far as that's concerned, he'd rather we keep our female products behind closed doors in the medicine cabinet. "I have a few minutes. What's on your mind?"

He scours the sink briskly and then rinses and dries it quickly. I know that he's in a hurry. But what I want to say—what I have to say—is going to take time. "Well, I wanted to tell you that, well, *I remember*," I whisper.

My father takes his powerful aftershave and pours a bucket of it onto his hands. It fumigates the whole room, and I reach over and crack open the bathroom door.

"Awww. You should," my father says, dousing his face and neck with the stinky stuff. "You should always remember your mother. She loved you, you know."

I want to tell him that's not what I meant, but he reaches behind the door and takes down his shirt, putting it on, then lifting the collar as he looks at himself in the mirror.

"Well?" he asks.

"You look great," I say.

"No," he says, looking down at me with an indulgent smile on his face. "I meant you. What did you want to talk about? I have to get out of here in a few minutes, but I'm here now."

"A few minutes?" I ask, wondering why he's leaving so soon after just getting home late. "You just got here. Where are you going now?"

My father turns around. He opens the door and walks out, saying, "Out. I have things to do . . . you know, gente to see."

"What people?" Guelita Rosa asks when she sees me trailing behind my father as we make our way into the living room.

"I'm on the hunt, Mamá," my father says, leaning down and giving my grandmother a quick kiss on the forehead. "A man has to do more than feed his family. A man has to be a leader. A paramount. We'll talk more later. Okay, Graciela?"

Sitting sideways next to Guelita Rosa, I put my arm over the back of the couch and watch through the living room window as my father gets his work stuff out of his truck. "He's acting strange," I tell my grandmother. "I wonder what's going on."

"Quien sabe," Guelita Rosa says, pulling on the pink yarn on her lap and turning back to work on a round doily. "Andará noviando."

I roll my eyes. "Ay, Guelita, why does everything have to be about that! He is not dating. He's too old for that."

Guelita stops crocheting and puts her project down on her lap. "Graciela Inés Torres. How dare you dismiss your father like that," she chastises. "He is not too old to date. My son is still strong, virile."

"He's forty-five," I say.

"Exactly," Guelita Rosa says. "He's in the prime of his life."

Outside, my father jumps off the bed of his truck and runs around to the front with the energy of a young man, and I have to admit he is not too old to date. But he is acting strange.

My father's odd behavior, however, is not the only thing amiss in our lives. There is something else going on in our house. Although Mercy is still refusing to speak to me, suddenly and without explanation, I notice that she is happy again. After my father leaves, and I am ensconced in a book, I hear music coming from her room as she gets ready for work. I open my door, step lightly over the pattern of white orchids on the faded linoleum floor, and press my body against her door, listening to the sounds of joyful verses coming from her lips. I can't believe my ears. On and on she goes, singing along to an old Selena tune the way she used to when she was in high school, before Jose—*before Alexander*.

When she stops, I bolt down the hallway and dash into the kitchen where Guelita Rosa is having a cup of coffee in the breakfast nook.

"What's with you?" Guelita asks.

I shrug and stare at the raggedy fingernails on my

right hand, thinking that I should stop biting them. It is a nasty habit, born out of stress and my inability to deal with it.

"She was singing," I whisper after a short pause.

Guelita Rosa puts the purple pill in her hand back on the saucer in front of her. It trembles next to its colorful neighbors.

"Mira," she says, nodding at something outside.

I pull the curtain aside. A strange guy has pulled into our driveway, and he is sitting in his idling car, waiting. I can't quite make out his face, but he has big tattooed forearms that rest on the ledge of his closed car door.

Mercy comes out of her room, and before I can get up the courage to ask her what is going on, she flies out of the house in a showy red dress I've never seen before. The skirt is short in the front, but the back is long and flowing. And when she runs down the porch steps into the driveway, it floats off her calves, billowing behind her—a scarlet blur, a bright red kite floating freely in the breeze.

CHAPTER SIXTEEN

Three Years Earlier

WHEN I WENT BACK OUT, I set Abuela Estela's plate in front of her on the patio table, laid a napkin next to it, and sat down on the porch steps. She didn't start eating right away. It wasn't until I got up and pushed the plate closer to her that she started to cut into the single egg with her fork.

On the steps, I sipped my coffee and watched my grandmother move that egg around on her plate over and over again, separating the yolk from the white, shoving one to the right and the other to the left, parking her fork between them. No matter how much I tried coaxing her to eat, Abuela Estela just kept moving the egg parts around, making a different arrangement with the two parts every time she picked up her fork to play with them.

After I while, I decided not to bother her anymore about it. "I'll be right back." I picked up my coffee cup and went back into the kitchen to rinse it out and put it on the rack. I'd eaten earlier, so I didn't fix myself anything else. But when I went back outside, my grandmother was gone. Her chair was pushed in and the momma cat was hunched over on the table licking her plate clean.

I shooed the cat away and picked up the dishes. The coffee was cold, so I tossed it into the grass, and then I called out to my grandmother, "Abuela?"

When I went looking for her inside, I heard the television murmuring softly in her room. She was sitting in the rocking chair watching reruns of an old telenovela that used to run when I was a child. Mercy and I had watched it when it first aired. We'd disliked the main character because she was too nice, and we hated the male lead. He was very handsome but so very wrong for her.

"There you are." I stood next to my grandmother's rocking chair. "Do you need anything else?"

My grandmother put her arms around herself. "This house is too cold," she said.

I took the throw off the back of the rocker and wrapped it around her shoulders. "There," I whispered. "Is that better?"

My grandmother ignored me again.

I didn't mind. I was beginning to get used to it. It had been naive of me to think there was some kind of cosmic reason I'd found her alive, out here with no one but Lucia to take care of her. There was nothing pre-destined about it. She was inaccessible to me, mentally and emotionally.

I sat beside her on the edge of the bed and watched the telenovela with her for a while. "I'm tired," I finally said. "I'm not used to staying up so late. Is there anything else I can get you?" When she didn't acknowledge me, I got up and walked to the door. "I'm going to take a quick nap. Just holler if you need anything. Okay?"

Nothing.

Abuela Estela's eyes were glued to the television, unblinking.

I had a sudden urge to turn it off, just to see what she would do, but that would have been rude. "Okay." I sighed. "I'll leave my door open. In case you need anything."

In my room, I fell asleep right away, resting so soundly that I didn't wake up for hours. When I opened my eyes, my grandmother was shuffling quietly away from my bed. "Abuela?" I called to her. "Did you need anything? Is it time for you to eat again?"

"We ate," she said without looking back at me.

I sat halfway up, putting my weight on my elbows on the bed. "Is Lucia back?" I asked. "Who did you eat with?"

When she didn't answer me, I sat all the way up. "Abuela? Is someone else in the house?"

"Yes," she said, as she pulled the covers away from me, folded them, and laid them aside on the cot.

"Who?" I asked. "Who's here?"

A draft whistled somewhere in the house and the follicles on the skin of my forearms rose up in tiny pimples. I could feel a chill seeping into my bones.

"Get up," she said. "You can't stay here anymore. What will people think?"

"What do you mean?" I asked. "You want me to leave?"

"Yes," Abuela Estela whispered. "Immediately."

"What?" I asked. "Why?"

My grandmother shuffled out of the room without answering me. I followed her into the hall, wondering what had prompted this sudden urge to have me out of the house. But as I stood in the hall, watching Abuela Estela walk to her room, I smelled flowers, fragrant and fresh, as if a summer breeze had suddenly come through a window. I stood very still, watching as my grandmother turned left at the end of the hallway and disappeared.

But someone else was in the hall.

From the corridor that led to the kitchen, I saw the misty, transparent form of a young woman come into view. She was wearing a pale, knee-length dress, and her form glided into the hall. Her long dark hair was swirling about her shoulders, and she was standing very demurely, her hands held in front of her, looking at me with shimmering, glittering eyes. She looked . . . she looked a lot like my mother.

"Mom?" I whispered, and she smiled and then the essence of her, her transparent mist form, disappeared.

I rushed forward, reaching into thin air, to the place where she had been standing, but there was nothing but the remnant of a floral scent, a whiff of lavender soap, and I knew it was her. I knew I'd just been visited by an earlier version of my mother, one with her beautiful, youthful face.

Tears pricked at my eyes, and I wandered around Abuela Estela's house looking for the ghost of my mother for about half an hour, with my heart in my throat—hoping to find her, but worried about what I would say, what I would do, if I did.

Finally, when I couldn't sense any trace of her, I went to bed and fell back asleep. After an indeterminate amount of time, I woke up and looked around, confused. *Did I dream it?* I got out of bed and pushed my feet into my sandals because the concrete floor was ice cold. I pulled the thin sheet off my bed and wrapped myself in it before I went through the house looking for the source of the cold air. It was summer. There was no logical reason why the house should be so cold.

I found the window above the sink in the kitchen wide open and reached up to close it. That's when I saw a shadow move outside.

I must have screamed, because the shadow jumped away. "Hey!" someone called quietly from the darkness. "Don't be afraid. It's me, Manuel."

"Manuel?" I stood on my tiptoes and peered out the window. "It's the middle of the night. You shouldn't be here."

"I know it's late," Manuel admitted, stepping closer to the window. In the moonlight seeping through the shadows of the night, I could see his dark eyes glinting up at me. "I couldn't sleep."

I looked at him for a second and then put my feet flat against the floor. *Close the window*—my rational mind whispered, but I couldn't do it. I was so scared I couldn't get my body to obey.

"That's too bad," I finally said. "But there's nothing I can do about that. Go home, Manuel."

"I can't," Manuel said.

"Yes, you can," I said. "Put one foot in front of the other and go. Simple as that." Then I reached up and closed the window as fast as I could without looking at him.

When I went back to my grandmother's room, Abuela Estela seemed to have forgotten about asking me to leave. She asked me to help her lie down for a nap, instead, but told me to leave the television on.

"Go back to your room," she said. "I can't hear with you breathing over me all day like this. Go on. Get out of here."

Confounded and more than a little unsettled by the night's events, I went to my room. I don't know if it was actual cold or fear that made me do it, but I wrapped myself up like a burrito in my sheet and curled up into a fetal position on my cot. Before I knew it, I was fast asleep.

When I woke up, it was morning again, and I wasn't cold anymore. I tossed the sheet aside and went looking for my grandmother. Abuela Estela was in the kitchen. The kittens were under her feet and the momma cat was eating something off a plate on the chair beside her.

"What time is it?" I slipped my hand under the momma cat's belly, pulled her off the chair, and placed her gently on the floor between us. I picked up the plate, put it in the sink, and ran some water on it. There was cheese residue sitting on the rim. "Why didn't you wake me? I would've fixed you something warm to eat."

"The sun's coming out," Abuela Estela said. She stood up, shuffled over to the window, and fussed with the curtains. "Help me close these things. My eyes are old. I can't have this much light."

"I know. I'm sorry," I said. "I forgot to do that after I closed the window."

"I'm going to my room," she said, and she shuffled out of the kitchen. I tried helping her, but she kept slapping me away. She sat in the rocking chair and watched the television set intently.

Alone in the kitchen, I scrambled some eggs and ate them standing at the sink. I could tell the roofers were back, because I could hear them talking as they worked on the gardener's shed again. I was a bit sad to see them out there, because it meant I wasn't going to be able to go outside until they left. After his creepy behavior the night before, I wasn't about to give Manuel another opportunity to speak to me.

That day, I worked on the kitchen, cleaning the pantry, scrubbing the refrigerator and stove inside and out, and washing every dusty dish in the cupboard. I didn't go outside for two days, until I saw that the roof on the shed was completed, and Manuel and his co-worker were nowhere in sight.

Relieved, I took a few dollars from my wallet and walked down to the postecito at the corner and bought some fresh vegetables and a fragrant papaya. The calabash-looking fruit was so big, it would probably take me days to finish eating it, and that was if I ate from it every day.

The young blonde woman at the postecito asked me if I was visiting, but I didn't feel like being social, so I said, "No speak Espanish."

The girl glared at me from behind the cash register, scoffed, and rolled her eyes. When she gave me my change, she waved at me and said, "Hasta luego, pinche pocha."

I waved back and smiled and pretended I didn't know what she'd just called me.

When I got to my grandmother's house, I put the small bag of groceries away. Then I went into the garden. It was such a beautiful day, I sat on the grass and ate a plateful of papaya slices, savoring every sweet bite of orange flesh while I stared at the rust-colored sunset.

When I was done, I put the plate aside and leaned back, my elbows anchored on the bed of purple petals. Their light, delicate fragrance perfumed the air around me, and I closed my eyes and let the sun kiss my face. I could have stayed like that, frozen still in that beautiful moment forever, but I heard a noise and when I opened my eyes, I saw Manuel standing on the gardener's roof, staring down at me intently.

I sat very still, regulating every breath, every blink, so as not to make him think I was doing anything but enjoying my day—by myself.

For myself.

Then, without dropping his gaze, Manuel reached down, undid his toolbelt, and let it drop at his feet. It rolled off the side of the roof and fell to the ground with a heavy thud. I sat up then, intending on going inside, but before I could stand, Manuel descended. Taking giant steps, he bounded across the roof, slid off the side, climbed down a ladder, and ran toward me. When he jumped over the fence, I scrambled to my feet and ran toward the house. I hurried through the nearest entrance, which led straight into my bedroom. I slammed the door shut, locked it, and then immediately collapsed against it.

My body shook, my legs felt like weak rubber bands, and my heart knocked against my sternum like a trapped cardinal inside a glass cage. *Did that really happen? Did Manuel really rush at me? Or did I imagine the whole thing?*

I was ready to believe I was having one of my echoes when suddenly I heard a small tap, a quiet knock on the door. I stood very still and listened as Manuel tapped lightly on the door again. The only other sound in the room was the thumping of my bewildered heart, beating numbly against my ribcage.

"Cha-ta? Cha-ti-ita? Let me in, muñeca." Manuel's voice was gentle, beseeching.

I stood pressed against the door and didn't answer.

My body stiffened, I stayed very still, pushing my left shoulder against the door, wondering what I could do, where I could go, if he chose to push his way through.

CHAPTER SEVENTEEN
Eagle Pass, Texas
August 2011

I AM STARTING TO GET MORE AND more worried about Mercy. She's spending more evenings out than in since she's gone back to work, and she's always got somewhere to go after work. Even more telling is the fact that a different car is bringing her home every night. I mean, I'm all for dating, but she needs to slow down. She doesn't have to go through the whole town to find a new husband.

Because it hasn't escaped my attention that my sister has so many guys around now, I can't keep track of who's who. It is hard to tell if they're coworkers, platonic friends, or actual love interests because she acts the same with all of them. Night after night, she throws her arms around their necks and kisses every one of them before she gets out of their cars.

But it isn't just the dating that's bothering me. There is something else going on. This evening, I watched Mercy get out of an older man's car. It was a nice car. Big. Expensive. I don't know makes or models, but I could tell by the fancy hood ornament, the gold handles and trim, that it was either a Caddy or a Lexus. It doesn't matter. It's what happened next that is bothering me.

Mercy walked around the car and let the older man with the crooked red tie pull out a bundle of bags and hand them to her. When she tried taking them, he wrapped his arm around her waist, pulled her in, and kissed her. Mercy twirled the bags in her left hand and put her right hand out, palm flat against his chest between them, to keep him at a distance after the first kiss.

It was dark, after midnight, but I could see them clearly in the moonlight. The man smiled and shook his head, but then he pulled out his wallet and gave her a few bills out of it. Mercy stared at the money sitting on the palm of her hand and laughed. Then she wrestled his wallet away from him and pulled out the rest of the bills from it. He took his wallet back and leaned in to kiss her. Instead of pushing him away again, Mercy put her skinny arms around his neck and leaned into the kiss. I squeezed my eyes shut, hoping to erase what I'd witnessed. Then I closed the curtain too, and slipped back into bed while Mercy came in, acting all quiet and innocent.

Now I'm lying here, quietly listening to Mercy move around in her room, putting up her wares in her closet, hiding her treasures, afraid I might want to borrow something, completely unaware of just how repulsed I am by every single ill-gotten item in her room. But no matter how hard I try to ignore what I have seen, I can't reconcile it in my mind, so I get up and walk to her room.

When I burst through the door, Mercy shoots up in bed and pulls a fuzzy red sleeping mask off her face. "Grace!" she screams. "What the hell!"

"Don't!" I say, my voice trembling with rage. "Don't tell me to leave!"

"What is it?" she asks. Her eyes are luminous, beautiful, even without all that makeup she globs on every morning. "What's wrong?"

"What's wrong?" I ask, my breath coming in great big huffing gulps. "Look, Mercy. I'm your sister, and I know I'm younger than you. But I'm not too young to set you straight."

"Grace, get out of my room!" She waves the stupid-looking sleeping mask in the air, toward the door. "Now!"

I tear the sleeping mask out of her hand and brandish it in her face as I yell, "Look, Miss Universo! I don't care how smart you think you are, you're not some sexy movie star. What you're doing is wrong and I'm not going to stand by and watch you throw your life away anymore!"

"Give me my mask back." Mercy holds her hand out.

I toss the flimsy mask aside. It clinks against the closet door. Mercy opens her mouth like she is about to say something important, but I don't let her talk. "I saw you," I hiss. "I was right there, watching you from the window. I can't believe you, Mercy. Taking money from that old man. It's disgusting. It's—it's . . . immoral!"

"You're spying on me?" Mercy pushes the bedcovers aside and gets out of bed. "Why are you spying on me?"

"I'm your sister. That's my job," I say. "I can't just stand by and watch you become a—a . . ."

"Go ahead," Mercy taunts. "Say it. You can't say it, can you?"

"That's not what I meant," I whisper, because I don't want Guelita Rosa or my father to hear us arguing about this. I could be wrong. I don't want to be right. Mercy's my sister. I love her.

"Think whatever you like, Grace," Mercy says, picking up her face mask and putting it back on top of her head. "You always do anyway. You never give me credit for being smart."

"What if you get caught?" I ask. "Have you thought about that? It's illegal, what you're doing."

"Oh my god!" Mercy blusters. Her eyes are shining, and I worry that she might start crying. That she might break down and say I'm completely right about her.

"Tell me I'm wrong," I whisper. *I want to be wrong. I do.*

"Get a grip, Grace. They're gifts, all right! Gifts!"

Mercy crosses the room, slides the closet door open, and shuffles the clothes across the rack one by one, showing me their tags. "See? There's nothing illegal about getting gifts from men. I go out with them and they buy me nice things. I can't help it if men like to buy me nice things."

"So, you're for sale now?" I ask. "Is this what you're going to do from now on? Instead of going to college with me like we planned, you're becoming someone's mistress?"

Mercy picks up a Gucci purse and traces the golden letters on its clasp. "I'm not a prostitute, if that's what you're implying," she whispers. She sounds so small, so young, it's hard to believe she is a whole year older than me.

"Then why did he give you money?" I ask.

"For Alexander," she whispers. "So, I can get him a nice grave marker. We went there this afternoon, and he saw that stupid tin plate the funeral home put up. He's a good guy, Grace. He cares about me."

I reach out and touch her shoulder. "I'm sorry. I didn't know," I whisper.

"Don't!" Mercy slaps my hand off her shoulder and hugs the huge purse up to herself like it's a shield. "This is all your fault!" she cries. "Get out of my room!"

"Mercy, please," I whisper. "Don't push me away! Let me help you. Can we talk, please? We need to talk about school."

Mercy shakes her head. Tears burst from under her downcast eyes and start streaming down her face, and she wipes her cheeks and nose with the sleeve of her pajama top. "No," she says. "Everything's messed up and it's all your fault. I hate you, Grace! I really, really hate you!"

Tears start to slide down my face too, and it breaks my heart seeing her so torn up, so broken, because of me. Because I wasn't paying attention. Because I wasn't present. But I'm present now. I am. And I want to make things right, but it's clear to me that this isn't working. I need to find a way to connect with her again—to make her see how important she is to me. How much I love her.

"Mercy, please," I whisper. "Please, don't push me away."

"Just leave me alone." Mercy moves away then. She turns around and yanks the door open. "Go!" she screams. "Get out! Now!"

CHAPTER EIGHTEEN

Three Years Earlier

IN THE EARLY EVENING, ABUELA ESTELA sat at the picnic table, cooing and throwing bread crumbs at a couple of gray pigeons milling around the edge of the porch, while I watered the plants. Just then, something caught the corner of my eye.

The rusty latch on the fence gate squealed and I froze. Manuel entered and came down the side yard. He stepped up onto the porch and nodded his acknowledgment to my grandmother, who acted like he wasn't there and went back to cooing at the birds.

"I'm sorry I scared you this morning," Manuel said.

He was standing so close to me that I started to tremble. Angry at myself for feeling so vulnerable, I put my thumb over the mouth of the water hose and sprayed the plants, making sure Manuel's feet got a good hose down in the process.

"You were trespassing," I reminded him. "That's against the law."

"Yes," he admitted. "I'm sorry about that too."

Manuel stepped back and shook the water off his boots, but he didn't say anything else. He just stood there waiting for me to acknowledge his pathetic apology. But I wouldn't give him the satisfaction. I put my thumb back on the lip of the hose and sprayed everything around me. Every plant on the porch, every pot of ivy hanging from the hooks on the side of the house, got a forceful, violent shower.

"Be careful." Manuel pointed at his boots. "These are new."

Like I care, I thought.

I kept watering the plants because I didn't have the words to tell him what I was feeling. I wanted him to know that rushing at me like he'd done that morning was not okay, but I didn't know how to say it without sounding like a scaredy-cat. The last thing I wanted this guy to think was that I was a weakling—that I didn't know how to defend myself. Because I did.

"Are you done, Abuela?" I called back to my grandmother. "You ready to go back inside?"

I needed to move, to get away from Manuel, to let

him know that he wasn't welcome in my grandmother's yard. Soaking him down wasn't doing the trick. "It's late," I said. "We should go in."

"So that's it?" Manuel asked, putting his hands on his hips. "You're not going to talk to me."

I sighed. "I have nothing to say to you."

Manuel threw back his head and laughed. Then he put his hand on his chest and said, "Come on, now. You're breaking my heart, mamita. I came all the way back just to chat with you. Is this any way to treat your friends?"

"Friends?" I dropped the water hose and turned to twist the knob off at the spigot. "Don't be ridiculous. We are not friends. I don't even know you."

"Well, that's why I'm here," he said. "To get to know you."

"I don't have time for this."

I walked over to the patio table and picked up my grandmother's cup and saucer. I tossed the coffee into the grass and reached for her dishes. The single egg on her plate was scrambled up and swirled beyond recognition. I couldn't tell if she'd even tasted it, but I was sure she wasn't going to eat it. She was too busy feeding the pigeons bits of bread. I tossed the eggs at the kittens lying about under the table and nestled the saucer and cup over the plate. "Come on, Abuela Estela. Let's go," I told my grandmother, taking hold of her arm.

Abuela Estela stood up and shuffled back to the house. I opened the door for her. Manuel stood on the porch, hands on his hips, watching us as we entered the house. I closed the door and locked it behind me. I don't know how much longer he stayed there. I refused to look.

CHAPTER NINETEEN

Eagle Pass, Texas
August 2011

THE SUMMER GOES BY FAST. BEFORE I know it, it is time to start the fall semester at the community college. I have the horrible feeling that losing Alexander has derailed Mercy completely, because starting school never enters her mind. We had planned to do the college thing together, sign up for rotating schedules, and take turns watching Alexander while the other one was in class. We'd talked about sitting in the student center watching the giant television screen and munching on French fries between classes. But those conversations can never be had again. They are gone. Dead and buried with Alexander.

But even though Mercy and I never talk about

school anymore, I do what I have to do to make sure she is all set to go, because, to be honest, I don't want her to depend on this new guy to save her the way she depended on Jose. I want her to be her own woman, to get an education, to build a career and be able to support herself.

Besides buying her books, which I can't afford to do, I pick up two of everything when I go to the bookstore. I pick up two of every flyer at the student-life office too, always making excuses about how my sister is at work but I am taking things to her.

Since the course selections can be done on one of the two computers there, where no one really knows or cares what's going on, the student adviser never catches on, and I register Mercy for classes without a problem.

I make sure there is nothing else Mercy or I will need to do to get the refund on our financial aid. Mercy and I are good at forgery. We'd been signing our father's name on all our school forms since we hit middle school— even though he was perfectly capable of reading English and filling out forms, my father hated doing it.

I toy with the idea of letting Mercy know that I am choosing her courses for community college. So many times, I've walked across the hall in the middle of the night with our printed course schedules trembling like maple leaves in my hands. But then I stop in front of her room and chicken out. I consider rapping gently and slipping hers under her door, but I just never do.

Doing that seems even more cowardly than standing night after night holding those papers in front of her door. The whole thing is too burdensome, too emotionally draining, so I just keep doing things on the sly and hoping she'll understand when the time comes to start attending classes.

The weekend before school starts, I begin to wonder how in the world I am going to tell Mercy that she's enrolled in twelve hours at Southwest Texas Junior College. I sit on the dating bench my father built when Guelita Rosa decided Mercy and I were of age and think about what I have done. How will Mercy take it when she finds out I've gone as far as picking out her semester schedule for her? Will she be angry because she'd rather pick the times herself?

I sit there pondering how to approach Mercy about starting school while Guelita Rosa and her comadres ramble on and on in their seats on the porch. Most people's grandmothers are nice. They bake pies and cookies and drink iced tea as they rock back and forth on their porches. Not my grandmother. Guelita Rosa can be cruel as an old urraca.

On Saturday afternoons, she perches herself on

a wooden bench on the porch surrounded by her comadres: Doña Sofia, La Nena, and Las Gemelas, Luisa and Olivia de Leon, twin sisters with twin bulbous moles trembling on the side of their noses. The two of them talk, and talk, and talk, smacking their prunish lips as they wheeze, spit, and blow their noses violently into the handkerchiefs on their laps. Guelita Rosa says the twins never got married because of those moles. I say they were too busy digging into other people's lives and sharing it with the neighborhood to find someone to marry them. Who wants a snotty, snooty chismosa for a wife anyway?

Eventually, the comadres close the gate and part ways, going toward their respective homes. "You know what I think?" Guelita Rosa asks as she sees them off. "I think the twins are right. That new woman next door, Connie, is up to no good. Luisa said Connie walked into the Walgreens yesterday and picked up some of those contraceptions, you know for putting over the man's privates."

"Grandma!" I say, blushing at her words.

"What?" My grandmother huffs. "Oh, please, don't pretend you don't know what I'm talking about. Contraceptions are nothing new. Those things have been around for centuries. Cleopatra used to use them, you know."

I shook my head. "They're called contraceptives, not contraceptions," I say, sighing and looking down the road toward the intersection of Williams and Brazos Streets, where the Gemelas are waiting for the city bus to pick them up.

I look at our neighbor's house. Daniel's mother couldn't have been buying condoms. She is new in town and, as far as I can tell, she is a shy woman who keeps to herself. She has no need of contraceptives. I keep my eyes on the horizon. The Sacred Heart Church is on the next block. I can see the pale outline of the white steeple against the azure sky from where I sit. How many years has it been since we've set foot in that church for anything other than a funeral?

"Well, it's true. That's what they're for!" Guelita says. "It's shameful, really. Back in my day, women didn't need such things. We just crossed our legs and kept our goodies to ourselves. We didn't go around looking for trouble the way women do now."

I put my hand on my forehead and close my eyes. My grandmother claims she can say whatever she wants because she doesn't have any hair on her tongue. She always says what's on her mind, even when nobody wants to hear it.

"Please, Guelita!" I say, shaking my head and shifting uncomfortably on the narrow courting bench.

"What?" Guelita Rosa asks. "It's true. I'm not making it up."

"I know," I say, taking a deep breath and releasing it slowly, because our neighbor's sex life is not even on my radar. I have bigger fish to fry. "I just wish Mercy would do that more often. Keep her goodies to herself, I mean."

"Hmm. Your mother was like her, you know," Guelita Rosa says. "That poor girl—God rest her soul— was always looking for man trouble. Starved for affection, she was, when she was young, before she married your father. Dear Lord, before he took her in and put a ring on her finger, your mother made ojitos at every man that crossed her path. I told your father all about her, about the way she'd been carrying on before he came home, when he was working up in Nebraska, but he didn't care what she'd done before he met her. He loved her and wanted to marry her—said he'd make an honest woman of her."

"That's not true," I say, horrified.

Why haven't I ever heard this before? Is Guelita Rosa's medicine messing with her memory, or is she just being her usual spiteful self? I've heard her say some mean things before, like that thing she said about Mercy having no business having a baby, but this is way out there. It seems the older she gets, the more pill bottles crowd each other on her dresser, the meaner she's becoming. This, however, is beyond anything I ever expected from her.

"You're lying!" I hiss under my breath, fighting back my tears.

"No, it's true," she insists, fixing her cloudy old eyes on me in a way that makes the tiny hairs on my arms stand on end. I shiver with rage. "That's where your sister gets it."

Now there's a stab between the ribs! There is no denying Mercy's always been boy-crazy. But that's normal. My eyes burn as my grandmother's words swirl around in my head. *Could it be true? Is Mercy just like my mother? She doesn't have the don. I got that. But what does it mean, this impulsiveness, this waywardness?*

I remember Abuela Estela telling me my mother left home, that she never saw her again, and I wonder if this is the reason they became estranged, the reason Mom never told us about Abuela Estela, the reason she told us she was dead.

The possibility shakes me to the core, and I push the whole thing out of my mind, because I can't deal with it right this minute. "Well, even if it is true and my mother was the same way, I really don't want to hear it. So keep it to yourself, okay?"

"I will not. It's time you grow up, Grace. Your sister is not wicked. She's just starved for affection. Just like your mother was." Guelita Rosa's voice quivers with emotion. "'*Why are you like this, Isabel?*' I asked her once. '*Why are you so starved for affection?*' And you know what she said?"

I slide sideways in my seat, away from Guelita Rosa. "I should get dinner going!" I start to haul myself off the dating bench, but Guelita Rosa puts her hand on my shoulder and pushes me back down. It isn't that she's that strong, but if she wants to keep me there, to torture me with *revelations* about my mother, there isn't much I can do about it. As my elder, I owe her my attention. She knows I am too good a granddaughter to disrespect her by walking away while she is still talking to me, so she goes on.

"She told me a story," Guelita Rosa says. "About her mother." Her eyes shine as she speaks. "She sat at my kitchen table and said her mother had been her tormentor, a horrible, abusive woman who threw her out of the house when she was a young woman—refused to see her again, disowned her. I can only imagine that's what hardened her, made her so cold, so bitter."

My heart pounds against the walls of my rib cage, crying out, raging. My vision blurs with unshed tears, and my mind reels the longer I sit there. *Was my mother really as cold in her youth as Guelita Rosa is portraying her?* It's hard to tell what is what. I have very few memories of my mother. And most of them are tainted by my own echoes, like the bloody fistful of flowers that I saw in her hands a few days before she was murdered.

Suddenly I have a terrible headache.

I close my eyes, shake my head, and try to ignore what is happening, but the wind is blowing now, a warm breeze hits my face, and a strange scent engages my senses. It creeps up into my nose, curls itself behind my eyes, and begins growing tiny, invisible arms, a series of fragrant floral notes that overwhelm me, an echo so strong, so vivid, that I can't shake it off.

A woman is standing a few feet away from me in a long gray nightgown. Her white hair, wild and disheveled, hangs over her face like a hazy curtain, and she is all slapping hands and angry, blood-shot eyes. I can't quite see her face as much as I see her hair flying around that loud, screaming mouth.

Her lips move angrily. They purse after every question, then open immediately, to scream and shout, over and over again.

"What are you doing?" she screams.

And the boy—the boy is slapped off me—he scuffles away, gets up, his long legs sticking out from under the khaki shorts, naked from knees to ankle socks, brown and wiry and covered in dirt as he runs off into the grass, away from the wall of the house, where I am pinned down by the screams and slaps of an old, angry woman.

And me—I am clutching two flat copper pennies, shiny and new in my hand, wondering what is so wrong about playing with him for a few minutes.

"What were you doing?" the woman screams. Her lips are an angry, jagged line running crookedly across her wrinkled face. "What were you doing with that boy?"

"I was cradling him," I say, because it's the truth. That's all I know. That's all I understand of what's happened.

"What?" she screams. "Tell me the truth, Graciela! What were you doing with him?"

"I wasn't doing anything wrong," I cry. "He was the baby. I was the mami. I had to love him. I had to kiss him."

"Who told you that?" The woman's hands grip my arms, and she shakes me. Hard. "Who told you he was your baby and you should kiss him? Did he tell you that?"

I open my hands and show her the two shiny coins, coppery brown and beautiful in the morning sunlight. "Yes."

She slaps the pennies out of my hand.

They go flying, bounce off the dirt, and land somewhere in the weeds, disappearing into the bright green blades of grass higher than the boy's knees. "You don't do that, Graciela!" she screams. The words flutter out of her angry mouth like frightened red birds. "You don't let boys climb all over you like that. Never, ever let anyone do that again!"

"He was my baby," I explain. "I was cuddling him."

The woman slaps me. Again and again her hand slaps

me, on the cheek, on my arms, and on my thighs, as I scrunch up, hide my face, and cry into my hands.

"You're not a carnival ride!" she screams, pulling my hands away so I look at her. "¡Me entiendes! You. Don't. Do. That!" she screams. Her angry lips make out each word again deliberately, shaking me while her hands threaten to snap my wrists and pull my hands off the ends of my arms. "You-don't-do-that! Do you understand?"

Then, because my face is hurting, I cry out, "Yes! Yes!"

Slobber dribbles down my lips, past my chin, and onto my hands. "I don't do that! I don't! Never!"

"And you don't take money from boys!" She takes my hands and holds them inside hers, squeezing them hard, crushing my fingers, collapsing them against my soft palms. "Do you hear me? Never. Ever. Take money from boys. You understand? Tell me you understand!"

"I understand," I nod, sniveling out the words obediently.

Then my mother is there.

"What are you doing?" she says, pushing the woman away, picking me up, and holding me tight. "She doesn't know what this is! She's a child, for God's sake. A child."

I close my eyes tight and fight the echo with all my willpower. *Stay in the moment. Be present. Stay present,* I keep telling myself as the woman's words swirl around in my head over and over again.

"She's a child! A child!"

"Graciela!" Guelita Rosa slaps at my cheek a little too harshly. "Graciela! Can you hear me?"

"What?" I ask, focusing on Guelita Rosa's lips. I touch my cheek where she slapped it as I try to make sense of what's happened, because in that very moment I am not sure if what I've just experienced was an echo or a very deeply embedded memory.

It felt real enough.

I could call it a memory if I could be sure that was Abuela Estela slapping the pennies out of my hand and yelling at me, but the sights and sounds had been so distant, so foggy and convoluted by the terror they brought out in me that I couldn't be sure if it was a memory, an echo, or a visitation—because my mother was there. She'd come to my rescue. But I was young, so it had to be some sort of repressed memory.

Guelita Rosa looks down at me intently, a frown puckering the skin between her thin eyebrows. She shakes her head. "I swear, child. You give me pause."

"Pause? Me? I don't see why," I say, playing the whole thing off, pretending it didn't happen, at least until I can recall it and try to make sense of it. "I'm the good one, remember?"

My grandmother lets out a sigh and purses her lips as she looks at me and shakes her head again.

"What?" I ask, pushing my hair out of my face

and turning to look at her directly. "How am I bad? Tell me."

"Where were you right now?" my grandmother asks. "Where did you go?"

Where were you?

Where?

Where?

I push the rambling questions out of my mind and tell myself I can't have another echo. Not one after another.

When I don't answer her, when I cast my eyes down and pick at the fringe of my jean shorts, Guelita Rosa starts up again. "How far you go when you get one of your echoes gives me cause for concern, child. I have to worry—because of your mother. You understand, don't you, that I had to slap you?"

"I guess," I say, glaring at her, because her slap reminds me again of the echo I just had, and I shudder at the thought of it.

"I had to snap you out of it," Guelita Rosa says. "I had to make sure that thing didn't take over you, the way your mother used to let hers dominate her life. We don't have to repeat the bad patterns of those who birthed us, you know. You have the power to control this thing—this gift. Please tell me you won't let it take over your life, Graciela. Promise me that."

"I'm not," I say, rubbing my stinging cheek. "I wouldn't—"

"Mercy has to learn to control herself too," Guelita Rosa says, letting out a long, deep breath. "But she's being stubborn. We have a lot of work to do on that one."

"Can I go now?" I ask, inching away from her on the bench. "Mercy's getting off work soon, so I should really get dinner started."

"I wouldn't worry about her!" Guelita says.

"Why not?"

Guelita smirks, a crooked little uplift on the left side of her mouth. "She put one of those things in her purse this morning."

"What things?" I ask, putting my hand on my brow to block the sun as I look up into my grandmother's shimmering eyes.

She winks at me then, and laughs. "You know," she finally says, leaning down to whisper it, like it's our little secret. "One of those contraceptions."

"Argh!" I stand up and move to walk away, refusing to discuss with my grandmother what I know is probably true. "I don't want to hear this!"

"But you will," Guelita Rosa says, taking hold of my wrist and keeping me there. "I need to tell it and you need to hear it. You're not a child anymore, Grace.

From now on, we speak truth to each other. Plain out. No more secrets. Understood?"

"Yes," I whisper.

"Good," my grandmother says. "That's the way it should be. The way it should have been all along, generations and generations ago. We haven't done each other any favors, keeping secrets from our own."

As I consider her words, something stirs inside me, and the question that has been hanging in the air between us for years suddenly comes out. "Guelita? Why did she do it? Why did she leave the house that night?"

Guelita Rosa takes a deep breath and sighs. A sickly little breeze blows by and the leaves on the mulberry tree rustle sadly overhead, and she slumps over a bit.

"No clue," my grandmother says. "You probably know more about it than I do. I just wish your father had been able to stop her. She'd still be alive if he had. Haunted by her echoes, by the thing she couldn't have stopped, but alive nonetheless. ¡Ay, qué pena! ¡Qué pena!"

CHAPTER TWENTY

Eagle Pass, Texas
August 2011

BECAUSE MERCY IS STILL PRETENDING I don't exist in her world, I do the only thing I can do to let her know about school. I sneak into her room and put the red backpack I bought for her at the college bookstore on her bed and lay her class schedule on top of it.

Satisfied, I go back to the kitchen and put the big acero on the stove and turn the heat on low. As I take out all the ingredients for enchiladas, I think of what I'm going to say to her when she finds the backpack and schedule on her bed. She'll have to rethink her dating once school starts, but I made sure her classes were all in the evenings, so she won't have to stop working during the day.

She'll also have to go pick up her refund from her

financial aid at some point, but I figure I'll tell her about that once she gets over me signing her up for school. It'll probably soften the blow when she hears we qualified for a needs-based grant, which means everything is paid for and she even has a few hundred dollars coming back to her.

I am browning rice in hot vegetable oil, getting it ready for the herbed chicken broth that'll soak into it and make it tender and soupy the way Guelita Rosa likes it, when Mercy comes bouncing into the house. She lays her purse on the coffee table by the door and rushes off to her room. I hear her door slam and stop stirring, staying as silent as possible, listening for a clue as to how she is taking the news of being enrolled in school for the fall.

I don't have to wait very long.

A few minutes later, Mercy opens the door and comes walking into the kitchen holding her schedule with both hands. "Where did this come from?"

"I . . ." The words get caught in my throat and I can't get them out no matter how hard I try. "I . . ."

"You did this?" she asks. Her perfectly styled brows are two beautifully painted birds facing off low on her forehead as she frowns at me. "Answer me, Grace!"

I clear my throat. "Well, you've been so busy—" I start, but then nothing else comes out. Her eyes glisten, then narrow, and her lips tremble as she tries to talk. "You had no right!" she finally cries, tossing the schedule onto the table.

"School starts Monday," I say quietly, so as not to scare her away. I know this is going to be a big step for her. But she can do it. I know she can. "Don't worry, we don't have any classes together. I made sure of that."

Mercy's nostrils flare, then quickly collapse against the sides of her nose, again and again, like the hooded flaps of a tiny cobra. When she finally speaks, she chooses her words carefully, deliberately. "You little worm!" she screams. "Where did you get my information? How did you do this? Did you forge my signature?"

"Someone had to," I say, offended by the comparison to a slimy thing. "It's not like you were ever going to do it. You've been too busy making the rounds!"

"You witch!" Mercy screams.

Then, before I have time to get away, she goes for my hair. I try to pull away from her, ducking out of her reach, but she spins around, loses her balance, and pushes me backward with the force of her movement. I slam hard against the counter. I reach back, trying to catch myself. I don't remember the pan of frying rice on the stove, and the palm of my hand lands on the handle of the skillet. The movement jostles it just enough to splatter oil and rice all over the top of my hand.

I must have screamed, because Mercy grabs my arm and yanks it away from the grease fire the oil has started on the stovetop. She wraps her arm around my waist and pulls me away from the flames instinctively.

"Oh my god!" she cries as she holds up my hand and stares at it. "Oh my god! Oh my god!"

"Get some water on it!" Guelita yells. She is holding on to her walker as she stands just inside the kitchen door. "It's okay, Graciela. You'll be all right. Mercy—listen to me. Put her hand under the cold water. You need to stop the hot oil from soaking through."

The pain eating away at my hand radiates up the length of my arm, like a relámpago, an electric shock wave that makes me howl like a wounded animal. The sounds coming out of my mouth scare me, and I try to stop, but my body starts to do things I can't control.

I shake and shiver all over. My knees give out and I lean against the counter. Tears pour down my face, and saliva drips out of nose and mouth. I grab my elbow and squeeze my arm, trying desperately to make the pain go away even as Guelita Rosa and Mercy place my hand inside a bowl of icy cold water.

"We need to go to the hospital," Mercy finally says, pushing my hair out of my face and looking at Guelita as she speaks.

"No," Guelita says, shaking her head. "It's not that

bad. We can take care of it here. Bring me one of those pots of aloe vera from the rack on the back porch. I'll need some gauze too, from the top shelf in my medicine chest. Now, Mercy! Move it!"

Even after Guelita plasters the cooling, gooey aloe vera slivers all over my burns and wraps my hand in gauze so that it looks like a giant puffball, I can't control myself. I cry and cry, losing my mind from the pain and the shock of it all. I know I am not taking it well because when I go to my room and lie down, I can't keep my body from writhing on the bed.

"Stop squirming." Mercy opens a medicine bottle and shoves two blue pills into my mouth. Then she puts the bottle on my nightstand, so she can hold the glass of water to my lips. I try reading the label on the bottle with my peripheral vision, but the letters are too small. "It's a sedative," Mercy explains. "The doctor prescribed it to me when . . ."

"It hurts," I whisper, closing my eyes against the pain.

"Just lay back," Mercy says. "Let the medicine take effect. The prescription says to take one, but I gave you two—so you can rest."

Mercy lays my arm very gently on a pillow beside me. Then she picks up the bottle of pills and the glass of water and walks out of the room. But she doesn't apologize for my injury. She doesn't even acknowledge that it was her fault I am in so much pain. She just lowers her eyes and closes the door quietly behind her.

Tears roll down the sides of my face and into my ears, and I use the hem of my shirt to wipe them off. After a while, the medicine starts to take effect, and I start to calm down.

The pain in my hand is a dull, throbbing sob, and I feel myself drifting away. I am almost asleep when Alexander crawls out from behind my dresser and comes to watch over me. He stands beside me, staring at my wrapped hand, blinking, not sure if he should touch it or not. "Coco?" he asks, pointing at my swaddled hand with his tiny index finger.

"Sí, coco," I say, closing my eyes, hoping Alexander will stay with me, watch over me with those large brown eyes, soft and dark as wet earth.

"Don't cry," Alexander whispers. "It'll be all right."

I want so much to hold him and kiss him and tell him how much I love him—how much I will always love him. But I can't. The sleeping pills are taking effect, and I can feel myself slipping away.

"I'm sorry, Alexander," I whisper. "I'm sorry I hurt you, baby."

"I not hurt," Alexander says, lifting his hand and showing me that, unlike my own, his is fine.

"You're not?" More tears slip out of the corners of

my eyes and spill down the sides of my face onto my pillow as I turn sideways.

"No. Not hurt." Alexander shakes his head and smiles. "Sleep now?" he asks.

I nod. "Yes, sleep," I whisper.

"I go?" Alexander asks.

"No," I say, forcing my eyes to stay open. "No. Please don't go. Stay here with me, baby. Stay with me."

"Okay," Alexander says. Then he lays beside me and wipes the tears from my cheeks and sighs. "You bees all right."

"Thank you," I whisper, my eyelids heavy over my eyes.

As the blue pills start to take effect, I wonder how this will change Mercy. *Will she feel guilty and stop ignoring me altogether? Will she be more inclined to forgive me for enrolling her in school after tonight? More important, will she go to class on Monday?*

I want to believe this accident will change things. But the truth is, there is no telling how this whole thing with my hand will affect her. At this point, I'm not even sure *I'll* be in school on Monday myself. But I don't care anymore. My hand feels like it is dying inside that pocket of goo and gauze, and I ache all over. I just want the earth to stop spinning, to freeze on its axis. I want the world to revolve backward. I want to travel back in time and make everything all right again. Because no matter how bad I thought things were back then, at least we had Alexander.

At least my sweet little sobrino was alive.

CHAPTER TWENTY-ONE
Three Years Earlier

The banging and clattering had stopped at around three o'clock in the afternoon, and there was no one out there now. The roof was finally all done, and I was glad, because I had been cooped up for days in my grandmother's house trying to avoid Manuel.

The sun shone glorious and magnificent in the sky, and I wanted nothing more than to take a long, luxurious walk and let it bathe my skin in warmth. Wondering where Lucia was, when and if she was ever coming back, I decided to check out the warehouse she mentioned before she left. I went back to my room and looked through the summer dresses in the old wardrobe.

They were all so pretty. And they looked like they would fit me. I took the yellow one out. The delicate lace on the scooped neckline was handmade, and I wondered how old it was. I wasn't sure, but I thought it might be vintage, circa 1970s. *Could this be my grandmother's?* I put the dress up against myself and flounced the skirt back and forth in front of the mirror, trying to get a feel for how it would move when I walked. It was longer than I was used to wearing, but that was part of its charm.

I took the dress and went to Abuela Estela's room, hoping to get her permission to wear it. The room was dark and unusually cold for a summer day, but she was fast asleep in her cocoon of blankets, so I didn't bother her. The rest of the house was dark too, but I didn't dare open up any windows. My grandmother's sensitivity to light dictated our living conditions, but I was free to go outside now, so I put the dress on and left the house.

At the warehouse, I picked up some mangoes and smelled them. I thought a mango salad would make a nice dessert if I put it on bread over the last of the goat cheese in the refrigerator. I put some vegetables in the little green mesh bag I brought along with me.

There was a warm breeze when I left the warehouse, and I lifted my face and closed my eyes for a moment. The red soda pop in my hand was sweating, and I took a swig of it. I'd thought about finishing it at the warehouse so I could leave the glass bottle there, but I didn't want to linger in the dark, musty store any longer. I wanted to walk in the sunlight, move my muscles, enjoy some of the freedom I'd been missing the last two days.

I was rounding the corner toward Abuela Estela's house when I heard a familiar, unwelcome sound. The slow, long-winded whistle sent a shiver down my spine, and I turned around. The sight of Manuel grinning at me as he walked slowly behind me made me drop the bottle of soda. The sturdy, round bottle landed at my feet, bounced, and thumped over on its side, then started rolling in a semicircle around my shoes, drawing a jagged red line on the ground as the liquid spilled.

My vision blurred and I started to shake.

Somewhere in the distant recesses of my mind, a woman howled, a deeply pained, ear-piercing wail that shattered the bottle before me, a starburst of red blood. The woman's soul-wrenching sobs turned into words and the sobs turned into my mother's familiar voice, crying out. *"Help! Help me!"* she screamed. *"Someone please help me!"*

My legs buckled under me, and I caught myself just in time before falling to my knees. The bottle dropped again and again from my hand. The glass clinked against the small pebbles on the dirt road, rolling sideways and spewing out lines of red liquid around me again and again. Somewhere, in the distance of time and space, my mother screamed, over and over again. The bottle, the burst, the blood, and my mother's scream became a series of sights and sounds that repeated again and again before me and inside me, echoing feverishly in my mind.

"No," I whispered, pushing the echo aside. "No."

My heart was racing.

My stomach lurched, and I thought I might throw up.

Calm down, I told myself. *Breathe. You're having an echo. That's all. There's no real danger. Nothing's really wrong. You're fine. You're okay.* But no matter how hard I tried to make myself believe what my mind knew to be true, I had no way of stopping my body from reacting violently to my surroundings.

"Where have you been?" Manuel asked, calling out to me from about ten yards away on the other side of the narrow dirt road. "I've been looking for you."

My vision steadied, but my heart was still beating so fast I couldn't think straight. "Stay away from me." I was aware that my words might anger him, but unable to do anything else other than what my instincts demanded, and my instincts were screaming for me to move, to walk away as quickly as my legs could manage and get away from Manuel.

So that's what I did. I dropped the mesh bag. I let the groceries spill all over the ground and swiveled on my heel and started walking off. Fast. As fast as my legs would take me. Abuela Estela's house was half a block away on the other side of the street, where Manuel was walking now.

If I hurried, I could get ahead of him. If I hurried, I could cross the road up ahead and beat Manuel to the gate. If I hurried, I could get there in two, maybe three minutes. If I hurried, I could save myself.

"Why are you running off? Wait for me, girl," Manuel called after me.

I cast my eyes on the rutted ground and walked faster, pumping my arms as I went along. My hands were oars, my sleeves sails on a fleeing ship.

"Cha-ta! Cha-ti-ta!" Manuel called out the repulsive nickname from across the street, torturing me with its lilting, singsong notes.

"Leave me alone!" I screamed, quickening my pace.

"What's wrong, Chatita?" Manuel asked. "Why are you so skittish? I'm not going to hurt you. I just want to get to know you."

I bolted. Ran as fast as I could. But his legs were longer, stronger, and he made it to Abuela Estela's gate before I did. My breath ragged, shaky, I stood under a huisache, looking up and down the narrow country road, hoping to see someone, anyone, I could call on if Manuel tried touching me. But there was nobody out there. The country lane was bare.

Who would hear me if I screamed out here? Nobody.

The nearest neighbor was at least a quarter of a mile away. Too far for my voice to carry. My mind raced. I could always keep walking, head back to Las Cenizas, to the postecito. I could admit to the blonde girl that I did indeed speak Spanish and ask if her if I could hang out there for a while, until Manuel lost interest and left.

No. I thought. *That would send the wrong message. It would show him I'm scared. I need to stand up for myself. I need to set him straight!*

I kept my eyes on the ground as I crossed the street, making sure I knew where his shadow was moving, how his feet were positioned.

Manuel flipped the latch on my grandmother's gate and swung the wrought-iron door open with a ridiculous flourish of his hand. "Come on in, my darling," he whispered as I stepped through the gate.

He leaned in for a quick kiss and I pushed him away before his lips could touch my cheek. "Stop it!" I said. "Go home. I don't like you like that."

I ran toward the front door of my grandmother's house, but once again, Manuel ran around me and beat me there. This time, I refused to play his game. I stepped off the gray flagstone path and ran as fast as I could over the grass, toward the backyard.

This time, Manuel didn't go around me.

This time, Manuel ran after me.

He wrapped his hulking arms around my waist and hauled me off the ground, twirling me in the air.

"Let me go!" I said.

Manuel turned me around and held me just above ground level. "Calm down!" he whispered. "Shhh . . ."

"Let me go!" I pounded on his chest with my fists and his chins with my feet. When that didn't work, and he tried to kiss me again, I scratched at his face, digging deeply, making him bleed. The crimson shred marks on his left cheek smeared, and I pushed and shoved at his arms, trying to extricate myself from his grip. But he was strong. Stronger than I'd expected.

"Put me down! Put! Me! Down!" I cried.

My heartbeat roared in my ears and pounded at my temples and I couldn't breathe. Manuel's arms around me made it hard to inhale deeply, the way my body demanded as I fought for my life.

"Let her go!" a man's voice called out.

I twisted in Manuel's arms and looked behind me. An old man was standing on the threshold of the gardener's shed. His wiry frame was barely discernible in the shadows of the half-open door, but he was there, witnessing Manuel's unwelcome advances. He looked like he couldn't pick up a shovel, much less fight off Manuel, but I was never happier to see another human being in my life.

"Stay out of it," Manuel said. "This is none of your business."

"I take care of this place," the man said. "Anyone living here is my business. Don't make me come out there, boy. Let the girl go. Now."

When Manuel didn't put me down, the gardener reached behind the door and brought out a rifle. The long barrel was worn, and the weapon looked like it had seen better days, but that didn't make it less threatening. Manuel looked into my eyes; he deliberated for a moment before he slackened his hold on me.

I put my feet on the ground and steadied myself. But I couldn't just let it end there. I made a fist, turned around, and punched Manuel square in the face. Then I took off and ran into the house through the door that led to my room.

Every muscle in my body vibrated, as I stood inside my room trembling. I locked the door and gave the knob a good jiggle to make sure it was working, that I was really safe. Then I crossed the room and took a good look at myself in the mirror. My hair was disheveled, and there were a couple of blood smears on the yellow dress, under my breast.

But I was safe.

I was safe.

CHAPTER TWENTY-TWO
Eagle Pass, Texas
August 2011

I WAKE UP EARLY. MY HAND IS throbbing, so I unwrap it and take a look at it. There is some blistering and redness, but not so much that I feel like I need to go to the hospital. Wrapping my hand back up, I leave my room and go sit in the breakfast nook, next to Guelita Rosa, who is already eating her oatmeal. My first class isn't until the afternoon, so I have an open day ahead of me until then.

"Oh, you're up. Come here, let me look at your hand," Guelita says, pushing her bowl aside and patting the table in front of her.

"It's okay. You can look at it later. After you finish eating."

"Want some coffee?" she asks. "Mercy, get your sister some coffee."

Mercy pours a cup of coffee and places in front of me without saying a word.

Seeing that Mercy has taken over my breakfast duties fills me with hope, and I smile at her when she comes over and clears away Guelita's dishes. But to my dismay, Mercy glares at me before she shuffles back into the kitchen in her fuzzy slippers.

After Mercy leaves for work, Guelita Rosa calls me into her room and smears more aloe vera goo on my hand and wraps it up again. She does this every few hours, saying that if we keep up this treatment, I won't have any scarring. I want to believe her, because I really don't want to have any reminders of my altercation with Mercy. We have enough bad feelings between us already. We don't need to add this to the mix.

"Aloe vera is a gift from the gods," Guelita Rosa had said this morning as she slathered my hand with the goey substance again after breakfast. "It was given to the people of our valley to help them deal with the merciless sun back in the time when they first came over the ice patches on the North Pole and settled in the Americas, way back in time, thousands of years before the Europeans 'discovered' this continent." She says the word *discovered* like it's a curse word.

My grandmother is full of interesting stories like that. She didn't go to school past the third grade in Mexico, but she's watched all the shows on the National Geographic and History Channels, so she has a lot of theories about our culture and how we got here. Like everything else that comes out of her mouth, some of it is fact and some of it is fiction, but most of it is somewhere in between.

It doesn't take long for me to figure out that Mercy's attitude toward me hasn't gotten any better. If anything, I would say it's gotten worse. She doesn't ignore me anymore, so much as look at me like she loathes me. Every time she comes in and out of the house, she makes it a point to stare at me with those same dark eyes, as large and beautiful as Alexander's but dangerous as obsidian daggers.

Don't you dare talk to me, those eyes say, and I listen to them. I keep my mouth shut even though my whole body hums with the need to scream at her for making it hard for me to go to school today.

Before I leave the house for class in the afternoon, Guelita Rosa cleans my right hand, smearing it with aloe vera again and bandaging it. Because I refuse to take anybody else's prescription medication anymore, the little blue pills Guelita Rosa offers me from her plate, I'm wondering if I'm going to be able to function today. The throbbing pain comes in unexpected waves, especially when I move my hand too quickly. But I have to do this. I have to go to school.

I can't use my right hand at all, so I have to use my left hand for everything—zipping up my jeans, throwing books into my backpack, slinging it over my arm, pulling myself onto the city bus. Everything feels extra difficult.

By the time I open the door of the room for my English class and go inside, I am beyond exhausted. I am sweaty and flustered and just plain out of sorts as I push my hair out of my face and look around the room for a place where I can sit all by myself, away from all the shiny faces, happy and hopeful about the new school year. And I swear if someone tries to talk to me, I'll scream.

As I scan the room, one face stands out at me. Daniel Perez's smile is so sweet, so bright, I feel the last of my fight slip out of me like the last breath of hot air slips out of a deflating hot-air balloon.

"Grace!" Daniel calls, waving at a desk beside him.

I look around the room for alternative places to sit, but the place is packed. So, I shift the weight of my backpack from my shoulder to the crook of my elbow and then down into my good hand before I make my way through the row of desks. Walking over to where he is sitting, I take the seat behind the one he's offering me.

"What happened to your hand?" he asks, eyeing the bulky bandaging.

"It's nothing. Just a small burn," I say. He leans over to help me get my books out of my backpack. "I didn't know you were in college."

"Second semester," he says. "I started back in California, but then my father passed away, so I dropped out to help my mother. Then we moved here. And, well, here I am. Back on track."

The professor comes in, and I shift away from Daniel to pay attention to Professor Romero, a Latina who seems nice enough. She doesn't look at me when she says we should feel free to let her know if we have any specific needs, but I look down at my paper when she says it because I don't want to call attention to my hand. But I feel like an idiot, because everything I've written in my spiral notebook about Dante's *Inferno* is unreadable.

Daniel watches me struggle, but he doesn't say anything. I think he knows I don't want anyone making a big deal of my temporary handicap. I don't really remember much about what Professor Romero says, because I just want to make it through the class and get home again.

It's not that I don't want to be there. I just don't want to be there with a gauzy hand. And I am worried, wondering if Mercy got in her car and came to class like I did. I had no way of knowing, because she wasn't home when I left the house.

When Botany, my second class of the evening, is finally over, I walk down the sidewalk to see if I can spot Mercy. If she didn't come, I'm going to have to call Dad for a ride because the bus stopped running about two hours ago. There is a beautiful oak tree behind me, so I step back and rest against it. Despite the fact that the sun has already set, it's still a hundred degrees out here. I look for Mercy's car in the parking lot, but it is nowhere to be seen. After a few minutes, Daniel drives up in his black Camaro and rolls down his window.

"Do you want a ride?" he asks.

I look over at him briefly and really consider it. "No, thank you," I say.

"You sure?" he asks. "There's no bus coming. Not this late."

"I'm sure," I say.

Daniel looks at the road ahead for a moment, and then he shrugs. "Okay," he says. "See you later."

He waves, but I don't wave back. One, because I don't want him to think we're friends now, just because we're in the same class. And two, because I am busy squeezing the wrist of my burned hand, trying to keep the pulsating pain at bay. A few minutes later, I give up and start walking back to the college office to call my father.

"I looked like a fool today," I tell Alexander when I finally make it through the door of my room and lie back on my bed. "Today, my handwriting was worse than yours. What do you think about that?"

Alexander looks up long enough to smile at me before going back to playing with his red fire truck in the middle of my room. I put my injured hand gingerly on top of my stomach, stare up at the ceiling, and sigh.

"You're not staying up, are you?" Guelita Rosa asks when she comes to the door to check on me. She opens it just enough to look in on me and then reaches in to flip the light switch off when I shake my head. "Good. You need your rest. Do you want one of my pills?"

"Again with the pills," I say, and I turn on my side, away from her. "No, thank you."

Guelita closes the door behind herself, and I focus on Alexander in the dark. He is just sitting there, in the middle of the room on his knees, watching me for a moment longer before he disappears, his tiny form dissipating into the shadows. "Good night, Alexander," I whisper.

From somewhere in the darkness, I hear him whisper, "Night-night."

His voice, soft, faint—gone.

∾

When I wake up, I open my eyes and look at my gauzy hand. I take the wrap off gently, peeling it layer by layer until my hand is completely exposed, and I let it breathe. It isn't so bad. The skin bubbles have deflated, and the redness has begun to lighten to a dull pink hue that covers most of the top of my hand.

I am settling in on the couch to write the first essay for Professor Romero's English composition class when I hear a knock on the door. I shift uncomfortably, trying to get the new backpack I bought with my financial aid off my lap with one hand so that I can answer the door, when Guelita comes walking out of her bedroom. "I'll get it," she says. "It's that nice young man from next door."

"Oh, please don't open the door," I say, feeling sick to my stomach at the thought of having to talk to Daniel. I also don't want him to see my exposed hand and start asking questions again.

"Why not?" Guelita asks. "It's not like he comes over every day. Besides, what makes you think he's here to see you?"

I let out a frustrated breath as I look at my grandmother. "Really? You think he's here to see you?"

Guelita Rosa lifts her right hand in midair and flips it, palm side up. "Maybe," she says. "I won't know until I open the door."

"Guelita, please! I'm busy," I say. "I have to concentrate."

As usual, my grandmother does whatever she wants. She opens the door and greets Daniel with a wide smile, asking, "Yes? Can I help you?"

Daniel stands at the threshold with his hands shoved deep in his jeans pockets, looking into the house as if he isn't sure exactly what he is looking for. "Uh, no," he says. "I was just bored, and I thought I'd come over and talk to Grace. See how she's doing."

"Well, she says she's busy," Guelita says, cocking her head toward me. "But if you're bored, I have things you can do. There's a whole yard of work that needs to be done out there. You got a lawn mower?"

"I—I, ah . . . I don't," Daniel says. He looks sideways at the front yard on both sides of the door, then he takes his hands out of his pockets and shoves them under his arms as if he doesn't know exactly what to do with them. "I'm sorry."

Guelita Rosa frowns at him. "Then what good are you?" she asks, and I cringe. She can be so rude. I can feel Daniel's devastation as he looks across the threshold at her.

"We have a wheelbarrow," he says. He smiles then. I look away because something about that smile makes me very uncomfortable. I don't want to feel sorry for him, but I can't help it. He has no idea who he's messing with. Guelita's a handful.

"A wheelbarrow, huh?" Guelita considers this for a moment. "Is it big? Can you move those rocks for me?"

"Rocks?" Daniel asks, turning to the left and checking out my father's handiwork, the huge pile of rocks that was supposed to become a fountain, but which has become rooted to the earth, like a mountain in the making. "What do you want me to do with them?"

"Leave him alone!" I cry, louder than I intended, because I feel so bad for Daniel. My grandmother is really taking him for a ride now.

Guelita turns around. She looks at me as if I've just sprouted horns and hooves and snakes for hair. "What's the matter with you? Why are you yelling?" she asks, waving Daniel into the house. "Come in, son. Grace didn't mean to yell at me. Did you, Grace? She has more respect for her elders than that."

The fact that my grandmother is letting Daniel into the house angers me, and suddenly I don't feel so well. My heart starts beating fast. My breath becomes ragged, like I've been running. And the room starts to spin. I close my eyes. Fighting it. But it's no use. The echo filters in.

A soda bottle drops again and again from my hand. The glass clinks against the small pebbles on a dirt road, rolling sideways and spewing out lines of red liquid around me again and again.

Suddenly I am there again, in my grandmother's yard, being lifted up in the air and spun around like a child.

"Put me down!"

"Put me down!"

I hear myself screaming, but I fight the echo, push it out of my mind, and open my eyes in the present to look at Daniel as he comes in. Because I've deliberately spread out my books and notebooks around me, to give the impression that there is no room for anyone to sit beside me on our big saggy couch, he has to sit on the love seat across from me.

"Well, I have things to do," Guelita says, and she makes her way back to her room.

When she leaves, and Daniel and I are alone in the sala, I stop fussing with my papers and glare at him. "Well?" I ask. "Did you need something in particular? Because, as you can see, I have a lot of work to do."

Daniel sits forward. The love seat squeaks as he settles into position and stops moving. His elbows on his knees and his hands clasped in front himself, he looks at me. Then he interlaces his fingers and clears his throat as if he is a presidential candidate about to answer an important question on the campaign trail.

"Come on, spit it out," I say. "I don't have all day."

"Why don't you like me?" he asks, lifting his chin and fixing me with a clear, penetrating stare. "I mean, I haven't been anything but nice to you, and you keep shoving me away. Every time I try to become friends, you shoot me down. What is it? My hair? My eyes? My skin color? I'm half Mexican, you know. I mean, I look like my mother, but my father was from Eagle Pass. I'm not all white, if that's what's bothering you."

I'm shocked. Of all the things I'd expected him to say to me on that couch, that was the last thing I would have guessed. "What?" I ask. "I don't care about that. I just don't have time to get to know you. Unlike my sister, I have things I'm trying to do with my life. Graphic design takes time and skill, not to mention a degree."

"Okay," he says. "I get it. You're busy. But everyone needs a break every once in a while."

"I can't take a break," I say. "I haven't even started on my first essay."

"Okay, fair enough," he says. "But later, when you're ready. Could we go get a burger or something? Everyone needs to stop to eat, right?"

I put my good hand on my forehead and rub my temple. It's exhausting, having to talk to him. Why doesn't he get it? I just want to be alone. "Yes," I say. "People often do that, but they kinda have to get started first, which I can't do because you're still here, on our sofa, distracting me."

Daniel's eyes soften then. He grins and looks down at the floor for a moment. "I can't win, can I?" he asks. "No matter what I say, no matter what I do, you're just going to keep shooting me down."

The silence thickens and stretches between us, like distended taffy, and I shift uncomfortably on the couch. "I'm not trying to be mean," I finally say.

"But you *are* being mean," he says. "You know that, don't you?"

I sigh and glance over at the open book sitting beside my crossed legs. My head is throbbing from the echo, but also from the sheer stress of having to talk to him. If I was Mercy, if I knew how to handle boys like him, this would be fun, but I am not Mercy and I don't know what to do, how to deal with a nice guy like Daniel. He's not doing anything wrong. I'm just not ready for this.

"This is exhausting," I whisper, more to myself than to him. "You're exhausting."

"Well, thank you for your time. I'll let myself out." Daniel stands up, walks over to the door, and pulls it open.

Guilt springs up inside me. I am about to call Daniel back when Mercy steps through the front door. "What are you doing here?" she asks.

"Leaving," Daniel says, his voice low and terse.

Mercy stares after Daniel, who bolts out the front door, letting the screen slam behind him as he flees across the yard. I watch him rush up to the chain-link fence that separates our yard from his. He puts both hands on the top bar and flings his body over it, quick and agile as a bobcat, and I shudder.

The memory of Manuel jumping over a fence in another time, another place, far, far away from here, makes my stomach lurch and I swipe it away—erasing it from my mind, quickly, before it can overwhelm me. Daniel doesn't look back. He runs up his porch steps and disappears into his mother's house.

"What was that about?" Mercy's eyes narrow as she watches me close the curtain behind me and settle back on the protesting couch.

I shrug. "I don't know," I lie. "Something about a wheelbarrow. He's going to do some yard work for Guelita or something. I'm not sure."

Mercy turns away and walks toward her room.

"Mercy," I call, my voice warbling, nervous. Mercy stops and halfway turns to me, keeping her eyes averted. "How was school?" I ask.

My sister lets out a quick, frustrated sigh. Then she throws back her shoulders and turns to face me head-on. "I'm not going to school, Grace."

"What?" I ask. "Why not?"

"Because I don't want to, okay?" she asks. "Listen. I need you to just leave me alone about that. I don't need you harping on it. I've made up my mind. I'm not going to college. Not now. Not ever. Understand?"

"But if you don't go to school now, you'll lose your financial aid for good," I say. "You can't just ignore this, Mercy. That's not the way things work."

"Stop!" Mercy screams, a loud, reverberating scream that startles me. "Just stop! Don't you get it? I'm not you, Grace. I'm not interested in school!"

"You used to be," I cry, slamming the book on my lap closed and pushing it to the floor. "You used to say we'd go off to college together, when we were young, remember?"

Mercy puts her hand on her hip and stares at me for a second. Her left leg shakes nervously. "Yeah, well. That was a long time ago," she admits. "You just have to accept it, Grace. I don't need to go to school anymore."

"Don't be ridiculous," I say. "Everyone needs to go to school. You need to think about your future. You think just because you kiss those guys in their cars they're going to take care of you? They're not, Mercy. Those guys don't care about you. They're just using you."

"Shut up," Mercy yells, her mouth twisting in rage. "You're just jealous," she continues. "You've always been jealous. Face it, Grace. You *have* to go to school. It's the only way you're ever going to get a life. You're never going to get a man to marry you. Guys just aren't interested in you. Not that way anyway."

That's not true! You don't know anything about me, what I've been through, I want to scream, but I don't. I know it's just her immaturity talking back to me then, so I don't say anything. Instead, I just stare at her, as mad at her as she is at me.

A moment later, Mercy turns around and leaves the room. I sit with my wounded hand on my lap, staring at our closed front door, wondering what is to become of us. We are so messed up. Both of us. For different reasons.

CHAPTER TWENTY-THREE
Three Years Earlier

"**Y**OU SHOULDN'T GO INTO TOWN BY yourself, child,"
Don Baldomar, the gardener, said to me at the kitchen
table that evening. He'd come by to check on me at my
grandmother's house in Mexico.

"I was just trying to get some exercise," I whispered,
looking over at Abuela Estela, who was sitting by the
window absently petting a black kitten on her lap.

"Las Cenizas is not safe," Don Baldomar continued.
"Not safe at all."

"The world is not safe," Abuela Estela said, sighing.
"As long as men roam the earth, nobody is safe."

I turned to look at my grandmother then, shaking
my head. "That can't be true," I said. "Not all men are

bad. You don't really believe that, do you? I mean, Don Baldomar is a good person."

"Don't be upset," Don Baldomar said. "Your grandmother doesn't mean to be so fatalistic. She's just had a hard life."

"Hard life," my grandmother repeated the words. Then she turned around to look at Don Baldomar. "I did. I did have a hard life. Until you brought me here. Remember? You saved us, Balde. You saved me and the baby."

"What is she talking about?" I asked Don Baldomar, but he waved the whole thing away and started toward the door.

"Just don't leave the property," he said. "If you need something from the store, write a note and pin it up on this clothespin, here." He tapped a weatherworn clothespin tacked on the outer frame of the front door with his index finger. "I'll go into town and get it for you. Understand?"

"Thank you for interceding," I said. "But I'm not going to let that guy make me a prisoner. I refuse to shut myself in for him."

"Well, I understand that. Just be careful when you go out," he said, and then he left, closing the door behind him with a gentle nudge.

"Guelita?" I asked, when I was alone with my grandmother. "What did you mean, Don Baldomar saved you and the baby?"

"He saved us," Abuela Estela whispered, kissing the black kitten's head and speaking softly into its ears. "Balde saved us. He took us away from the bad man. He did. Didn't he? He did. He did."

"You mean my grandfather?" I asked. "Is that what you meant by that?"

But it was no use, no matter how differently I worded my inquiries, Abuela Estela never quite answered my question. I had no idea what baby she was talking about. But since I didn't grow up with any aunts or uncles from her side of the family, I had to assume that the baby she was speaking of was my mother.

Chapter Twenty-Four
Eagle Pass, Texas
October 2011

FOR THE LAST FEW WEEKS, AS the semester's moved on, Daniel's been showing up at the house more often. It started with him asking me to edit a paper and just took off from there. Now we're sitting around doing our homework together on the couch a couple of times a week when he's not at work.

We're getting to be good friends, but I suspect he wants more than that. I'm not sure whether I'm interested or not. But he's a nice guy, so he's not pushing for anything more than the easy friendship I'm offering him.

I get the feeling, however, that I'm going to have to make a decision about that soon. Because when I get home from my last class of the day, I see that Daniel is sitting on the dating bench in front of our house. It is after nine, and the porch light is off, but the moon is very bright. Enough of its light is piercing through the dense branches of the mulberry tree that I can see he's not alone.

Mercy's there too.

She is very close to him. Her right leg is crossed over her left leg, and her skirt is riding high up on her thighs. As if that isn't obvious enough, she's thrown her shoulders forward, and she's resting her crossed arms over her knees. To top this off, she looks like she is entranced by whatever is coming out of Daniel's lips.

The sight of them sitting so close together on the dating bench sends a strange sensation coursing through my body, a heat that rises and rises inside me, making me feel flushed and faint all at the same time. I can't quite place what I'm feeling. And though I know it's not an echo, I also know I don't like it. So, I take a deep breath and push back against it.

As I near the house, slipping into the yard quietly through the open gate, Mercy pulls away from Daniel. Then she stands up and walks around the bench. She slinks away without looking back at me.

"What's going on?" I ask Daniel when I step up to the bench.

"Oh, nothing," he says. "Just getting to know your sister a bit."

Something unfamiliar, a tiny pain like a pin, pricks at my heart, and I push it away. "What do you mean?" I ask. "What did she say?"

"Nothing really," Daniel says. "She just wanted to know what I did, where I worked. You know, small talk."

"Small talk?" I ask.

Daniel shrugs. "Yeah. I told her all about the hospital, how hard it is to work there sometimes. Then she kind of teased me a bit, you know, about being an orderly."

"She did?" I ask. I'm not sure why but I'm feeling a little mortified by the fact that Mercy wants to know more about Daniel than I do. *Could this mean . . . does this mean . . . she's interested in him? I'm not sure I like that.* On the bench, Daniel nods and I smile wearily. "She'll do that," I say, and leave it at that.

I don't have the heart to ask him what I want to know. Had she told him about our argument, the reason my hand is bandaged? I don't want Daniel to start asking questions about my complicated relationship with Mercy, especially because I'm still not sure how I feel about him.

Guelita Rosa says he's trying to win me over, but I don't think so. I mean, sure, he comes over often, but most of the time we're just hanging out. Sometimes, he brings something sweet to share, pan dulce, ice cream bars, peanut butter cookies his mother has baked, things like that, but most of the time we really do just sit around doing homework.

I put my books on the bench between us.

"You cold? Man, you're freezing," Daniel says, taking my hand and cupping it inside his. He lifts it to his lips, blows warm air on it, and rubs it vigorously. The intimacy of it sends a strange tingle up my arm, and I try to ignore it, but it's so pleasant that my heartbeat quickens. I feel it throbbing in my eardrums. When he is satisfied that I am sufficiently warm, he stops. I pull my hand out of his grip and push it into the pocket on the front of my pink hoodie, hoping he can't see how flustered I've become.

"You going to the carnival?" he asks, moving my books to the left of him on the bench so he can scoot in and get closer to me.

"I don't know. I hadn't given it any thought," I say.

"You want to go with me?" he asks. "I could ask your dad if you need me to."

"My dad?" I ask, shifting on the bench so we are not so much facing each other as sitting side by side. "Why would you need to do that?"

"I mean, if he needs me to," he continues. "Like an official date. Although it doesn't have to be a date . . . if you don't want it to be."

I scrape the shriveled chrysalis of a leopard moth off

the apex of a branch from the mulberry tree beside me. "You don't have to ask my dad."

"You sure?" he prods.

"I'm eighteen," I say, pushing at the leaves underfoot with the tip of my tennis shoe. "I don't need his permission."

"I know," he says, shrugging his shoulders. "It's just that it's the right thing to do, you know—ask him, I mean. He strikes me as being a pretty traditional guy."

I look at the dark pile of rocks sitting at the other end of the moonlit yard. In the night shade cast by the surrounding huisache trees, it looks like a grave site. I shiver. "He's not. He made this bench."

"What?"

I roll my eyes. "It's a dating bench. So, we can have somewhere to sit," I say. Then, because he still looks confused, I add, "With boys—you know. Anyway, you don't have to ask him."

"You do want to go, don't you?" Daniel asks. Then, when I don't answer, he half-heartedly pushes his shoulder into mine, nudging me gently. "Come on. You know you want to."

"I do like carnivals," I admit.

Daniel grins. His teeth gleam in the moonlight, and he looks like James Dean in one of those old black-and-white movies. "But . . . ?" he asks.

I make a face, because this is hard. "It's just that . . . Well, I haven't dated much—I mean, I haven't dated at all, actually. So, this is kind of weird for me."

"Are you saying you've never . . ." Daniel's eyebrows rise high on his forehead.

"Been on a date." I finish his sentence for him.

"Like ever? That's crazy!" Daniel turns away to look out into the street, where my father's truck is slowing down in front of the house.

"Oh, God." The words leave my lips before I can censor them.

"What?"

"Nothing," I say. There are so many reasons I don't want to talk to Daniel in front of my dad, so many reasons why I shouldn't, especially since my father doesn't even know Daniel's been coming around. He's usually already at work by the time Daniel shows up. I don't know how he'll react, what he'll say, if he thinks Daniel and I are *getting close*. Unlike Mercy, I've never been in this position before. But I don't have time to even begin to explain the complex nature of my relationship with my father to Daniel because, at that moment, my dad pulls into our driveway.

"Daniel, you should go home now," I say.

My father slides out of the truck and reaches back inside the cabin to pull out his jacket from the passenger seat. Then he goes around the front and starts walking to the house.

"Why?" Daniel asks before standing up to face my father, who is coming up the walkway with his head down. "Hello, sir, how're you doing?"

I stand staring at Daniel as he steps toward my father.

"Hey! I must be tired. I didn't see you two out here." My father stops a few yards in front of us. He is wearing a ball cap. The short bill is throwing a shadow over his face, so that I can't quite see his expression, but I can sense the tension in his back muscles as he straightens up. His shoulders shift, and he turns and walks toward us slowly.

"Hello, son." My father reaches out to shake Daniel's hand. "How have you been?"

"Just fine, sir, just fine." Daniel takes my father's hand, shakes it, and then puts his own hand back inside his pocket. He throws his weight onto his heels and rocks himself back and forth a bit.

Fine?

I'm not fine!

My head is spinning. My stomach is twisted up into all kinds of knots, and I have the intense desire to run down the street, screaming into the night. More than anything else in the world, I want to get as far away from the situation Daniel has created as my legs can take me.

But instead of running, I stand there, frozen beside the dating bench—*how did I end up here?* I ask myself as I look up at the last of the weathered, caterpillar-eaten leaves clinging to the branches of the old mulberry tree.

My back is stiff, my hands are tight balls inside the warm pockets of my hoodie, and the muscles of my face are stiff from the cold breath of the dark October night.

"Good. Good. And your mother? She getting along? Can't be easy for a widow, to start a new life," my father says.

"Yeah, she's fine," Daniel says. "She's all excited about the carnival this weekend. Her art students have a face-painting booth. She's really looking forward to running it."

"Hmm." My father pops the cap off his head and scratches his head, looking sideways at our front door before putting it back on. "That's good."

"I asked Grace to come to the carnival with me," Daniel continues. "She hasn't decided if she wants to go."

My father looks over at me. He smiles and rubs his beard stubble vigorously. "Well, I'm sure you two will figure it out."

I roll my eyes and wonder why I am still standing there when all I really want to do is get back in the house.

"We will," I say. "Good night, Dad."

"Good night." My father nods. I shift my weight from one foot to the other and watch my father step back, turn around, and leave.

"Well?" Daniel asks. "Are we? Going to the carnival?"

I take a deep breath and fight hard not to roll my eyes again before sitting back down on the bench. *Why are you doing this?* I ask myself. *Say something. Tell him you don't want to go. Be honest for once.*

I look at the kitchen window to see if my grandmother is looking at us from inside. Then I scan the other window, the one in Mercy's room. I remember that she was out here, teasing Daniel earlier, and suddenly, I realize—*she was flirting with him! I'm sure of it.* The thought makes my heart race, and I wonder . . . *Am I jealous? Is that what I felt when I first saw her with him? Jealous? Really? Why?*

No sooner has my father gone back into the house than the light goes out on the porch. "Nice!" Daniel says, sitting down close to me on the bench. "That's a sign, you know? He's okay with this."

I wiggle uncomfortably. "Okay with what, exactly?" I ask, unsettled not so much by Daniel, but by my own thoughts, my own uncertainty.

"Us." Daniel rubs his hands together and smiles at me as he tries to warm them against the October chill.

Us.

One word, and suddenly my heart is aflutter. How does one word bring up so many unchecked emotions? *What is this?* I ask myself as I try to figure out what is happening to me.

"There's an *us* now?" I ask, allowing the strange little smile twitching at the corners of my lips to take over my face.

Daniel stares at me for a moment. His gaze lingers on my lips. Then he reaches over and takes my hands in his. "I'd like there to be," he says, in a quiet, shy voice. "If . . . if you like me as much as I like you."

My heart starts pounding furiously. My face feels flushed. My palms are sweating, and I'm . . . Well, I'm embarrassed because we're holding hands—we're actually sitting on the dating bench, holding hands! Not for warmth. Not for friendship. We're holding hands *like people do when they're in love.*

"Well?" Daniel asks. "Do you—like me?"

"I . . . I think I do," I whisper. My breath leaves my lips in a frosty little cloud and I laugh, because I'm more surprised by my response than he is. "I do. I like you very much."

"Awww, Graciela Inés Torres," Daniel whispers as he reaches up and takes my chin in his hand and pulls it gently toward him. "You're falling for me!"

I turn to him. His breath is warm and balmy against

my cheek as he leans in close, closer than I've ever let any boy get before.

I hold my breath and debate whether to let him kiss me or not. If he were any other boy, I'd probably jump up and run off. But I'm not afraid of Daniel. He's sweet. And I like him. I do. I'm sure of it.

As our lips meet, I catch a whiff of a strange scent.

Wet earth, dark and pungent.

Rain?

Dark and elusive, the scent enters my nostrils and makes my nose twitch. I break off the kiss and open my eyes.

"Are you okay?" Daniel asks.

I nod and rub the goose bumps rising on my forearms inside the long sleeves of my hoodie. It isn't the crispness of the evening breeze that's made my skin react, but rather that strange scent of stagnant water clinging to the night air.

"You still cold?" Daniel puts his arm around me then. He places his hand against the waistband of my jeans and pulls me toward him. I feel the heat of his breath on my face as he leans in to kiss my temple.

The smell of rain lingers, clinging to the molecules in the air, penetrating my lungs. But there is something else coming to the surface, mingling with it—the scent of freshly cut flowers, crushed and crumpled, attacks my senses. I see them clearly in my mind. Pink phlox underfoot. Violet geraniums and pansies bent over, trampled, collapsed. Purple jacaranda blooms set against the brightness of a blue-white sky. I shake my head to get rid of the images, but the scent remains.

Daniel leans down and kisses me again. Somewhere in the recesses of my mind, an old memory creeps in—the image of a dark woman lingering on the other side of the fence of our front yard. Disheveled hair flying all about her head. Dark and stagnant water. Flowers.

Daniel's tongue on my lips shocks me, and I jerk back and press my hand on his chest, to put a bit of distance between us.

"Too much?" he asks.

"No," I say. "It's just—do you smell something? Rain?"

Daniel sniffs and shakes his head as he looks out, into the swarthy shadows of night. "No. I don't think so," he says.

That's when I see it.

In the darkness, something lingers—a shadowy semblance made of moonlight and dark, angular swatches of night. The dark thing shifts and moves on the balls of its feet, ready to pounce, like a caged beast.

Beyond the pile of rocks, on the other side of the fence, the dark silhouette begins to move faster. It rocks back and forth and side to side—the dark moth woman from the funeral raises her arms and yells at me.

"Run!" she screams. *"Run, Grace, run!"*

Her voice is a roar that billows and blows over me like a blistering, cold wind. I jerk back, pushing Daniel away so hard he almost falls off the bench.

"Whoa!" Daniel says.

The porch light flickers and sputters as it comes back on, and the dark woman disappears—vanishes as quickly as she appeared. I stand up and step away from Daniel. "I'm sorry. I have to go!"

Mercy opens the screen door and comes out of the house. She leans on the porch railing. Daniel stands up too. He takes my hand and squeezes it gently. "It's okay. You're a virgin. I get it," he says.

"What?" I ask. But I don't have time to unpack what I am thinking, how what he just said makes me feel in that moment, because my sister puts her fingers on her lips and whistles loudly, like she's calling out a foul on an amateur basketball game.

"It's getting late, Grace!" she calls. "You coming in?"

"Yes," I call back. Mercy looks up at the full moon, staying in her place at the top of the steps, letting me know she isn't going in without me.

"Don't. Not yet." Daniel squeezes my hand when I try pull it out of his grasp.

"Let me go," I say, more forcefully than I intend.

Daniel releases my hand and I run up the walkway and up the porch steps, keeping an eye on the stairs as I go along. When I pass Mercy at the door, she smirks. "So you're going on a date," she teases, so only I can hear her.

"Yes. No. Maybe," I say, putting my hand on the cold handle of the screen door.

The moon shines brightly on Mercy's face, making her brown eyes glisten and sparkle darkly under the shade of her long lashes. She lifts her chin and sighs. Her breath forms a white-gray cloud as it leaves her lips, rolling out and dissipating into the night. "Just don't get into his car," she warns.

"Stop it," I say. "He's not like that."

But is he? My mind reels with doubt. *How do you know? How do you know if a man is good or bad?* I pull the screen door open and walk inside.

"They're all like that," Mercy says, following me inside and walking behind me as I make my way to my room. "Make no mistake about that. If you get into his car, he'll put more than his tongue down your throat. He'll put his hands up your shirt, grab your—"

"Shut up!" Her words taunt me, and I turn around halfway down the hall. "Just shut up, Mercy! Not everyone's like you, or those nasty guys you date!"

"Don't be naive, Grace. All men are pigs. Every single one of them wants one thing," Mercy says, grabbing my arm. She digs her long, lacquered fingernails into the soft flesh of my good wrist. "You haven't told him you're a virgin, have you?"

"Shut up!" I yell, ignoring her because I feel a sharp pain in my burned hand. "You're disgusting! Disgusting!"

I rush to my room and slam my bedroom door behind me. Then I throw myself on my bed, pulling my bedclothes to my chest and hugging them while tears escape my crushed eyelids.

As I lie there, weeping into my pillow like a child, I hear and then feel Alexander crawl into bed with me. He sits quietly beside me and listens to me hiccup and cry myself to sleep.

"Disgusting! Disgusting!" Alexander keeps whispering as he reaches up and rests his tiny hand on my cheek.

I wipe the tears out of my eyes and look up at him. "Don't say that, baby," I whisper.

Alexander strokes my face lightly. "I love you, Grace," he says.

I swipe a string of snot off my nose and hiccup. "I know," I say. "I love you too. Very much. You know that, don't you?"

Alexander nods.

The scent of flowers comes back. It takes over my

senses, and my vision blurs. *Purple blooms. Lavender. Soft. Relaxing.* And I close my eyes.

"Go mimis?" Alexander asks as he continues to stroke my cheek softly.

I want to smile, but I can't. My sister's taunting. That horrible, penetrating scent. The dark woman calling my name. Daniel's kiss. It is just all too much for me.

Too much.

CHAPTER TWENTY-FIVE

Three Years Earlier

IT WAS NOON WHEN MANUEL KICKED the door open and came at me, a mass of muscle and rage hovering over me. I cringed, trapped between him and the dresser. "I'll scream," I said, but he didn't seem fazed by my threat.

His hands on my arms were vises, and my throat was suddenly closed, so that when he said, "I'm in love with you. Don't you know that?" and kissed me, all I could do to fight him was bite into his bottom lip.

I tasted blood in the kiss, but it didn't stop him. He only kissed me more deeply. And when I struggled and pushed and shoved at his jaw, he pulled my hands down and wrapped his arms around me, imprisoning me in his embrace.

I fought and fought.

"Help!" I yelled. "Abuela Estela!! Help me!"

"Shut up!" Manuel covered my lips with his hand. "I love you. Why can't you understand? It didn't have to be like this."

I pushed my knee into his groin and my hands on his chest and shoved with all my might. Manuel groaned and fell to his knees. He lay on his side on the floor, grabbing between his legs.

I rushed out of the room through the open door. Outside, I looked at the empty country road and screamed, "Help!"

Then, seeing the gardener's shed door flapping back and forth, open in the wind, I ran toward it, screaming, "Don Baldomar! Don Baldomar! Help me!"

But when I got to the gardener's shed and stood breathless at his door, I saw that the dwelling was empty. "Help!" I cried out, into the woods, hoping that Don Baldomar was out there somewhere, close enough to hear me.

Manuel caught up to me. He grabbed me. Wrapped his arm around my waist. Then he grabbed the hair on the back of my head and said, "I love you. Why can't you understand that? I love you. Stop fighting me."

"Let me go!" I cried.

He didn't try to kiss me again. He just hung his head and pressed his face against my cheek. "I'm not trying to hurt you. I love you. I love you," he kept whispering as a deluge of tears rolled down his face. "Please don't fight me."

"Let her go! Now!"

I turned to the left and saw Don Baldomar stepping out of the woods. He was armed with a large tree branch, a thick, bulky weapon that he pointed at Manuel. "Don't make me hurt you, son. Let the girl go."

Manuel laughed. He looked at me briefly—resentfully. Then he wiped the tears off his face with the back of his hand harshly, like he was angry at himself for having wasted them on me.

"Go away, old man," Manuel told Don Baldomar. "I told you before. This is none of your business."

"But she is my business," Don Baldomar said. "Isabel is like a daughter to me."

"Isabel?" Manuel asked. "Is that your name?"

Because I wasn't about to tell my attacker that Don Baldomar was talking about my mother, that he was looking out for me because I reminded him of her, I shoved Manuel. "Let me go, you filthy beast!" I screamed, and I scratched his face.

When he didn't let me go, Don Baldomar ran toward us, screaming and wielding the thick branch up in the air like a battle-ax. But Don Baldomar was too slow. Before the old man could bring his weapon down over

Manuel's head, Manuel tossed me aside and charged at him.

I hit the ground hard, scraping my right knee against a rut. Blood oozed out of the torn skin, and I pressed my hand to it. When I looked up, Manuel was taking a swing at Don Baldomar.

Manuel's fist made contact with the old man's ear. The branch flew out of Don Baldomar's hands and he went down sideways, falling to the ground with a thud so loud, so finite in its density, I thought he might be dead, especially because he didn't move. He just lay on his side, arms outstretched, limp, eyes closed, mouth agape, like an old felled tree.

CHAPTER TWENTY-SIX
Eagle Pass, Texas
October 2011

THE DAY OF THE CARNIVAL, I dress carefully, choosing a long-sleeved knit red dress with tiny white buttons that go all the way down the front of it until it reaches my calves. The night is chilly, so I throw a pink cardigan over the dress. It is soft and plush and feels so good against my skin. I slip my feet into a pair of slate-blue flats because there is no point in wearing high heels if we are walking up to the mall and back. The carnival is set at the top of the hill, to the left of the theater, but we approach it from behind, through the empty parking lot.

"This is going to be the best date you've ever had!" Daniel teases, reaching out and taking my hand in his.

"Ha ha," I say as I sniff the air, taking in the smell

of buttered popcorn and cotton candy coming from the carnival stands up ahead. Daniel swings our clasped hands in the air and lets them fall naturally back and forth as we walk down the empty parking lot in the dark with the dim, foggy light of half a dozen light posts to illuminate our way.

"No, seriously. I'm really looking forward this," Daniel says, squeezing my hand gently.

"Me too," I say, scanning the parking lot. "I guess everyone parked on the other side, huh?"

Daniel nods. "Yeah, well, there's more light in the front, with the street and the cars going by, so it makes sense. People want to protect their assets."

We walk by a broken light, and Daniel stops to look up at it. I look up at it too, "I see what you mean," I say.

It feels nice, holding hands with him without sweating. I haven't felt this at ease with a boy since kindergarten, when Joey Zamora took my hand and pulled me toward the merry-go-round because I was afraid of getting on it. That didn't turn out very well. He told me to sit on the axis, so I wouldn't get scared, and then spun the thing so quickly I fell back and hit my head on one of the metal bars. Worst of all, I was wearing a dress, so everyone saw my underwear. Embarrassed, I'd cried, and my head had hurt the rest of the afternoon.

I let Daniel lead the way toward the end of the mall

where the lights from the carnival create a halo over the one-story building and the psychedelic Ferris wheel spins slowly off in the distance. As we approach, I hear the soft echo of carnival music intermingling with the high-pitched sound of squealing children and the murmur of hundreds of effervescent conversations.

When we turn the corner, the carnival lights eat up the moon and we are suddenly bathed in rays of golds and greens and blues so bright we have to squint as we walk around looking for Daniel's mother and her art booth.

"There she is," Daniel says, pointing to a tiny box structure squeezed between the Spider and the Floating Teacups. "Come on. Let's go say hi."

"Hey!" Connie says, turning around from her work on a young girl's face. "What do you think? It's my first dragon of the evening."

"Very cool," I say, leaning in to get a better look. She's got some beautiful lines going. The dragon's tail along the girl's jawline is masterfully drawn.

"You want to help us?" she asks. "We could use another pair of hands. Can you draw, Grace?"

"Maybe later," Daniel says. "It's our first time out."

"Oh, right!" Daniel's mother laughs. "Leave. Get out of here. Go do what kids do on dates these days. I'll see you at home."

"We'll check on you later, okay?" Daniel says. "After we've done the rounds."

Connie nods, and Daniel takes my hand and pulls me away from his mother. "Come on," he says. "Let's go get bracelets. That way we don't have to keep getting tickets."

The bracelets are fifteen bucks each. Daniel counts out every dollar aloud in front of the old lady in the ticket booth before handing her the stack of bills. "It's all there," Daniel says when the woman counts the money before having us extend our arms into the booth so she can put the flimsy bracelets around our wrists.

"Keep those on," she warns. "If you take it off, you have to buy another one."

"Thank you," Daniel says as we step away from the ticket booth.

"I don't understand why she had to count the money twice," I tell Daniel. "Do we look like swindlers?"

"Forget her." Daniel pulls at his bracelet, trying to stretch it out. "She's probably seen a lot of characters in her day."

"I guess," I say. "What should we get on first?"

"Whatever you like," he says. "As long as we get on the Hurricane at some point. That ride looks vicious."

"Let's start off easy, okay? We have all night," I say, because I know myself. If I go on the craziest ride first,

I'll never make it through the night. My body needs to build up resistance, and I need to gather my courage before I tackle the big rides.

After the Ferris wheel, we go on the Sidewinder, which is scarier than it looks because it moves faster than expected. My stomach does a couple of somersaults while we are on it and, afterward, I need to recover. So, I suggest we try our hand at throwing rings over the ducks in the kiddie pool. Daniel insists on winning a toy for me and tries half a dozen times to land a ring over the golden goose to no avail.

"It's not as easy as it looks, is it, son?" the burly man taking his money for another three rings asks.

"Come on," I say, pulling Daniel away from the duck pond. "I'll get you some cotton candy to help smooth your ruffled feathers."

"My feathers are fine," Daniel says. "It's my ego that took a beating."

When we get to the cotton candy booth, we stand in line behind an older couple. "Oh, hi. Back for seconds?" the girl at the aluminum cotton candy kettle asks, giving Daniel a wink. "Can't stay away, can you?"

Daniel blushes and gives the girl a quick smile before he looks back at me. "Uh, yeah."

The girl looks at me then. Her red lips flash me a tight little grin, but the smile turns into a grim line as she sweeps me from head to toe before she asks, "Pink or blue?"

"Excuse me?" My voice quivers a little and I clear my throat.

"Which flavor?" she asks, looking to Daniel again and smiling broadly.

"Pink, two of them," he says.

"No!" I hadn't meant to yell. The girl stares at me, and I cross my arms in front of my chest in a lame attempt to regain my composure. "I mean, blue. I don't like pink—blue, please."

"You don't like pink?" the girl asks, confused. "It tastes like bubblegum."

I shake my head. "No, I do. I do. But I like the blue better."

"O-kay . . ." The girl's eyes widen, and she peeks over at Daniel again. "Blue, then. Two?"

In the end, we get both pink and blue cotton candy, a small bag of popcorn, and two soft drinks. We wait in line for the Whirlpool while eating our treats. Our turn comes faster than I expected, though, so I scarf down the last of my blue coconut-flavored cotton candy and chug my soda pop too quickly, and I end up getting sick after our ride.

"I'm so sorry," I whisper, turning away from Daniel, who is nice enough to hold my hair back while I puke my guts out in the small section of grass between the Whirlpool and the Hurricane.

"It's okay," he says, moving aside and giving me room to step away from the mess in the grass. "It's the sign of a good carnival ride when you toss it all up like that. Wanna go again?"

"Are you insane?" I ask, walking slowly and heading away from the rides altogether. "I almost lost a lung back there."

"I was kidding," Daniel says, chuckling. He catches up to me but gives me room so I can catch my breath as we stroll past the Ferris wheel. We walk all the way to the edge of the carnival, where a slight breeze is blowing.

"Come on, let's go see if my mom has anything to help with the nausea," Daniel says, pointing left, beyond the duck pond and the petting zoo with its sad little saddled ponies and bleating goats tied along the fence.

We walk quietly for a few more yards, me with my arms crossed low against my stomach because I'm not sure I'm done throwing up, until we get back to his mother's art booth.

"You look like a ghost," Connie says, putting a hand on my forehead to gauge my temperature. "Here. Sit down a minute. What happened?"

"The Whirlpool got her," Daniel says.

The effort of leaning over and sitting down makes my head spin and my stomach lurch, and I shoot up, intent on running to the nearest bush. But I don't quite make it and I splatter blue swirls of puke all over Connie's sandaled feet.

"Oh my god! I'm so sorry!" I say when I look up from the mess to see Daniel, his mother, and several of her art students turn away, disgusted.

"It's fine. You're okay." Daniel's mother steps back and away from the mess in front of her. "I'm a mom, I've been puked on more times than I care to admit."

"But your beautiful shoes," I say, looking down at the ruined gold-and-silver art deco sandals on her feet.

"They're old," she says. "There's a water hose back there, by the port-a-potties. It'll rinse right off. I'm more worried about you. Are you okay? Here. Have some water."

"Thank you." I take the small bottle of water she hands me. "Can you excuse me for a minute? I just need to rinse my mouth."

"Oh my god, of course. Why didn't I think of it first? Daniel, darling, go to my car. I have a travel kit in the glove box. There's a new toothbrush and toothpaste in there." Connie picks through her purse to find her car keys. "You can give her a ride home after she's had a chance to clean up."

"No. No more rides," I say, waving a hand in her direction. "I need to walk."

"All right," Daniel's mother says. "But you should at least take the travel kit and wash your mouth out. You don't want those stomach fluids floating around in there longer than they have to. They can damage your teeth. Here. Take my keys. Go with Daniel. And if you should change your mind, he can take you home. Okay?"

"Thank you," I say. "I'm sorry about the mess."

"Don't worry about it." Connie shrugs it off. "It's a carnival. Kids get sick. Go on now, let Daniel take care of you."

Daniel takes the keys, and we walk silently around to the back of the mall and down the poorly lit parking lot. When we get to his mother's car, he sits on the passenger seat and rummages through the travel kit he finds in the glove box. "Aha," he says, and hands me a toothbrush and a travel-size tube of toothpaste.

He waits while I reach into my purse, find a piochita, and roll and pin my hair back into a loose bun at the nape of my neck. I put a generous dollop of toothpaste onto the toothbrush and lean against the car's fender to brush my teeth.

Daniel sits sideways with his feet on the ground, fiddling with the radio while I brush vigorously until, satisfied, I rinse my mouth out with the leftover water in the bottle. Then I clean the toothbrush and put it in my purse. "I'll get her a new toothbrush," I say, handing the toothpaste back to Daniel.

"Don't worry about it." Daniel puts the toothpaste back in the glovebox. "She has fifty of these things in different places in the car and all over the house."

"Really?" I ask.

"It comes with being a free spirit," he says, smiling as he nods. "There's always some show or artist colony she wants to go to on the spur of the moment. So yeah, she's always ready to hit the road."

I pull the strap of my small purse over my head and lay it on my shoulder and across my chest, pulling my hair out from under it and flipping it aside. "Shall we go?"

"You still want to walk?" He pokes his head out and clings to the roof of the car by his fingertips. "I could take you home."

"Walk. I think," I say, biting my lower lip. "It won't take long."

"I don't mind if it takes long," Daniel says. "We could take the scenic route, go for a long ride, before I drop you off."

"No. I think I'm ready to go home," I say.

I don't want to admit it, but I'm not sure I'm done throwing up. I pull at my purse, adjusting it under my left breast. "I need to walk. It's just a few blocks. I have to get out of these clothes. I'm pretty sure I stink."

"Well, I wasn't gonna say anything," Daniel says, getting out of the car and coming around to take my hand.

"What?" I lift my collar up over my nose and give my breath a sniff. "Really?"

Daniel laughs and places his hands on my waist. "Of course not. I'm messing with you."

I am completely conscious of his arm around me, but I force myself to loosen up, to live in the present, to forget the past. Daniel's a nice guy. What happened with Manuel in Mexico is history. Gone. Never to be repeated, much less revisited.

"Are you sure?" I cup my hand over my mouth and sniff again.

"Calm down," he says. "You smell nice. Promise."

"We should really get going," I say, but Daniel doesn't budge. Before I know what is happening, he leans into me, closes the space between us and embraces me, snuggling against my cheek.

"What are you doing?" I ask as he wraps an arm around my neck and pulls my face inches from his.

"What does it look like I'm doing?" he asks. "I'm kissing my girlfriend."

"When did I become your girlfriend?" I ask, a little put off that he's getting all handsy when I just threw up.

"Girlfriend? Did I say that?" Daniel asks. "Sorry, didn't mean to imply anything. Unless, of course . . ."

"Stop," I say, turning away when he tries to lean in for a kiss again. "This isn't the time for that."

"Why?" he asks, still holding me by the waist.

"Because." I put my hands on his chest and push, lightly but firmly. "We're in public and I just . . . puked."

Daniel takes my hands, kisses them, and places them on his shoulders before putting his arms all the way around me again and pressing me against the car. "We're alone, Grace. There's no one else out here. So we're not actually in public, and you just brushed your teeth."

"I mean we're in a public place." I pull my cardigan close and hold it in place over my chest with my right hand. "A parking lot is like the definition of a public place."

"Awww, come on." Daniel lets out a sigh. "You really wanna do this?"

"Do what?" I ask.

"I'm into you, Grace," Daniel says, pressing against me so that my back is flat against the front door of the car and he is hovering over me.

"Stop it!" I scream. But I am too late. Daniel has me pinned between the fender and the mirror and I have to push to get him off me. "Let me go!"

"Just one kiss." Daniel's breath is hot against my neck as he puts his mouth on my skin. "Nothing more. I promise."

My vision blurs and suddenly I am somewhere else, somewhere dark and humid. I smell flowers. And I taste dirt between my teeth. Rain pelts my body and bruises my face. I shiver from the attack on my senses, but I know it isn't real. None of it is real. I shake my head, trying to clear the echoes out of it.

Then I reach up and pry Daniel's fingers off my neck.

"Ow! Ow!" Daniel says, because I am crushing his fingers in my hand. "Sorry. Sorry."

I let his hand go and step back.

I try to take a breath, but my lungs hurt.

The maniacal carnival music roars in my ears, wild and confounding, and I can see my maternal grand-mother again. I can hear her screaming. *"What were you doing?" she asks. Her lips curl cruelly around her teeth, and she slaps me again and again. The pennies go flying out of my hand, and she screams, "Who told you to do that? Who? Who?"*

"Grace?" Daniel reaches for me. "What's wrong?"

"Stop! Stop it!" I put my palms on Daniel's chest and shove him away hard. He stumbles back. I move away from the car and circle around him. "I didn't ask for this. I didn't ask you to climb all over me. I'm not a carnival ride, Daniel! I'm not here for your enjoyment! I am not! Not! A carnival ride!"

"I know. I know," Daniel says. "I'm sorry, Grace. I really am. I didn't mean to make you feel that way. That's on me. My mistake."

Sobs rack my body, but I can't help it. I am crying like a child, a confused little girl who can't understand how a grandmother can be so cruel—a girl who can't understand how men can be so, so bad. I touch my cheeks, which are hot and wet. I feel tears rolling down my face, and I swipe them off with my trembling fingertips.

Daniel stares back, toward the carnival. "What can I do? How can I make it up to you, Grace?"

"I have to go. I have to get out of here," I say, and I take off running.

"Grace!" Daniel yells after me. "Where are you going?" he asks. "Your house is that way!"

I hear him yelling something else, but I'm not listening anymore, because I'm running. Running and running. And running. As fast as I can. As fast. As fast. As I can.

CHAPTER TWENTY-SEVEN
Three Years Earlier

WHEN I SAW DON BALDOMAR LYING prone like that, I jumped up and ran. But glancing back, I saw that Manuel was running after me. I couldn't go out to the road again, so I ran the other way, through the ornamental pink phlox, past the white gladiolas, past the lavender reeds, and jumped over the bed of dainty daisies.

But Manuel was too fast for me.

Or maybe I was too slow.

I ran until I reached the gate of the fence at the end of the back yard. Grabbing the lock in my hands, I twisted and pulled. I jerked and struggled and cursed, but it was no use. The gate was locked. Hearing him, I stepped away, looked for somewhere else to go, somewhere else to run, but I was too late.

Madly, he broke through the beds of purple geraniums and pansies. Standing before me, he pushed untamed locks of his hair out of his eyes and grinned. I stepped back, stumbled, almost fell, but caught myself and leaped over the bed of petunias.

Manuel smashed the flower beds, crushed tender vines, and cornered me between the jacaranda tree and the high wooden fence. His coarse hands grazed my cheeks. His rough knuckles scraped the length of my face, and he wrapped his thick fingers around my neck.

I arched back, pulling away, but he forced me down. Down. Down.

Down.

Until I was lying on a thick bed of pink phlox and strewn jacaranda blossoms. I blinked at the brightness of periwinkle light piercing through the purple blossoms of the tree above, so beautiful, so soft against my bruised skin.

My lips moved, made sounds I did not recognize as I wept, begged—implored—but Manuel was deaf to my supplications.

Desperate, I grabbed at the thin branch of a flowering shrub, pulled, tugged, tried to pull myself up. To get away from him.

The periwinkle and green of pinnate leaflets collapsed and stripped off in my closed hand, cutting through my skin and flesh. All I had to show for it was a handful of blood-soaked purple blossoms crushed within my fist.

Disgusted, I pressed them against his face, shoved them in his thick nostrils, pushed them inside his gaping mouth to cleanse his foul breath with the perfume I held in my wounded hand.

My tears were salt.

My voice, as I begged for my life, was a muffled breath.

His hands, as he silenced me, were earthy loam, the grit of grime and muck.

As the periwinkle light faded and dimmed, the scent of purple blooms overwhelmed me.

I couldn't hear my blood roaring in my ears anymore.

The tears were dry in my eyes.

I couldn't feel my body.

My throat closed.

Breath left me.

But the purple-pink scent, the smothering perfume of crushed jacaranda and pink phlox blossoms, lingered in my lungs. It was the only thing I had left. The last breath I took . . . The last thing I sensed before I lost consciousness.

CHAPTER TWENTY-EIGHT

Eagle Pass, Texas

October 2011

I RUN DOWN BRAZOS STREET, PAST THE Kentucky Fried Chicken, all the way down several blocks until I reach the far end of the Colegio Biblico. I don't stop until I find myself staring at a muted-gray three-story building.

My mind registers my location. *The old folks' home.*

Cars inch by, hundreds of them, backed all the way down Main Street. The fumes from their exhaust pipes, mingled with the heat of the night, sweep up to my face and clog my lungs as I breathe in and out, trying to appease my raging heart.

Headlights, like judging eyes, stare back at me in different shapes and configurations, as the cars wind their way around me. I think of Mercy then. I see her standing there, holding the door open for me as I made my way into the house. Her lips move, and she says, *Just don't get into his car.*

I reach up and touch my face. The tears have dried and crusted on my cheeks. My mind races as I think about Mercy again—Mercy, who told me I could tell her anything when I used to crawl into bed with her after our mother was murdered. Mercy, who would understand. Mercy, who could help me make sense of this.

"Mercy!" I cry, out loud. "Mercy! Where are you?"

The wind whips my hair, and I push it away from my eyes again and again as I walk up and down Main Street, peering into every car, scanning every face, looking for my sister—my beautiful, intelligent, lost sister. She had been right about Daniel, but so wrong about everything else.

If only she knew. If only I'd been honest with her. If only . . . if only I'd told her about Manuel. Horns blare, and I realize I am walking in the middle of the street. I am so close to the cars, drivers are rolling down their windows to wave and scream at me.

"Get out of the street! What's wrong with you?" a teenage boy yells.

A man leans his head out of the car. "Pos que tienes?" he screams.

I spot the Dairy Queen to the right, and I step onto the sidewalk. I stand there, thinking and watching cars go by for a moment longer before I realize Mercy wouldn't be in a car. She would still be at work, at the theater, doling out tickets to the late show.

I start walking back.

Staying on the sidewalk, I take a right at the Popeyes and head down Bibb Avenue. I am sweating now, and my face is burning, but I am determined to reach Mercy, to tell her everything. She needs to know—she *must* know what happened to me in Mexico. Maybe then she'll understand—we are better than this. We deserve better, and going back to school with me—well, there is hope in that.

Hope is all I have as I trek down Bibb Avenue, back to Mall de las Aguilas, to the other end of it, away from the carnival grounds, away from Daniel and his octopus hands, but closer and closer to my sister.

I walk through the mall and go right into the theater. The scent of popcorn is strong, overpowering, but that isn't the reason my stomach hurts. Something else is wrong. Mercy is not behind the counter. There are three workers back there. Jalissa, the manager, looks up at me from her tablet as I approach the register.

"You just missed her," she says. "It's slow tonight, so I sent her home ten minutes ago."

"Umm, okay." I linger in the lobby a moment. The lights are so strong, they hurt my eyes. But I need to stop and think.

"Honey?" Jalissa taps me on the shoulder. "Are you okay?"

The words register.

They twist into my gut, and I feel myself roll forward on my feet.

Breathe, I tell myself. *It'll be all right. She's probably back at the house, getting ready for a late date. You can still catch her if you hurry.*

"You need me to call someone?" Jalissa asks when I just stand there, staring at her. "You look like you've seen a ghost."

"I'm okay," I say, and I turn and leave the theater. I take a side door and walk out the back of the mall. The parking lot is practically empty, but Daniel's mother's car is no longer out there.

Relieved, I pull my cardigan close to my chest and take a deep breath as I continue walking down Williams Street, past the Sacred Heart Church, past the Salon de Colores and San Luis Elementary.

I am walking quietly, with my head down, when I see a light curl up around my feet, casting a shadow across the asphalt. I hear tires braking, a car door slams, and I start to run. I pump my arms and legs, using every ounce of energy I have to get away from whoever is following me.

"Graciela, wait!" a man calls out.

I keep running without looking back, but I don't get very far. The man following me is taller than me, and naturally his long legs let him catch up to me. He pulls at my arm and slows me down, stops me, swings me around and catches me in his arms.

"Get away from me!" I yell.

"Graciela, m'ija," the man whispers, holding me against his chest. "It's okay. You're okay. I'm here. I'm here."

"Papi?" I ask. Confused, I look up and focus on the man's face. *Yes. Yes. It is my father holding me. Not the dark woman. Not Manuel. Not Daniel. Just my father. My dad. My papi.*

"Graciela, hija, talk to me," my father says. "Is it an echo? What's going on? What do you see? You can tell me."

"I can't," I whisper.

I feel weak. My legs are burning. They are liquid lava, and my life is pouring itself out of me through them. I am on the verge of fainting. I know it. I can feel it.

My father pushes the hair out of my face and looks

intensely at me. His eyes scan my forehead, my eyes, my lips. "Graciela! Graciela! Can you hear me? Stay with me, baby. Stay with me."

Where were you?

Where?

Where?

I open my eyes. Move my lips. Whisper—

"I remember."

CHAPTER TWENTY-NINE
Three Years Earlier

AT FIRST, ALL I SAW WERE shades of green, rays of jaded light, piercing through the emerald shadows. Chartreuse phosphorescence. Olive dapples. Lime twists—*beautiful*. Then, magically, the hues took shape and form, a thousand throbbing hands of gold and silver green waved at me—*so beautiful*. My head throbbed, but my mind registered the names of things.

Trees.

Limbs.

Foliage—*all so beautiful*.

Leaves on trees came into focus, gained definition, and I knew that I was lying in a garden. I sat up and my head swam. My throat hurt, and my lungs felt heavy as they toiled inside my chest to take in and redistribute oxygen. I anchored myself against the trunk of the tree and stood up. My knees shook, my legs wobbled under me, and I thought I would throw up from the dizziness.

I looked toward the house and took a step forward, but my head swam again, and I fell forward. I braced myself with my hands, but I didn't quite catch myself because I felt my face hit the ground hard.

"Hold on," a man said, and I felt his hand on my shoulder, turning me over gently.

"Help," I whispered.

"I've got you," the old man whispered, his voice calm, soothing. "Just put your arm around my shoulder, like this." He put my arm up and around his neck. "Now hold on. Can you hold on? You have to help me. You have to hold on."

But I couldn't help him.

I couldn't hold on for one more second. My body simply wouldn't do what I asked it to do, so he put one arm around my back and the other one under my knees and lifted me up carefully. "Who . . . ?" I asked.

"Don't talk," he said. "Save your energy. You're safe now."

"Who . . . are you?" I asked. His blurry face looked familiar.

"Baldomar, the gardener," he said, and he started walking, hauling me back to the house. I lay my head against his shoulder and let him carry me into my room and lay me down on the cot.

He yelled out into the interior of the house as he stood over me. "Doña Estela! Doña Estela! Your young woman is hurt!"

I turned sideways to look at him standing by the door that led to the rest of the house, and the room started spinning again. I closed my eyes. When I opened them, my grandmother was sitting on the side of the cot beside me, holding my face in her hands and looking intently into my eyes.

"Oh, good. She's back," Baldomar whispered from behind her.

Abuela Estela patted my cheek. "Child? Can you hear me?"

"Yes," I said. "But my head hurts. Everything hurts."

Everything was spinning, spiraling, swirling.

I closed my eyes.

Shut it all out.

"Do you remember what happened?" a strange voice asked when I opened my eyes again, and I turned to the left and saw that a short, thickset man in a wrinkled police uniform was standing beside Don Baldomar.

"He chased me," I whispered. "Caught me."

"Who?" the police officer asked. "Do you remember who chased you?"

"He was too strong," I said. "Too fast. I couldn't get away."

"His name," Abuela Estela said. "Who was it? Who caught you?"

Hot, angry tears started welling in my eyes as the memory of the attack came flashing back in swaths of purple and white fragrant colors, and I blinked them away. "Manuel . . . ," I whispered.

The police officer leaned over me. "What?" he asked.

"Manuel," Don Baldomar confirmed. "I tried to stop him, but he knocked me down."

I took a deep breath and let it out. It felt like a chore, breathing, staying focused—the scent of lavender was overwhelming my senses. "He was fixing the roof . . . said his name was Manuel."

"So you know him." The police officer stopped scribbling. "And how did you know him? Is he *your boyfriend*?"

"Don't be ridiculous!" Don Baldomar said. "Can't you see she was attacked?"

I put my hand down and tried to sit up. "He was working on the roof. That's all—that's all I know."

It took me a while to explain the circumstances of Manuel's attack to the policeman. My grandmother gave me a glass of water. I sipped at it every few minutes while I tried my best to answer the officer's questions.

He grilled me until I was so exhausted that I thought I would pass out again.

"I'm tired," I told my grandmother. "I want to go home now."

"She can't leave," the police officer told my grandmother. "She has to stay here for a while. We need her to be available, to identify her aggressor when we catch up with him."

"Do you think you'll find him soon?" Don Baldomar asked from the other side of the room, where he'd been sitting down on a folding chair while the officer questioned me.

The officer tapped his pencil on his pad. "We have his name. We know who he worked for. Should be easy to trace. It's a matter of days, I think. The girl should rest until then. She needs to recover."

"And then?" Abuela Estela asked, looking up at the heavy policeman. "What happens when you catch him?"

"Depends," the police officer said.

"On what?" my grandmother turned to look at him.

The policeman took a breath and let it out quickly. "On what he says, Señora."

Don Baldomar cursed. "And what does that mean, exactly?"

"Well, I'm not sure." The policeman shifted his weight from one foot to the other. He pulled at the lapels of his shirt and tamped them down before running his hand flat against the front of his shirt, as if he was trying to press it with his fingertips. "There are several ways this can go. He won't admit his guilt right away. No one ever does. But if he's guilty, he'll fumble around, try to give us some story or other. Then again, he might say this was something else, something more than what I have been told so far."

"Something more?" I asked. "I don't understand. What else could he say? He broke in here. I didn't give him permission—I didn't—"

Behind the police officer, Don Baldomar cursed and stood up. "There's nothing he can say that I can't negate. I was there. I tried to stop him."

The officer cleared his throat and looked at his notepad. "Don't get upset, Señorita. I believe you when you say you were attacked, and it helps that you have a witness. It's just that I have to take his statement, and of course find out what he has to say about the nature of your relationship—about what might have led to this. We will go from there. We will look at everything and go from there. Okay?"

"The nature of the relationship?" I asked. "There was no relationship! I smiled at him. Once. But nothing else. Never again. He stalked me."

"Stalked you?" the policeman asked. "When?"

"He came to the window. Followed me from the store," I cried. "But I told him to let me go! To stay away!"

"It's true," Don Baldomar said. "I was there for that too."

"But you said you smiled at him?" the policeman asked. "When was that?"

My grandmother looked back at me, and then something hardened in her. It started in her eyes and moved down to her nose, making her nostrils flare even as her lips thinned. "Does it matter?" she asked, keeping her eyes focused on me.

"It might," the policeman said. "I don't know."

"That's enough!" Don Baldomar yelled. "I think you've got enough information to make an arrest. It's time for you to leave. The girl needs her rest."

When Don Baldomar and the policeman left, my grandmother got up and locked the door behind them. But something was different. She was more mobile, more agile than before. In the bathroom, she helped me run a hot bath before excusing herself. She left me alone to tend to my hygiene.

When I was done rubbing the dirt out of my hair and off my face, digging it out from under my broken fingernails, I slipped under the stream of the shower and let the scalding-hot water pelt me while I stood there shivering, numb and colder than I'd ever been in my life.

I'd just finished rinsing the soap off when I heard someone come into the bathroom. I stood frozen in place under the stream of water when suddenly the intruder pulled the curtain back and screamed, "Filthy harlot!"

It was my grandmother, standing a few feet away from me in her long gray sleeping gown. Her grey hair, wild and disheveled, hung over her face like a hazy curtain, and she was holding a broom in her raised arms. "Get out of there! You dirty whore! You don't deserve to live here!"

"Abuela!" I cried when the first blow struck my shoulder, hard and brutal and much more forceful than I'd expect from a woman her age.

"Filthy rat! Get out!" she kept screaming as she beat me with the broom again and again. "Get out! Get out!"

Covering my breasts, I scooted around her and ran out of the bathroom. I hurried into my room, wet and stark naked, frantically looking for something to cover myself. I had just gotten a hold of a T-shirt when my grandmother was behind me, hitting me with the broom again and again.

"Please," I cried. "Stop. Stop."

"I saw you." Abuela Estela stood holding the broom in the air. It trembled in her hands because she was crying so fiercely. "I heard you! The other night! You were talking to him through the window!"

"No," I said. "I wasn't. I didn't."

"I heard you!" she cried, hitting me again, making direct contact with my left shoulder blade. "You were smiling and cooing at him. I heard you. I saw you showing him your teeth!"

"What's going on?"

Suddenly, Lucia was in the room, standing behind me. I had no idea she had come home early. But there she was, and I couldn't be any more horrified by my naked state.

"Please," I begged my grandmother. "Please, let me get dressed."

"What for?" my grandmother screamed, and she began raining blows on me again. "You're shameless! A shameless, shameless harlot!"

Lucia stepped in and wrestled the broom out of my grandmother's hands. When she had taken it away, she threw the broom aside and held my grandmother back. My grandmother snarled. She bent forward and clawed toward me, enraged.

"Por favor, Doña," Lucia begged. "Don't hit her anymore. Whatever she did, she's sorry. Aren't you sorry? Aren't you?"

I didn't answer. Tears were streaming down my face, and I was trembling as I pulled my arms and head through my T-shirt, pulled it down, and covered my nakedness. Sniveling, I looked around for my jeans. Lucia put her arms around my weeping grandmother and walked her out of the room.

"She was flirting." Abuela Estela wept bitterly as she walked away shaking her head. "I saw her, Lucia. I saw her talking and smiling at that boy in the backyard. I saw her. She was smiling—*smiling*."

Putting on my jeans made me dizzy again, and I sat on the edge of the cot waiting for the room to stop spinning. But then the muscles in my abdomen contracted and I started heaving. Nothing came out at first, but I knew it was coming. I could taste the beginnings of it, right there, in the back of my throat, and I got up and wobbled over to the bathroom.

I sat on the floor by the toilet and threw up the water my grandmother had given me to drink during the interrogation. Lucia rushed in and knelt beside me. "I'm so sorry," she whispered as she pushed my hair back and held it with her hand at the nape of my neck. "Please don't let them upset you. I know you're telling the truth. Don Baldomar knows it too. We'll testify if we have to—we'll say whatever we have to say to make sure that beast gets what he deserves."

"I want to go home," I cried. "I just want to go home."

Lucia put her arms around me and cried with me. "Let it go," she whispered as she stroked my hair and held me against her chest. "Listen to me. This pain is not for you. This is *not* happening to you. This is someone else's pain, someone else's burden. Release it. Let it go. Let it go."

Then, when I was quiet again, Lucia put a blue hand towel under the faucet, ran cold water on it, and pressed it against my face. "Come on," she said, speaking low and soft. "Let's get you back to bed."

"Can you help me up?" I asked. "I'm still dizzy."

"You probably have a concussion." Lucia helped me back to my room, and I lay down on my cot. "You need to rest—stay in bed. I'll go down to the pharmacy and ask them what to do. They'll give me something for the dizziness. I'll be back before you know it. Okay?"

"Don't!" I grabbed her arm as she started to leave. "What if . . ."

"She won't. I won't let her," Lucia said. "I'll wait until she's asleep before I go. Okay?"

I nodded. "Thank you."

Lucia fluffed the pillows and set them behind me on the cot. "Now close your eyes and rest. Please."

CHAPTER THIRTY

Eagle Pass, Texas

October 2011

A DEEP, DEPLETING EXHAUSTION TAKES OVER MY limbs, and I drop my hands at my sides and close my eyes for a moment. Guelita Rosa, sitting beside me on the couch, takes a deep breath and whispers, "It's okay. You've been through a lot. Take your time. Just tell us what you remember as you remember it."

I've been talking a long time, telling them most of what happened to me in Mexico that whole week I was gone, but for some reason, I stop short of telling about the rape. I tell them about the attack—*the assault*—about Don Baldomar falling to the ground, like a dead tree trunk, but I don't tell them the rest, don't go into details.

It's all so *confusing*.

I feel vulnerable.

Exposed.

And I just don't have the energy to get into it right now. Maybe someday, when I'm stronger—when my head is not throbbing, and my mind is not a whirl-wind—I'll sit down with my grandmother and tell her the rest of this thing I just remembered.

I know I'll tell her first, before I tell my father, before I tell Mercy even. When we're alone. When my father and Mercy are out of the house, I'll tell her. Because I know I can trust Guelita Rosa with this dark thing that's weighing on me, threatening to drag me down with it.

"That's it," I say, looking across the room at Mercy, who is sitting forward on a chair with her fingertips clasped over her mouth. Her eyes are watering, and she's sniffling. "That's the last thing I remember."

"So when did you go to the church?" Guelita Rosa asks.

"I don't know," I say.

My father, who's been pacing the room, angry and frustrated, like a caged jaguar, presses his hand against his eyes, and then he wipes his face and comes over to the couch to crouch in front of me.

"I'm sorry this happened to you, chiquita," he cries. "I'm sorry I wasn't there to protect you. We looked everywhere for you! If only I'd known. If only . . ."

"I'm okay, Dad." I reach over and caress the hair on my father's hanging head. "I'm all right."

My father takes my hand, kisses it, and massages it for a moment, examining each finger before he looks up at me again and says, "Listen. I don't have a lot of money, but if you need to see someone, to talk to a psychiatrist about all this—"

I shake my head. "No," I say. "They wouldn't believe me. They'd think . . . well, you know what they'd think."

"I do," my father admits. "We went through that with your mother too, when things got bad. Not that this isn't real. That's why I don't want you to ignore this, Graciela. It's traumatic—what you've been through."

"But there are specialists," Guelita Rosa says. "In Mexico, medicos who could help you sort this out."

"Do I have to go? I mean, what if I don't want to?" I ask her, and my grandmother sighs and looks at my father, resigned.

My father doesn't answer right away. His lips twist sideways on his face, and he shakes his head. "No," he admits. "You don't have to go. Not if you don't want to. But you'll tell me if you change your mind? Okay? I'm here for you, Graciela."

"I'm here too," Mercy whispers from across the room.

"We're all here," Guelita chimes in.

"I didn't mean to freak everybody out," I whisper when I remember why they're scared. They had been looking for me because so many people called the house, telling them I was running amok down Main Street, weaving in and out of car lanes, like a zombie. "I'm sorry if I did."

Then, because I am still confused about everything I've remembered and I want desperately to figure it all out, I look up at my father and ask, "Why didn't you ever tell us our grandmother is alive? Why didn't you take us to visit her?"

"Because she's not," my father says.

"But I was there," I say. "With her—I remember."

"That's not possible. That house is abandoned. Es una ruina—it's uninhabitable," my father says. "Grace . . . I know you think you stayed there a whole week, but you couldn't have been there more than a few hours, a day maybe. The fact is we might never know how long you were there. Maybe what happened to you, the trauma you experienced there, distorted things for you."

I close my eyes.

I don't want to alarm anyone, but something's happening to me as I sit here, looking up at them. I hear something outside, thunder maybe, and the questions from the past are all starting to spin around in my head again.

Where did you go?
Where were you?
Where?

But there is something else going on. The living room is spinning, and I smell rain again—damp, stagnating rain—cold, dark rain—pelting rain—pounding rain. That's when I see it. Out of the corner of my eyes, a shadowy silhouette drifts into the living room. It creeps through the window and lingers, wavering and wafting, ever so gently beside the curtains in the dining room.

Somewhere in the fogginess of my mind, I hear Guelita Rosa say, "What is it, Grace? What's going on?"

I fight hard to stay present—to ignore the dark entity that has entered the room. "So what happened to Abuela Estela, then?" I ask my father.

"I don't know. They were estranged," my father says. "Your mother told me—well, let's just say they parted ways long ago and she never looked back."

"So you never met her?" Mercy asks.

"No, I did not," my father says, turning to look at Mercy.

I'm not convinced that he's being completely honest with us. He looks uncomfortable as he shoves his hands in his pockets and looks down at the floor.

"So it's possible then," I say, "that she's still alive?

"No, it's not," my father insists, taking his hands out

of his pockets and pressing aggressively at the space between his eyebrows, as if he's trying to erase whatever is up there—*whatever he's not telling us.* "Your mother wouldn't have . . . she wouldn't have lied. Not to me."

The entity in the room starts to vibrate, making a thin hissing noise. The sound of moths beating their wings against a searing light so elusive to others is loud and debilitating to me. It feels like it's piercing my eardrums, and I have to concentrate hard to focus—*to stay present.*

I close my eyes.

Ignore it.

"What about you?"

"What about me?" My father's face tightens. I see a ligament twitching under the rough skin of his jawline. "What are you implying, Grace?"

"I heard you," I say, looking at him and only him, because I don't want to give power to the thing that is looming in the corner, beside the window.

"What did you hear?" my father asks, scowling at me as if I was still a child. "When?"

"I heard you arguing," I tell him, fighting the urge to back down, to rescind my question. But I've gone this far, and I need to see this through. "The night she left. I heard her say she wanted to warn her mother. She said Abuela Estela was in danger. Why would she say that if she wasn't alive?"

My father lets out a burdensome breath and his shoulders drop. He looks at me and sighs. "She was having an echo," he says after a while. "A bad one. That's what you heard. That's what happened that night."

"It was happening a lot back then," Guelita Rosa says, echoing my father's dejected tone. "Your father tried so hard to keep her safe. We even took her to a clinic. To get her help."

"It wasn't the first time I had to stop her from leaving the house," my father says. "You understand, don't you? Why we're concerned for you. This thing in Mexico, with your grandmother, maybe it wasn't real. Maybe it was an echo. Like the ones your mother used to have."

My heart twists in my chest as I remember the horrible thing that happened to me in Mexico, and I feel trapped all over again. But I know my father loves me, just as I know what this sounds like, what this looks like to him. "Are you saying that I wasn't really there, that Abuela Estela, Don Baldomar, and Lucia were not real—that Manuel didn't attack me?"

I turn to look sideways and see the dark silhouette in the room shift and start to gain shape. It mutates, forming and reforming itself until it becomes the dark woman who chased me at Alexander's funeral. A coldness curls itself around me, and I shiver.

"We'll never know what was real or not," my

father is saying, but it's hard to hear him because the silhouette of the dark woman is wavering, and I see that she's crying—silent, iridescent tears that roll down her cheeks and cling to her black dress like transparent pearls, seedlings that root into the fabric of her black dress and sit there shimmering, reflecting back a violet, phosphorescent light that hurts my eyes.

"It's been so long," Guelita Rosa says. "Even if we were to ask them to look at it again, what would they find?"

"An abandoned house," my father continues. "A police report that says you were sleeping in a church in Piedras when they found you. That's all they ever found back then."

The dark woman in the room wavers and throbs to the sound of a dull, aching wail that rings in my ears. But she doesn't move, she just lingers there, thrumming her vocal cords with a lament so remorseful, so sorrowful, it resonates all the way down to the pit of my stomach.

The scent of stagnant rain on sandy loam intensifies, fills the room, attaches itself to my lungs, and I struggle to breathe. But I'm not ready to die. There are so many things left undone. So many things left unsaid. *So* many questions unanswered. I open my mouth and I fight.

I fight to breathe. I fight to speak. I fight to be heard.

"How did she die?" The question shoots out of me, but I am glad. Because it's the question that's haunted me since I was six years old. It's why I went to Mexico that day. It's why I've been so lost all my life.

"Your grandmother?" my father asks, confused. "I told you. I don't know."

"No!" I cry, taking a rattling breath, pulling as much air as I can into my lungs in one big gulp. "No, how did Mom die? What happened to her that night?"

"Please, Grace," my father begs. His eyes are red, and I know he is trying not to cry. "Don't do this to yourself."

The dark woman in the room drifts, slowly coming forward, mutating and reshaping herself again and again, growing bigger and bigger, taller and taller, breathing harder and harder as she approaches—in—out—in—out—getting closer and closer, until she is looming over us like a giant dark moth made of shadow and sadness and malodorous must and muck.

The scent overwhelms me.

The smell of rain mixes with the scent of flowers—petunias, jacaranda blossoms, and honeysuckle vines, but there's something else, something new mixed in with them, something putrid. *Contaminated water! Yes. Stagnant, noxious, tainted water!*

I feel the festering scent emanating from the dark

mothlike shadow in the room like an infectious virus and my body twitches, repulsed. The dark shadow creeps along the wall until she is standing right behind my father.

I jerk and jump up.

"Stop!" I yell.

"Is she all right? Should I get my pills?" Guelita Rosa asks my father.

"Graciela!" My father stands over me and takes hold of my face in the vise of his hands. "Talk to me, m'ija. Tell me what's happening."

The moth-woman lingers behind him, moving back and forth and side to side, like a ravenous beast—a predator, waiting for its prey to move, to run, *to take flight*.

I want to scream, to tell my father what is hovering over him, but I know it is just an echo—seen and smelled and heard only by me.

"It's not real," I whisper, closing my eyes and breathing in the pungent scent. "It's not. Not. Not. Real."

The dark shadow of the moth-woman behind my father wavers and blurs, the way the horizon shifts and moves in the heat of the day, and the scent of rain is so strong in the room, my brain quivers in pain.

"Go," I whisper. "Go away."

"You have to do something, Fernando," my grandmother whispers. "She's covered in sweat."

My father stands and picks me up, hauling me into his arms. "Move," he says, and Mercy jumps aside.

As my father rushes into the bathroom and places me in the bathtub, I think I might faint. As the cold water from the shower hits my body, the light in the room starts fading, overwhelmed by the hovering, growing dark thing hovering over us. My father's face disappears—replaced by the sight of a fuzzy black caterpillar sitting on a child's hand.

"Alexander," I whisper.

The caterpillar throbs. Its soft, dark belly starts to quiver and palpitate. The white oleander wings blossom, burst through the caterpillar's back, shrivel, and drop off. Fragile yellow threads break through the tender segments of red belly flesh. They spiral upward and outward, growing and growing. The flesh darkens and dulls. The black bristles fall off and lie glistening on Alexander's hand.

"Alexander," I whisper. "I'm sorry."

Hundreds of tiny maggots, thin and spindly as bean sprouts, crawl out of the caterpillar's belly. They slide down the walls of its flesh and creep toward the shadowy figure of the mothlike thing standing behind my father and Mercy.

The maggots climb up and over the dark thing, giving it life, fleshing it out—until I can almost see a face. My brain quivers inside my skull, and I scream.

"Stop!"

My father puts his hands on my shoulders and shakes me violently. "Graciela! Graciela! Talk to me, m'ija!"

I want to speak, to tell him the moth-woman is standing behind Mercy now, building itself up, gaining strength, but I can't. I can't speak. I can't breathe.

Please! I want to tell the dark thing. *Please go away!*

"Grace?" Mercy's face comes into focus. She is leaning over my father's shoulder, crying. "Grace!"

Suddenly, I am there again, in the bathroom with my father and Mercy hovering over me. The scent of flowers claws at my nose as I inhale. I can taste it, pink and pungent and putrid, clinging to the walls of my lungs, suffocating me.

My right hand throbs, and I bring it up and look at the angry gashes running sideways against my palm, bleeding, stinging as rain falls on it.

I blink.

"Please," I beg my father. "Please tell me how she died. I need to know. No more secrets, Papá."

My father breaks down. "She was beaten—bludgeoned," he cries, and he covers his eyes with his hand and hangs his head. His strong shoulders shake violently, and he sobs like a child in Mercy's arms. Heartbroken. "He left her in a ditch," he cries. "On the side of the road. In the filth! Like a dead animal!"

"Who killed her?" Mercy asks my father. "Who did that to her?

"We don't know," he says, rubbing the tears out of his eyes with his knuckles. "They never caught the bastard."

"So he got away with it," Mercy whispers.

The rain comes gushing down the walls in sheets now, darkening the small, crowded bathroom, pouring down from the ceiling, falling all around us. It pounds down on the shadow of the dark moth-woman, and I watch her lift her head up to the ceiling. The scent of wet loam and the earthy waste, a decayed fox, a decapitated racoon, rotting rats, death, scents and images that fuse, intermingle with the scent of lavender—a soft, delicate scent that overpowers and decimates the stagnant air in the room.

The dark thing opens its mouth and screams—a loud woman's voice that fills the room, shattering the sound of pelting rain.

A loud thud, a cracking sound—and then, nothing.

Silence—dead and buried.

A closed casket.

CHAPTER THIRTY-ONE
Three Years Earlier

LUCIA CLOSED THE DOOR AND LEFT me alone in the room in the back of Abuela Estela's house. I closed my eyes and told myself not to think about what had happened. I must have fallen asleep, because when I woke up, Lucia was sitting beside me. She was holding my hand and soothing me. "It's all right. You're okay now."

I looked around the room, disoriented. "Was I dreaming?" I asked.

"It sounded more like a nightmare," Lucia said.

"Was I screaming?" I asked.

Lucia shook her head. "No, more like whimpering."

"Sorry."

I didn't tell Lucia what the dream was about, because I was foggy on the details myself. The best I could recall was a compilation of images. My mother, cringing in a dark corner, crying, begging forgiveness, over and over again. *"I'm sorry. I'm sorry."* A young child standing on a hill, yelling, *"Run, Grace! Run!"* Then my mother again, leaning down to kiss me, the scent of lavender on her skin, *"Don't be afraid. You're my little warrior. You'll be okay."*

I shook the visions from my nightmare away and focused on my surroundings. It was late, evening perhaps. My grandmother would be getting up soon. I wondered if she would be coming to check up on me. She hadn't been in the room since—since she lost her temper.

Lucia picked up a bag from the floor and searched through it. "How are you feeling? Still dizzy?" she asked. "The pharmacist said you could take one of these every twelve hours, and just keep movement down to a minimum until you regain your equilibrium. He said concussions usually go away on their own. All you need is rest, but to stay in bed or sit up in the sala until you're sure you're not going to fall and hurt yourself even further."

"Thank you," I said, taking the pill from her and letting it sit in the palm of my hand while she went to the dresser and poured me a glass of water from the small floral pitcher she kept there.

"You'll want to eat something light," she said. "He

told me not to give you anything heavy until we know how your body's going to react to these." She shook a small box of pills in her hand. "They're muscle relaxers, for the aches and pains, but he said they also help you sleep. I'm thinking it might help with the nightmares. Do you want one now, or later, before bedtime?"

I shrugged. "I don't know."

"Well, he did say to take these with food," Lucia said, reading the instructions on the package and then putting it back in the bag. "So how about I make you some soup? Then you can take one. What do you prefer? Chicken or beef?"

Nobody had cooked for me since I was a child, since Guelita Rosa first came to live with us, and I felt a little overwhelmed by the idea that Lucia was willing to make soup just for me.

"Chicken," I said, and before I could do anything about it, tears started rolling down my face. I tried to wipe them away, to control myself, but the emotional wave that had brought them on was a force unto itself, and I couldn't stop crying. "I'm sorry," I mumbled, and took another swig of water from the glass in my hand.

"Oh, it's okay," Lucia said, rushing over to hug me tight. "You've been through a lot. Why don't you sit out front on the porch and wait for me while I put together the soup."

"No!"

I hadn't meant to speak so forcefully. I just wasn't ready to sit out there. The scene in the garden was too fresh and just the thought of being outdoors made me want to throw up.

"Oh my god," Lucia whispered. "Forgive me. I wasn't thinking. You don't have to go outside. You can sit in the kitchen with me if you like."

"I need to lay down," I said. "My head still hurts."

"Okay. I'll come check on you after I put the pot on the stove." Lucia stood up. She took the bag of medicine and placed it on the dresser on the way to the door. "Call if you need anything. Okay?"

"Yes." I nodded. Lying sideways on the cot, I pulled the baby-blue sheet over my shoulder.

Lucia shut the door behind herself and I closed my eyes. When I woke up again, she was back in the room. She was holding a small wooden tray, and she smiled when I rubbed my eyes and blinked up at her. "Good evening," she cooed. "Did you have a nice nap?"

"Hi." I shook off the bedsheet and sat up. "How long was I sleeping?"

Lucia put the tray on my lap and waited until I had a good grip on it before sitting down next to me. "About three hours," she said. "As long as it took to cook that. You hungry?"

"Yes," I said.

"Sleep's good for you," she said. "Eat some soup."

"You didn't have to bring it in here." I picked up the spoon, loaded it with bits of chicken and vegetables and just a bit of broth. I blew on it before putting it in my mouth. It was delicious and piping hot, just the way I liked it.

Lucia watched me load another spoonful. "Good?" she asked.

"Perfect." I nodded and ate another two mouthfuls before I laid the spoon inside the bowl. "There's nothing better than chicken soup. It makes every muscle and bone in your body just melt. Doesn't it?"

"Melt!" Lucia giggled. "I never thought of it that way."

"Yes. Soup just melts things away," I said. "Like you could just die happy because there is nothing better in life."

Lucia frowned. "Die? You don't want to die, do you?"

I looked down at the bowl of soup and thought about my mother, about the way she'd gone, the way she was taken from us. *Murder.* The word just floated in my mind and I pushed it away. "Of course not." I fiddled with the spoon. "It was just—I don't know . . . I was just trying to say that I like it. It's good. Thank you."

Lucia took a strand of my hair and pushed it

back, over my shoulder and away from my face. "You shouldn't blame yourself," she said. "It wasn't your fault, what happened."

I couldn't talk, couldn't make sense of what I was feeling. There was something sordid and shameful in the way the police officer had said it would *depend* on what their investigation revealed. I'd wanted to hit him when he'd said he'd get back to us after they talked to Manuel. But there was more to it than that. I was humiliated by the way my grandmother had treated me after he'd left.

"I'm not," I finally said. "But that policeman got to me. The way he talked to me, well, it just made me . . . I was so embarrassed. I'm sure that's why Abuela Estela was so mad at me. She probably thought—"

"No," Lucia said. "You're not on trial here, so don't even think about that. I know you didn't do anything to cause that."

I pushed the bits and pieces of chicken and vegetables around in the bowl with the back of the spoon. "Thank you," I said. "I just want this whole thing to be over, so I can go home."

"Well, time has a way of slipping away from us here. You'll see. This will all be over before you know it," Lucia said. "For now, you should finish that soup and get some more rest. And don't worry about your abuela. She's probably already forgotten all about yesterday's misfortunes, and we'll deal with that police officer together when he comes back. I'm here, and I won't let anything bad happen to you. I promise."

I put the spoon down and pushed the tray aside. My head was throbbing again, and my heart and lungs felt heavy inside my chest. Lucia took the tray and placed it on her lap. "You okay?" she asked. "You need one of those pain pills?"

"I think I do," I said. "My headache is back."

CHAPTER THIRTY-TWO
Eagle Pass, Texas
October 2011

THE FOLLOWING MORNING, MY FATHER CHECKS in on me before he goes off to work and Guelita Rosa sits on my rocking chair, knitting a doily as she rocks herself back and forth gently.

"You should go back to your room," I tell her as I lounge in bed reading a novel for English class. "That chair can't be comfortable."

"It's comfortable enough," Guelita says.

I close my book and set it aside. "I'm all right, you know," I tell her. "You don't have to stay by my bedside. I don't need a nurse."

Guelita Rosa's eyes soften. "Can't an old woman pretend to be helpful?" she asks. "Let me have my moment, m'ija. It's not every day I get to be on the other side of this."

There's a light tap on the door, and Mercy pokes her head into my room. "Grace? Are you decent?"

"What?" I ask.

"You have a visitor." Mercy makes caras and mouths the words, *It's Daniel,* before she goes on. "Well? Can they come in?"

Remembering the last time I talked to him, I scrunch my face.

"No?" she asks, looking over at Guelita and smiling hopefully. "Too busy?"

"Oh, please, don't let me get in the way," Guelita Rosa says, shoving her knitting into the bag on the floor and standing up quickly.

Mercy steps aside to let my grandmother through. Then she pokes her head back into my room and whispers, "You don't have to talk to him, you know. I can ask him to come back in a few days."

"No, it's okay," I tell her. I know Daniel and I do need to talk. We can't just pretend that terrible first date didn't happen.

I check my reflection in the mirror of my dresser across the room. I look like a sleep-deprived scarecrow! There's not much I can do about the bags under my eyes, but I comb my hair back with my fingertips and straighten the pillows behind me so that I can at least sit up in bed.

Grace leaves and comes back with Daniel in tow.

"Fifteen minutes, bud," my sister says as she closes the door slowly behind herself. "She needs her rest."

Daniel walks in, smiles weakly, and says, "Hey. How are you?"

"I'm okay," I tell him because I don't know what else to say. It's not like I can just jump into what's really going on. I can't just blurt out why I freaked out and went running into traffic last night instead of staying there and sorting through things with him.

Daniel takes a deep breath and lets it out in a long, extended sigh. Then he scratches his head vigorously and turns around looking for a place to sit. After considering the rocking chair, he starts to pull it over, stopping two feet short of my bed. "Is this okay?" he asks. "Can I move this over?"

I shrug. "Yeah . . . sure . . . okay."

"I'm sorry you're sick," he says.

I can feel his awkwardness as he situates the chair and sits in it. His nervous energy matches mine, and I have to force myself not to fidget with the books on my bed.

"I'm not sick," I say, when he leans over to get closer to me.

"Really?" he asks.

I shake my head.

"Grace." Daniel says my name quietly. His eyebrows crinkle together in the middle of his forehead, and he looks at my hand on the bed for a long moment before he continues. "I wanted to say . . . Well, I'm sorry I caused you so much distress . . . It was wrong, what I did, the way I treated you last night. I was wrong. Very wrong. And I'm sorry."

"I know," I say, holding on to the book against my chest with both hands, because I've never been in this kind of situation before. "Thank you for saying that."

Daniel looks up at me then. His brown eyes are misty, and I realize he's really torn up about this. "I just wish—" he begins. "I wish I could take it all back. I wish I could turn back time and start that date all over again, do the right thing this time, you know. But I can't. And I know that. Which makes it all so very—"

"Daniel," I interrupt him because I know my echoes made things worse. I said some things that weren't necessarily in tune with what he was doing. The echoes amplified things for me, and I know that. I own that. But it's not something I'm ready to share with him. We're not there yet. "It wasn't right, what you did," I say. "But there were other things going on with me that made things worse—things I can't explain yet. Because I'm not ready to revisit it."

Daniel looks perplexed. "You didn't do anything wrong, Grace."

"You're right. I didn't," I tell him. "But I think you're onto something with that whole starting-over thing."

Daniel's lips lift up a bit at the corners. "You do?"

"I think so," I say. "I'd like to—start over. But I don't want that to ever happen again. If I say we slow down, we slow down. Okay?"

"Deal," Daniel says. "Because that's not at all who I want to be, as a man."

"I hope not," I tell him.

Daniel raises his hands and shakes his head. "I'm serious. When I told my mother what I did, how I messed everything up with you, she was so mad. I don't think I've ever seen her so upset. She said it would serve me right if you never spoke to me again."

I sit up straighter, shocked. A novel falls off my bed and hits the floor with a thud. Daniel picks it up and hands it to me.

There's a quick rap on the door.

"You all right in there?" Mercy calls from the other side.

"Yeah! We're fine!" I call out to her. Then I turn back to Daniel. "You told your mother?" I ask, horrified.

Daniel's eyebrows knit tighter than before over his glistening eyes. "Was that wrong? Did I mess up again?"

I look at him for a moment, mystified, because I'm learning new things about Daniel. I know he loves his mother, that much is obvious. He's always doing things for her. I just didn't know he was so open with her. It's definitely different from my relationship with my father.

"No. No. I understand. Mothers are special people." I sigh and plop back against my pillows, wondering how much his mother knows about my behavior last night and what she must think. "It just . . . well, it feels a little weird. But it's not like we're strangers or anything. I did throw up on her chanclas."

"Aww, she didn't care about that." Daniel waves his hand in the air dismissively. And when he puts his hand down again, it lands on my bed, so close to my own, that I can't help but reach over and touch the tips of his fingers.

"That was really bad," I whisper. "Can you tell her I really am sorry?"

Daniel turns his palm over and lets me put my hand inside his. "She knows," he says, and he squeezes my hand, but then the door flies open and Mercy stands looking at us.

"Time's up!" Mercy says, holding onto the doorknob and looking away into the hallway, pretending she didn't just catch us holding hands.

Daniel stands and looks back at Mercy before he leans toward me. Halfway down, he stops. Smiling, I lean over and give him a hug. He squeezes me tight before he asks, "Can I check in on you tomorrow?"

"I'll meet you on the couch at ten," I say, and he smiles and walks out of the room.

Mercy rolls her eyes and closes the door behind him. She comes around the bed, leans over me, and pushes the hair out of my eyes. "Grace, Grace, Grace," she whispers as she takes my face in her hands and shakes me gently. "What am I going to do with you?"

When I smile, she kisses my forehead and holds me so tight, I can't move. "Can you hear that?" I ask her. "That's my ribs cracking."

Mercy lets out a laugh and releases me. "How are things going? Everything going all right with him?" she asks as she fluffs the extra pillow and sets it aside so she can sit next to me on the bed.

I scan my room. The sunlight filtering through the pale curtains at my window is a bit bright, and I narrow my eyes and focus on Mercy's face.

"We're okay," I say. "We're just . . . figuring things out. Setting some boundaries. You know, dating stuff."

"Dating boundaries? I like that," Mercy says. "How about you? How are you feeling today?"

I shrug. "I'm good, I guess."

Mercy's eyebrows furrow, and she blinks nervously. "You freaked me out last night. I've never seen you like that before."

"What do you mean, like that?" I ask.

"You know," she whispers, averting my gaze. *"Like that."*

I watch her wring her hands in her lap. "Explain," I say. "What exactly was I doing?"

Mercy lets out a quick little breath, and she bites her lower lip as she looks at me. "Your head was wobbling," she whispers. "You looked . . . you looked . . ."

"Possessed?" I ask.

"A little bit freakish, yeah," Mercy says. Then she turns away from me and wipes a tear off her cheek. "You scared me! You scared Guelita Rosa too. And you know she's not scared of anything."

"Guelita? Really?"

"These episodes are getting worse, Grace," Mercy says. She looks around the room, but if she notices Alexander's toys piled up in the corner, she doesn't mention it.

"I'm fine," I say. "Really, I am."

Then I sit up and take her hand gingerly, because we haven't sat together like this in what seems like a lifetime, and I don't want to scare her away.

"You're getting worse," Mercy whispers, and her hand around mine tightens. "I just wish I knew what was happening."

"Happening?" I ask.

"In there." Mercy taps my temple. Her fingertips linger on my face and trace the curve of my brow. "What's goes on in *there*, Grace? Where do you go when you stop being *here*?"

I think about it, concentrate. Really concentrate. *Could I explain it? Put words to it?* I look at my sister. She pins me down with her worried gaze, and then her expression changes, shifts to that softness that I haven't seen in her eyes since before Alexander's passing.

"I know what you're thinking," I whisper. "It's true what Guelita Rosa and Dad say. I . . . see things. And smell things. And taste things, up here. In my head. But I'm not losing my mind."

Mercy stops frowning. Her face softens for a second and she takes my hand and rubs it gently between hers. "No" she whispers. "I wasn't thinking that."

"I see people too, Mercy," I whisper.

"See people?" Mercy takes a deep breath and lets it out. "What do you mean, *see people*?"

The memory of the rain and the dark thing comes back to me, and I feel the hairs on my arms rise into tiny bumps all over. I sit closer to Mercy on the bed and look around the room, scan the corners, to make sure it hasn't followed us.

"What is it?" Mercy asks. "What's going on, Grace? Talk to me!"

I look at her then, really look at her. She is so innocent, so complete, compared to me. "There's so much I want to tell you," I whisper. "So much I want to reveal."

"So tell me," she says, slapping her hand on her knee the way she used to when she was a child and couldn't get her way. "Because I really want to understand."

"Alexander lives here," I whisper. Because there is no way I could say that any differently. There's no other way of softening that blow.

Mercy's face goes very pale. She tries to pull her hand back again, but I hold it tightly. "Don't," she whispers. "That's not fair. I'm not ready to talk about that."

"I know," I say. "But you need to know, Mercy. You need to know that he comes to this room. That he wanders this house. Every day."

"Stop it!" Mercy cries out, and she jumps up and goes to stand by my rocking chair. She grips the back of it and uses it to hold herself up. When she turns to look at me again, her eyes are brimming with tears. "You can't say things like that, Grace. He was my son. Mine. If anything, he would . . ."

"He was ours." I toss the soft bedsheet aside, swing my legs over the bed, and stand up, so I can talk to her eye to eye. "Yours. Mine. Guelita Rosa's. Dad's—we all loved him, Mercy. That's why he comes here. That's why he wanders around following me from room to room. Para convivir. To be among us. To exist."

Thick tears run down Mercy's face. I watch her eyelashes flutter, as she tries to ignore them. But it is too late. Her shoulders shake with grief. "I hate you, Grace. I really, really hate you!"

"I know," I whisper, going over to put my arms around her. She lets me, and we lock in an embrace, two little caracoles, curled up together. I caress her hair. "I've wanted to apologize to you so many times before."

"Please stop," Mercy cries out. Her fingernails dig into the top of my scarred hand. I hold on to the pain, welcome it, as hot tears roll down my cheeks.

Something moves in the corner of my room.

I flinch.

It's Alexander.

He's poking his head out from behind the curtains of my window, looking very sad. His eyes tell me he doesn't want to intrude but couldn't help himself. The sight of him brings fresh tears to my eyes.

Mercy is wailing now, a low, soft sob that emanates from somewhere deep inside her, and I lean over and kiss her hand fiercely, the same way she used to kiss Alexander.

"I'm sorry, hermanita," I cry. "I can't bring him back for you. I wish I could, believe me, I do. But I can't, not really, not the way he was before. All I can tell you is he's with us. Always. I see him here, in this room, playing with his toys, rocking in his chair, looking at the birds, listening to us come and go in and out of this house."

Alexander scoots back behind the curtain again, and I know he is scared too. He's afraid his mother won't believe me—*won't believe in him.*

"Stop," Mercy sobs. "Please. You're hurting me."

"But it's true," I cry, caressing the top of Mercy's hand, putting it up to my cheeks. "Believe me. He's here right now, hiding behind the curtains, listening to us. I wouldn't lie about something like that, Mercy. I couldn't."

Mercy lifts her face and looks across the room. A breeze blows in from the open window. The pale curtain billows out gently and then slowly deflates, not quite settling back down, but bulging out slightly to the left of the windowsill.

"Is that—?" she asks.

"It was. He's gone now," I say. "But he was there. I promise."

Mercy exhales. The breath leaves her body in a series of shudders as she wipes her tears with her free hand. "Is that what happens when you have one of your episodes," she asks. "Is that what you do? You talk to ghosts?"

"Sometimes." I let go of her hand. "Although when Alexander comes, I think I'm in a sort of make-believe world. I can't explain it. It's like I call him into existence. I manifest him, and then he's here with me, but I'm the only one who can see him and hear him and touch him."

"Touch him?" Mercy's eyes widen. "You can touch him?"

"Sometimes, yes," I admit.

Deep in thought, Mercy rubs the mascara off her fingertips. "Are there others?" she finally asks, still looking at her stained fingers. "I mean, have you—seen other people, other entities?"

I think about the dark thing in the living room and shudder. "Yes."

"Mom?" Mercy's eyes meet mine, and she looks intently at me for a second.

"Yes," I say. "A couple of times. I think it was her. But she doesn't come all the time, like Alexander does. Oh, Mercy. And there's so much you don't know."

My strange answer shocks her, and Mercy averts my gaze again. "Then why don't you tell me?" she asks.

I think about what I want to say—how much I

should divulge. There is so much I want to tell her, so many secrets I want to disclose, but I'm just not sure if we're there yet. This isn't exactly what I had in mind when I said I needed to talk to her.

"It's hard," I admit. Then, because I remember the echo with the pennies, I stop and try to place that memory. "It's all so convoluted. But I'm remembering more things every day. Important things. They're tied together somehow. The echoes, the memories, the visitations. I know they are. I can feel it."

"Tied together," Mercy repeats, nodding as she thinks about what I am saying.

Suddenly, the thing with the pennies make sense, and I draw her close. "Oh my god, it's not an echo. It's a memory. Abuela Estela *is* alive. We used to visit her!"

Mercy frowns. "What?"

"We have to go back to Mexico, Mercy. I know that what I am saying sounds strange. That's why I'm whispering. Because I don't want Dad to get wind of it. But I think it's up to us. You and me. We have to find out what it all means."

"What *what* means?" Mercy asks.

"We have to go back to Abuela Estela's house and see this thing through—watch the real echo play out again—let it reveal itself completely," I whisper. "That's when we'll find out what it wants."

"What who wants?" Mercy asks, her voice a hushed whisper.

"The dark thing," I say.

"What dark thing?" Mercy asks, looking frustrated.

"The dark thing that turned into a moth in the living room," I explain. "I'm sorry. Let me start again. There's this dark thing, this dark mothlike woman, it's been following me around for months. Ever since I started remembering things. And last night, when she was in the living room, she was hovering over Dad. She was so angry. So mad. And she cried, Mercy. She cried when Dad told us what happened to Mom."

"Stop," Mercy says, rubbing her upper arms vigorously. "This is too much."

"Don't you see?" I ask. "It's all connected. The house in Mexico, Mom's murder, and the dark moth-thing."

Mercy starts to tremble.

"Grace, you're scaring me," she whispers.

"Don't be scared," I tell her, putting my arms around her and hugging her against me tightly, the way she used to hug me all those years ago. "It can't hurt us. If it could, it would have done that last night. No. There's something else going on here. Something bigger. Something more important."

"Maybe we should tell Dad," Mercy says, looking back toward the door.

"No!" I cry.

My tone startles Mercy, and she jerks back from me for a second.

"I'm sorry," I whisper. "But we can't tell him."

"Why not?" Mercy looks at me with her huge luminous eyes, so much like Alexander's. So much like our mother's.

"Because he lied to us," I confess. "He's been lying to us all our lives, Mercy, and he lied to us again last night."

"Lying about what?" she asks.

"Mom," I whisper. "He was lying about Mom."

"But he was crying, Grace," Mercy whispers. "Why would he cry if he was lying?"

"Trust me," I say. "He wasn't telling us everything."

"You're speculating," Mercy says. "You don't know that for sure."

"I can tell you that he knows more than he's letting on," I say, moving away from her and to my closet, where I keep my backpack. "I think he wants us to believe the house is abandoned, but *I heard them*, Mercy."

Mercy averts her gaze as I stand in front of my closet, strip off my pajamas, and put on a pair of jeans and a soft yellow sweater.

"Who? What did you hear?" she asks as I zip my jeans and pull my hair out from under the sweater.

"That morning—the day Mom left—they were

arguing," I say. "Mom told Dad she had to go to Mexico. She told him she had to warn her mother. She wanted to get her out of that house that very day. But Dad wouldn't take her. I think he was scared."

"Scared of what?" Mercy asks, as I shove my feet into my tennis shoes.

I think about what my father has said, that the house in Mexico is abandoned, that my grandmother is dead. But that's not my reality, that's not what I experienced, and I want to go see it all for myself. But I can't go alone. I need a witness. I need Mercy to go with me.

"I don't know," I say. "But that's what we need to find out. If the house is abandoned. If Abuela Estela and Lucia and Don Baldomar aren't there anymore, then what happened to them, huh? Nothing. They're still there. I know. I was with them."

CHAPTER THIRTY-THREE
Three Years Earlier

UNDER LUCIA'S CARE, I ATE AND slept so much that by the fourth day I couldn't take it anymore. I got out of bed and dressed, intent on doing something other than hiding in my room. I had slept most of the day away and the sun was almost gone. I wasn't ready to see the garden yet, but I thought I might be able to sit out on the porch in the dark if Lucia joined me after she took care of my grandmother.

In the bathroom, I let myself sink into a warm bath. I washed my hair and rinsed it carefully and when the water cooled, I got out and padded around the room in my towel, picking out a nice outfit. My bones still ached, but I had a feeling it was due to lying in bed so long.

I pulled out a pair of comfortable linen pants and a

pink shirt Mercy bought for me at the mall on my birthday. I slipped it over my head and pulled it down until it covered me all the way past my hips. It was nice and big and perfectly comfortable.

I was sitting on a metal chair in front of the dresser with nothing but the light of an oil lamp lighting the room, combing my hair absently, when out of the darkness I saw someone standing behind me in the mirror. As the image of a familiar woman came into focus, creeping out of the shadows in the room, gaining shape and form in the mirror as she came closer, I dropped the hairbrush. It clattered on the floor and then slipped away, gliding under the dresser in front of me.

Suddenly I smelled water. The mirror darkened, and I saw something move behind me in the reflection. But then the scent of lavender whiffed through the air, and I was there again, in my bed, the night my mother left the house in the middle of the night.

"Go to sleep, girls," she whispered.

"But I want to go with you," I said, pulling her close to me, inhaling the scent of her, the calming lavender from the soap she scrubbed herself with every night before she went to bed.

"You can't," she said, pulling my arms from around her neck. *"You have to stay here and wait. Okay?"*

"But what if I have a nightmare?" I asked. "Who'll be here to wake me?"

"I'll be back before you know it, cariño. I promise." My mother kissed me, pinched my nose, and tucked me back into bed.

As the memory faded, I focused on the mirror again. The woman I'd seen before was standing behind me. I could see her silhouette more clearly now. She was wearing a white gown as she stepped forth and came out of the shadows in the mirror.

Mom?

The word didn't leave my lips, but my hands trembled, and I clasped them together and pressed them against my chest, unsure of what to do, what to say to her.

"My child, my beautiful angel!"

The pale woman in the mirror lifted her hands, reached for me, and I jumped. I turned around in my seat, intent on leaping out of her way, when I saw that it was my grandmother and not my mother standing behind me.

"Abuela Estela!" I cried, putting my hands over my face and pressing my fingertips against my burning eyes.

"What is it?" she asked. "Why are you crying?"

"You scared me!" I swept the beginning of hot tears out of my eyes quickly. "I thought you were . . . I thought I saw . . ."

"A ghost?" she asked.

"Something like that," I said, pushing the hair out of my face and pulling my shirt close at the neck.

"Nonsense. No such thing as a ghost. It's the living we should be afraid of. It's real people who carry the darkness within them, not ghosts, not spirits."

Abuela Estela touched my hair, caressed it, pressed it behind my ear lovingly. "I'm sorry I interrupted you," she said, and she bent down to pick up the hairbrush. "Turn around. Let me do this."

She waved the hairbrush in the direction of the mirror. I turned around gingerly, not sure if I should trust her with a potential weapon, and watched her lift the hairbrush and place it gently against my scalp.

"Such a beauty," she said, as she took a lock of my hair and brushed the snarls out of it. I sat there and watched her comb one lock after another with such devotion, such love that, for a moment, I allowed myself to relax. I closed my eyes and pretended it was my mother doing the brushing. "What's the matter? Why are you so sad? A pretty girl like you should never be sad. You should be smiling. Smile for me, cariño. Come on, let me see your teeth."

I didn't know what to do, how to react to my grand-mother's loving request, especially when she phrased it that way, with the same words she'd used after attacking me. It seemed impossible to me that she should make such an odd request after everything that had transpired between us.

"Smile?" I asked, my voice quivering.

"Yes," she said. "Smile for me. But not too big. Just a little smile. A small smile, like a lady."

"I don't understand," I said, remembering how she had said that she had seen me smiling and flirting with Manuel in the backyard. I pushed the brush away from me and turned to look at her. "What do you mean, like a lady?"

"Don't be mad at me, child," she said, reaching up to stroke my cheek with her right hand. "You have a beautiful smile. Your father would be so proud. Smile for me. Please. Don't you know how much I love you? You were my first moon, my first star."

Her words startled me. But then I realized she wasn't talking to me. I was part of one of her delusions. "Abuela Estela? Do you know who I am?"

"Of course I know who you are," she whispered. "You're my first love."

I thought about it for a moment. Was she talking about my mother?

"There," my grandmother said, pinching my chin and then tapping my cheek lightly. "Just like that. Perfect. Small. Delicate. Like a lady. You understand, don't you?

Why you shouldn't show your teeth to any man?"

I shook my head.

My grandmother put the hairbrush on the dresser and took my hands in hers. "A smile is an invitation," she whispered. "An invitation into your life, into your heart. The bigger the smile, the wider the door opens. For a man. You understand? That's how they think. They think you're calling them inside. You can't do that, child. You can't smile too much or too often for men."

Just then, Lucia entered the room.

"The policeman is back," she said, coming over to my grandmother. She put her hands on her arm and started guiding her toward the door. "Come," she said, looking back at me. "He says he wants to talk to you both. He has news about the attacker."

My grandmother stepped back and shuffled out of the room. With her shoulders drooping, she looked as frail as the first time I saw her.

We met the police officer in the kitchen. He was standing by the front door, holding his hat in his hands. "Good afternoon, Señorita, Señora," he said, bowing his balding head slightly to us as we entered the room.

"Well?" my grandmother said after she sat down at the table and folded her hands in front of her. "Did you catch him?"

"Yes. Yes," the police officer said. "We have him in custody. He was not hard to find. The information you provided us made it easy for us."

Lucia lifted her hand in the air. "What did he have to say for himself? Did he confess? You didn't fall for his lies, did you?"

"No," the policeman said. "He confessed. We have it all in writing. He will be going away for a very long time, I suspect, especially since it wasn't the first time."

"Not the first time?" The news shocked me, and I felt myself sicken. "What do you mean? Has he been arrested before?"

The police officer nodded and put his hat back on. "Once before. Two years ago, in Nava. But they couldn't make a conviction, because the girl said she believed he was in love with her, so they had to let him go. Because these things happen between men and women, you understand?"

"No, I don't," I said, remembering that night at the window. The tiny hairs on my arms rose, and I rubbed my forearms. "Because he told me that too, but they're just words. I didn't want him to say any of those things. Anyone can say they love you. It doesn't mean anything."

The police officer stepped away from the door, came closer to me, and I shifted in my chair. "You don't really believe that, do you?" the policeman asked, looking down at me.

"Of course I do," I said. "He's a monster, a beast!"

Lucia put her hands on my shoulders and squeezed gently. "Thank you, officer," she said. "Is there anything else we need to do? Any papers we need to sign? She doesn't have to go down there, does she? To identify him?"

The officer pushed his chin out, making his lower lip stand out, like a spatula. He shook his head. "No. We have a signed confession. We don't need to put her through any more hardships than she's already experienced. I just wanted to let you know that we caught him and that you can sleep at night knowing he's off the streets and you're safe now."

Lucia and I thanked the policeman.

My grandmother, however, didn't say anything. She just stared at the wall in front of us, lost in time and thought again. When he saw that there was nothing more to be done or said, the police officer excused himself and walked back out. Lucia locked the door behind him. She turned around and sighed.

"I'm so glad that's over," Lucia whispered, turning around to look at us.

"Don't be a fool," Abuela Estela said. "This isn't over. Not until this one leaves."

"What are you saying?" Lucia was horrified.

Abuela Estela lifted her shoulders and sat straight in her chair for the first time since I'd arrived.

"You heard me. What's done is done. We can't take it back, but what you need to understand is that your disgrace brings shame and dishonor to all of us in this house. And I can't live with that."

Lucia gasped. She rushed over and put a hand on my grandmother's shoulder. "Doña Estela," she whispered. "You can't do that. What happened wasn't her fault."

"Don't argue with me, child! I won't stand for it!" Abuela Estela yelled. Then she turned to look at me directly. "You can stay through the rest of the night, but after that, you'll have to leave—you made a choice to throw your life away, now you'll have to find somewhere else to live. That is all. That is my decision. I won't speak of it again. Make sure you're gone by morning."

"Doña Estela!" Lucia put a hand on Abuela Estela's arm, to stop her. "You don't mean that. She doesn't mean that."

"And don't come back!" My grandmother shrugged Lucia's hand away. "I never want to see you again."

CHAPTER THIRTY-FOUR
Eagle Pass, Texas
October 2011

"¿Por qué tan calladitas?" Guelita Rosa asks, peeking at us from behind the rim of her empty coffee cup. "What's got your tongues tied up in knots?"

"What?" I ask, biting down on a piece of crunchy toast and dusting my fingertips against each other, acting like I have no idea what she means.

"Come on," Guelita Rosa says. "Spit it out. Where are you two going?"

"Going?" Mercy frowns, a little too dramatically if you ask me. "What makes you think we're going anywhere?"

"Well, let's see." Guelita Rosa looks at my back-pack resting against my chair on the floor, and then she reaches over to give Mercy's purse, which is hanging from the back of her chair, a tug. "It's Saturday morning, and instead of sleeping in, you two are all dressed up and ready to head out the door—like you ever go out together!"

When neither of us says anything, Guelita Rosa grins. She reaches over to each of us and puts a hand on ours. We let her hold our hands for a moment, before I say, "We can't get anything past you, can we?"

Guelita Rosa laughs. "You never could. Not that I disapprove." She squeezes our hands as she looks from Mercy to me. "It's good to see the two of you acting like hermanitas again. God knows, with all the darkness out there, we need more sisterly love than ever before."

"That's an understatement," I say, nodding as I pick up my cup and take a sip of my coffee.

"So?" Guelita Rosa prods again.

"So what?" Mercy asks, tossing her piece of toast onto her plate and staring at our grandmother.

"Okay, fine," Guelita Rosa says. "Don't tell me. I don't want to know."

"We should tell her," Mercy says. "In case . . ."

"Mexico!" I spit it out fast, before I lose my nerve. "We're going to Abuela Estela's house."

Guelita Rosa slaps a hand on her forehead and takes a deep breath, letting it out in a low moan. "Ay, pero what for?" she asks, shaking her head.

"I have to see it," I tell her. "If I'm going to believe that what happened in Mexico was an echo, I have to see that ruined place with my own two eyes."

"And if more echoes come?" Guelita Rosa asks, clenching her fingers and pressing her fist against the table. "What are you going to do then, Grace? Who'll catch you when you faint again?"

"I'll be there," Mercy jumps in. "Don't worry, Guelita. I'll stay with her the whole time. I'll make sure nothing happens to her."

Tears start rolling down Guelita Rosa's face, and she shakes her head and crosses herself. She cries openly—a slow, mournful wail that leaves her lips like a long, languid lament. Then she reaches out, puts her trembling hands up in the air, and Mercy and I look at each other.

"Demen un rezo," she whispers, and Mercy and I put our hands inside hers. She lifts our hands in the air and starts praying for protection. She invokes the Lord in heaven and the angels around us. She calls on the Virgen de Guadalupe and asks the santitos to keep us safe. She begs our ancestors to stay close to us, and then she pulls us in close and kisses our foreheads. Her tears baptize us, and I feel my fear dissipate.

"Remember," Guelita says, squeezing our hands in hers. "No matter what happens out there, what you find out, you are not that anymore—the sins inflicted upon us do not dictate who we are or who we become. Only you can do that. You own your futures."

"Thank you, Guelita!" Mercy leans down, hugs her, and kisses her cheek before she starts to clear the table.

"Can we get you anything else?" I ask her when she finally settles in her chair in the living room with her crocheting basket beside her. "Before we go?"

Guelita Rosa nods and points a crooked finger to her room. "Get me my rosary," she says. "Out of my Bible, on the nightstand. I can't go with you, but I can pray for you until you get home."

Mercy runs into Guelita Rosa's room and comes back with the rosary. She puts it in Guelita's hand and Guelita reaches up and hugs her one more time. I lean down and kiss her on the cheek.

"We'll be back this afternoon," I promise.

Deep inside me, something stirs. But I can't afford to be scared, not anymore. So I head out the door. The wind is strong. And there is a freshness to the cold breeze that gives me hope.

CHAPTER THIRTY-FIVE

Las Cenizas, Municipio de Guerrero, Coahuila, Mexico

October 2011

BECAUSE IT IS TEN IN THE morning, the sun is high up in the sky when Mercy drives her car south, past Piedras Negras, Coahuila. We go over potholes and beyond asphalt, until we veer off the road and enter Las Cenizas, the most impoverished colonia in the outskirts of the city.

"I hope you're not expecting much," Mercy says, looking sideways at me. "This neighborhood's pretty sad looking."

"I know," I say. "I stayed here, remember?"

She looks out at the postecito with the same blonde girl looking out its window as we pass through Las Cenizas. "Are you thirsty?" she asks. "It's hot out here."

"No," I say. "I don't want to stop there. The owner's not very nice."

"Okay," Mercy says as she steers the car where I point, around the corner, until we are on the narrow dirt road that has more bumps and ruts than a dead planting field.

The sun beats on the windshield and I squint as I sit forward, looking for my grandmother's house. "That's it," I say, pointing ahead. "Over there. See it?"

"I do," Mercy says. "Although I wish I hadn't."

When we get to Abuela Estela's house, Mercy stops, puts the parking brake on, and turns off the engine.

"Are you sure you want to do this?" Mercy asks, looking at my grandmother's dark house. "We could just drive back. Maybe have some taquitos at that restaurant you like in the plaza."

As I glance at the house, with its rotted roof, gaping windows, and overgrown grass, nothing looks the way I remember it. It's like I'm staring at a nightmare. A nightmare I didn't know was here.

We get out of the car and walk toward the broken gate swinging in the breeze, barely hanging on, creaking back and forth in the cold October wind.

Mercy takes my hand, and we walk across the high grass.

"It's abandoned." The words feel small, deflated, as they leave my lips.

"I can see that," Mercy says. We press the high burr

grass down with our feet as we go, trying to keep the stickers from getting on our clothes. "You stayed here? Deliberately?"

I hold Mercy's hand in mine as we stand at the wheezing gate, staring at Abuela Estela's ruined house. "I'll admit, I'm a little bit scared," I say. "When I stayed here before, the shrubbery wasn't overgrown like this, and the windows weren't bare. At least I don't think they were."

Mercy follows me as I step through the broken iron gate, and we walk into the yard. I stop before the front door, twist the doorknob, and push on it gently. When nothing happens, I push again, harder this time. But when it doesn't give, I walk off to the right, to peek around the corner.

I touch the cracks on the stucco wall along the side of the house, press my fingertips into the grooves. *Have those cracks been there all along? Because I honestly don't remember them.* I scoot along the perimeter of the house, looking in every window at the empty rooms, like my mother had done all those years before. Only back then, the house was not abandoned. At least that's not what I remember.

It's clear to me now that nobody has lived here in years. Mercy turns the doorknob on the side door. She pushes at it with her shoulder until it gives way, creaking wide open. She steps inside and peeks around. I follow her in. "Oh my god, Grace," she says, her pupils large and luminous in the darkened interior. "This is worse than I thought."

I tremble as I stand in the middle of the gloomy, dimly lit living room where I met Lucia that first night. Mercy wanders away from me and into the kitchen. When she comes back, she is holding two lit candles in front of her. "At least we can see now," she says, handing me the shorter candle. "Are you sure we're in the right place?"

"I'm positive," I say as we wander down the hall into the bedroom I slept in. "See, that's where I slept. Over there. On that cot."

Mercy stares at the rusted metal frame. "Ewww!" she says, making a disgusted face. "What possessed you to do that?"

"I wasn't possessed!" I complain.

Mercy lets out a frustrated breath. "I didn't mean it like that," she says, taking my hand and squeezing it gently. "It's just so weird—to think that you stayed here in this filth for a week."

"Who knows how long I was here?" I whisper. "I could have been here a day, or a moment, for all I know. I could have wandered the streets for hours trying to reconcile what I experienced here. I could have slept on that church pew for days before someone called the police. There's no telling how it all went down."

"That's true," Mercy says, letting go of my hand to wander around the room, peeking into the bathroom and shaking her body as she turns away from it.

I wander through the rest of the empty, wrecked house, with its cobwebs, missing interior doors, and broken, moth-eaten furniture. In my grandmother's room, I stare at her bed with its sagging mattress, and I feel a sharp pain in my chest. I move away and walk toward the side door, intent on going outside to get some fresh air, but then I spot Mercy in the living room.

"Look at this," she says, dusting layers of grime off an old entertainment console in the corner of the room and opening the lid to peer inside. She reaches in and pulls out a small stack of records. "Pedro Infante. Jorge Negrete. Lucha Villa."

I touch the album covers as Mercy goes through them. "I didn't see these before," I say. "When I was here."

"They must have been Mom's," Mercy says. "See the initials, here in the corner. These were hers."

"They're well preserved," I say. "You should take them."

Mercy leans down and opens the small door on the left side of the entertainment console and finds a huge stash of albums. "Jackpot!" she yells, and she dusts a space on the floor so she can sit in front of them. "Oh. My. God. This is so cool."

I look around the room and wonder what else I missed when I stayed here. Remembering the beautiful dresses hanging in the armoire, I leave Mercy sorting through her newfound treasure and walk back down the hall until I reach the room with the armoire, telling myself there is no way those would still be intact.

But when I open the armoire, something happens. My vision blurs, and the room starts spinning very fast. The sunlight coming into the room from the window filters out and the room becomes very dark. A chilly breeze swirls around me, and I am suddenly very cold.

The door leading to the back patio starts rattling, as if something wild and wicked is trying to get inside the house. I hear a woman scream in the distance, and I close my eyes, willing myself to control the echo. But no matter how hard I try, the woman's screams get louder and louder, and the rattling gets stronger and stronger, until I can't take it anymore and I put my hands against my ears.

The door flies open, and a young man comes rushing in. A girl standing in front of the mirror turns around. The skirt of her yellow dress billows out, a breezy blur that makes my head spin. I try to concentrate, but I can't see her face because she has turned away from me. But she is doing exactly what I'd been doing when Manuel kicked the door open that horrible morning.

A young, stocky man wearing filthy work clothes and thick, heavy boots comes crashing through the door and grabs the girl in the yellow dress. *Manuel!* my mind screams. Manuel tries to kiss her. She attempts to scream, but he puts his hand over her mouth and stops her.

"Shut up!" he says, and he puts his hand up and covers her lips. "I love you. Why can't you understand?"

The girl turns to me. Her eyes are huge, bulging spheres, full of fear.

Mom!

I open my mouth, try calling for Mercy, but my voice is gone. I try to move, to help my mother, but I am paralyzed. I scream—inside my head, I rage. That's when it happens. I'm able to move again, so I reach out to help my mother, but I still can't get close to her. I circle the bed and try to reach the door—to open it and call for help, but I can't reach the doorknob. It's like some supernatural force is keeping me from interfering.

My mother pushes and shoves at Manuel, until she manages to free herself. While he lays on the floor, grabbing his groin in pain, my mother gets up and runs toward me. I open my arms to her, but she doesn't make eye contact with me. It's like she doesn't know I am here. She can't see me standing right in front of her, between her and the door.

But when she goes by me, she doesn't pass by, but runs straight through me instead. And in that moment, in those few seconds when her body fuses with mine, I feel an intense electrical charge. Her body hits mine like a bolt of lightning. We fuse, frozen in time and space, and I quiver with the force of it.

As her spirit pierces through me, every nerve ending inside me sparks to life, and I feel everything she feels— know everything she knows—understand everything she understands. In that terrible, dark moment in her life, I am one with my mother. And I know that it wasn't me, but her that Manuel attacked, when she was a young woman, before she left here, before she met my father. And I understand why she brought me here three years ago.

I'd reached out to her at the church the day I ran away, questioned her love for me, and in response she'd brought me here to explain herself to me—to show me the secret she'd carried with her all her life—to share her woundedness, her sorrow.

The pain of it renders me helpless.

I can't breathe.

So I cry.

"*Mom!*"

"*Mami!*"

I call out, turning around to stop her from leaving again. But I am too late. My mother has passed through me and is now running out the door in a whirlwind of yellow fabric. Her long brown hair is flowing behind her like a billowing curtain, and she is gone, vanished into the brightness of sunlight and warmth.

The light fades, the space returns to normal, but I get the feeling this echo is not done with me. Because there is something else here. I can feel its presence, breathing quietly in the silence, lingering in the stillness, waiting in the shadows of the far corner of the room.

"Who are you?" I ask, taking a few steps backward, inching my way toward the door that leads to the backyard. A cold, chilly breeze rushes up from behind me, and I hug myself, shivering. My legs are weak, and I feel vulnerable, but I know I can't back down now. This is why I came here—to find the truth. "Show yourself!"

"Do you remember me?" the entity in the corner asks as it steps out of the shadows.

"Lucia," I whisper, as I recognize the hazy form of my grandmother's caregiver—my own caregiver those last few days before I'd left. "You know who I am?"

"Yes." Lucia nods her head. "I'm glad you came back. We need you."

"You need me?" My stomach twists, and I feel a strange pain in my chest. "What for?"

"To help us," Lucia explains. "Such horrible murders can't go unpunished."

"Murders?" I ask, putting my hand against the frame of the door behind me, because the word *murders* is bouncing off every corner of the room, echoing, until I think I might pass out. "How many murders?"

Lucia's ghost drifts quietly away from me and goes to stand by the small window that looks out into the backyard. "We were butchered," she says quietly, like it's a secret. "All of us. Your mother, your grandmother, and me."

"When?" I ask.

"Twelve years ago," Lucia says. "It was a nightmare. What everyone fears but nobody could ever conceive."

"Twelve years?" I ask. My mind spins and my stomach dips. *Twelve years! Twelve years!* The words echo over and over in my head. My mother was murdered *twelve years ago!* I put both hands on the wall behind me to balance myself. "No."

"Yes . . ." she whispers, turning away to look out the window again.

"Who did it?" I ask, pushing myself off the wall and stepping closer to Lucia. "Who murdered you all?" I ask, my voice coming out in shrills.

"Manuel," Lucia says, turning to look at me eye to eye. I step back and look around the room, because the scent of lavender is suddenly adrift in the air around us. "Days after he was released from prison. We'd gone to bed that morning. He slipped in through the back door. He cut Doña Estela's throat first. She bled out, right there in her bed, where she lay watching television. Then he moved down the hall. He found me asleep and did the same thing to me. Like lambs in our stalls."

"Twelve years ago." I repeat the words, because I'm trying hard to put it all together. "My mother died twelve years ago."

"Yes. She came to warn us," Lucia says. "But she was too late. We had already passed."

I flinch.

"Too late?" I ask.

"That's why we couldn't help her," Lucia explains. "We had passed away, but we hadn't crossed over. So we saw everything."

"Everything?" I ask.

"He hit her," Lucia says. "Knocked her out. Put her over his shoulder. There was nothing we could do. He took her away. Walked out with her. Into the rain he went. We couldn't do anything. We were too young in death—so we were still anchored here, helpless. But your grandmother. Your grandmother couldn't get over it. Her anger got stronger and stronger. And when she was able to go, she went out there."

My eyes water.

I smell rain. Dark, heavy rain.

And pink phlox and gardenias and daisies.

"That's why I'm here," I whisper, more to myself than to Lucia, whose shade is wavering, fading, like the light of my flickering candle.

The scent of stagnant water, the sound of pounding rain, the pain throbbing rhythmically in my hand, it is all too much, too much—the sweet, cloying scent of a jacaranda in bloom fills my nostrils, crawls up in my nasal cavity, and curls around my eyes, suffocating me.

CHAPTER THIRTY-SIX

Las Cenizas, Municipio de Guerrero, Coahuila, Mexico

October 2011

"OH NO. SHE'S BACK," LUCIA SAYS. "Graciela. Whatever happens, listen to your mother. Do you understand?"

But I can't answer her. I can't even move. The sound of a woman's wailing has entered the room. It swirls around me in the form of a dark swarm of moths that won't stop buzzing and hissing overhead. Across from me, Lucia is crying. Her form wavers and shifts against the swirling wind that's wound itself around us.

The mossy scent of tainted water and dead flowers swirls and swirls in the stagnant room. The door behind me opens and closes and opens and closes as if someone is kicking it in over and over again. In the far corner of the room, sitting on the little concrete step that separates the room from the bathroom, my young mother is crying; wet and naked, she shivers and covers herself with a bedsheet. Above and all around us, the sights and sounds and smells blend together, making everything incomprehensible.

The dark moths create a wall of confounding sights and sounds and smells that overwhelms me. I put my hands over my ears to muffle the sounds, but the scent of rain and flowers: pink phlox, petunias, daisies, and lavender, cloying and nauseating, penetrates my senses, wreaks havoc on my thoughts, and I drop to my knees because my legs can't hold me up anymore.

"Mercy!" I yell for my sister, grabbing at my chest in pain.

"This pain is not for you." I hear Lucia's voice, calling out to me from somewhere far, far away. *"This is not happening to you."*

"Mercy," I cry. But there is no Mercy.

No Mercy. No Mercy. No Mercy, the swarm whispers and whistles while my mind swirls and swirls.

Once again, Lucia's small and distant voice penetrates the chaos. *"This is someone else's pain, someone else's burden. Release it. Let it go. Let it go."*

"Stop!" I scream at the swarm. "Stop it!"

But the noise won't stop.

It won't subside.

It won't listen.

And when I look around, I see that the younger version of my mother is gone. There's nobody here but me. *Mercy*, my mind whispers. *Mercy. Mercy.* When I close my eyes, I see my mother again, an older version of her, leaning over us in bed before she left that night. *"You are my first moon, Mercedes!"* she says. *"You are my shining star, Graciela! Take care of each other, girls! Love each other always!"*

And then I see my sister holding Alexander in the street. *"Stay with me, baby,"* Mercy cries. *"Stay with me."* The pain is too much for me. My head is spinning, and my heart is breaking all over again. *Be present. Be present. Be present,* I tell myself as I shake my head and put my hands down onto the concrete floor.

I feel its coldness seep into my palms, shock my senses, awaken me. And I press my fingers against its glassy, crackled surface, feeling the tiny shards bite into my fingertips. Then I lift my right knee, anchor my foot solidly under me, and push myself up.

With all my might, I push myself up. My knees want to buckle, and I wobble a little, but I refuse to go down again. I refuse to let the echoes swirling around in this haunted place get the better of me.

Using every last bit of breath in my lungs, I extend

a word, as loud and as far as I can send it. "Mercyyyyy!" I scream.

The sound of my voice breaks through the sights and sounds, sends them flying outward, like glittering bits of shattered glass that drift away and disappear, snowflakes in slow motion. I stand in the middle of the room. Alone. My mother is gone, the swarm is gone, the sound is gone, even Lucia is gone.

Disappeared.

Vanished.

Mercy runs into the room. Her eyes are wild and she is breathless. "What is it?" she asks as she comes over and puts her hands on my arms and looks into my eyes. "What's wrong?"

"They're all here, Mercy," I say. "All of them. Together."

"Who's here?" she asks, still fighting to regulate her breath.

"Lucia, Mom, Abuela Estela," I start. "They're strong—but Abuela Estela, she's the strongest."

"But you're okay, though, you're fine?" Mercy asks vehemently. I can see she is trying hard to keep her promise to Guelita Rosa.

I look into her eyes and I realize that I *am* fine. That this gift—the don—didn't overwhelm me. It didn't defeat me. I am in control.

"I am. I'm all right," I say, and then I put my arms around my sister's shoulders and hug her to me. "But you know what?"

"What?" she asks.

"I'm stronger than her. I'm stronger than all of this," I whisper so only she can hear me. "Because of you— because you're here, with me."

"Of course I'm here," she says, pushing my hair back, away from my face. "I love you, Grace. I've always loved you. You're my baby sister."

Mercy kisses my cheek and I hug her tight. But then she pulls back, frowns, and looks about the room.

"Do you smell flowers?" she asks.

"Flowers?" I ask, because I do. The scent is definitely in the room with us.

"Lavender, I think," she whispers.

"Mercedes Aurora Torres!" I say, and a chortling, unexpected laugh escapes my lips. "Are you telling me you have the don too?"

"What?" she asks, letting me go and stepping away from me. "No. Seriously. I smell lavender."

She sniffs around the room.

Then together, we walk to the door because the scent is coming from outside. I put my hand on the doorknob and pull it open.

Sunshine. Beautiful, glorifying light startles the

eyes and shines through the darkness in the room, and beyond it, standing in the middle of the backyard, is our mother.

"Mom?" Mercy whispers.

"You see her too?" I ask, and Mercy nods.

Our mother cocks her head and smiles at us. Then she lifts her arm, turns, and waves for us to follow her.

We walk through the door and step out into the long, desolate stretch of land that used to be Abuela Estela's garden. I put my hand over my eyes to protect them from the sun, and my perception changes. The sunlight shifts and I see my mother standing in the midst of the desiccated weeds and brambles that are growing where the petunias used to bloom in summer.

Her dress is a light shade of yellow, and I recognize it as the garment I admired when I first came here. She waves us over, and we take a step toward her. But then, because I can't wait to be with her, to touch her, to hold her, I run through the brown patches of crabgrass.

From behind me, Mercy calls out my name. "Grace!" she says, running after me. "Grace! Wait for me!"

But I can't wait. I run until I am so close to my mother, I could touch her if I took two or three more steps forward. But she's put her hand out and stopped me in my tracks.

"Mom?" I ask quietly, unsure of what I am supposed

to do, why she won't let me get near her. "What can we do? What do you need?"

Mercy walks up behind me and takes my hand, pulls on it gently.

I turn to look at her. Her hair is disheveled, and her eyes are luminous in the morning light. "Don't be scared," I whisper.

"Come," our mother says. She motions for us to follow her and turns and starts walking away, toward the edge of the property behind the gardener's shed.

Mercy and I follow her through the tall grass. I am aware of the sting of several sand spurs as they anchor themselves against my legs, hitching a ride on my jeans, but I don't have time to stop and pick them off. I have to concentrate on following my mother, lest she disappear before I can figure out what she wants.

Behind me, Mercy stops.

"Shit!" she says, gingerly pulling an entire stalk of dry, clingy chancaquillas off her brown cargo pants before hurrying to catch up to me.

Our mother leads us over the crackling brown remnants of what was once pink phlox, past the withered stump of the dead jacaranda tree, past the wooden fence at the edge of the property, until we find ourselves pushing huisache and mesquite limbs aside as we make our way through the woods.

We go along like this, walking hesitantly through the thicket, moving quietly, carefully, one behind the other, until we come out on the other side of the brush and stand before a parched, barren field. In the middle of the field, we see an old cabin, torn and dilapidated, with nothing but empty, dry land around it, encased in destitution and blight.

"What is this place?" Mercy asks.

Our mother walks toward the cabin, ascends the porch steps, one at a time. The stairs creak, complain, call out their names, count her strides as she goes along—one, two, three—until she is standing in front of the cabin door.

Mercy and I follow her. My foot is on the first stair, when our mother reaches out and puts her hand on the rusty handle of the cabin door. When she pulls it open, a cloud of giant leopard moths burst out of the cabin. They swarm at us, a haze of white dust that hits me hard, like a strong gust of wind in a thunderstorm.

I fall backward, hit the ground. Mercy falls too, and she reaches for me as the speckled black-and-white moths fly out of the cabin and scatter themselves in all directions. They burrow deep into the battered field, clutching the crumbling weed stalks and clinging to the brown grass burrs all around us.

The door swings back and forth, squeaking

incessantly. I turn sideways and start to pull myself up, when I hear someone coming out of the cabin.

"What do you want?" a man's voice asks.

I look up.

An old, heavyset man with gray hair and dark, heavy-lidded eyes stares down at me. His wrinkled face is blotchy, punished by too much sun, and there are dark canker-sore scabs all around his mouth. He looks worn, defeated, lost—but I would recognize him anywhere.

"Manuel," I whisper.

"You!" Manuel yells, pointing a crooked finger at me and creeping down the steps. "You're dead."

And I realize that he's being haunted too.

I put my hands on the ground behind me and push myself up. "Come on," I whisper to Mercy. "Let's go. Get up."

My mother, waiting on the porch, stands in front of Manuel, attempting to block his progress down the stairs, but he passes her without even acknowledging she is there. Suddenly the light shifts, and another figure appears.

Abuela Estela places herself between us and Manuel, who is descending the stairs slowly, determined. She holds up her arm and says, "Stay away from them!"

"No!" Manuel says, swatting away the ghost of my grandmother. "No! You're not real! You're not!"

A hissing sound starts to build around us as the leopard moths rustle their wings, shaking the withered limbs of the weeds and grass they're sitting on. Louder and louder the noise gets. As Mercy and I stand up, the leopard moths abandon their stalks and fly all around us, hissing and buzzing and kicking up dust, until they gather around my grandmother.

They cling to her dress and hair and somehow fuse with her, building her up, growing her form, transforming her into the dark moth-woman of my echoes.

"What is that?" Mercy asks.

The dark moth-woman turns to look at us. Manuel steps away from her, trying to avoid her ascending form. "Not real. Not real," he says, shaking his head over and over again. Then, turning to us, his face changes. His nostrils flare and his eyes grow cold. "But you! You're dead! I remember! I killed you!"

The dark thing swings around and screams at us. *"Run!"*

"Run!" our mother yells as she soars past us, fleeing from the cabin, heading toward the woods.

"Run!" I tell Mercy, as I grab her hand and pull her along.

We run as fast as we can, bounding over grass burrs and crashing through the bramble weeds, breathless, scratched, and scared out of our minds. In the distance, at the edge of the woods, I see Lucia materialize beside our mother. They wave for us to follow them, and we shift direction and run to them.

Manuel runs after us, and the dark thing hovers over him, following close behind. As we get closer and closer to Lucia and our mother, I hear Alexander yelling from somewhere behind us, "Jump, Grace! Jump!"

Mercy must have heard it too, because she looks back at the same time that I look at the ground in front of me and see a large piece of wood, a rotting, crumbling brown plank, jutting out of the ground in front of me.

"Jump, Grace!" Alexander screams again, and without thinking, I gather all my strength and take a long leap over the rotten wood, twisting my ankle as I hit the ground on the other side of it. Mercy falls too, and she rolls off, cursing as her hands make contact with the bramble weeds and grass burrs.

Manuel, however, is not so quick to respond. He screams as he steps on the rotting wood and falls through the ground, hollering as he goes down. A loud, crashing thud comes from deep in the ground, bringing with it the foul stench of sewer water.

Mercy stands up and helps me as I try to put weight on my twisted ankle.

"Are you okay?" she asks, and I nod.

The dark moth-woman descends. She touches ground on the other side of the dank, naked hole in the ground. She stands very still, looking down into the exposed well with its broken lip of rotten planks.

Then the dark moth-woman starts to shiver; her whole form shakes. The giant leopard moths start to flitter and disengage themselves from her. They crawl down the length of her body, scurry over the desiccated grass, and disappear down the well, muffling Manuel's screams for help.

Abuela Estela is once again our maternal grandmother. Only she doesn't look the same. Her face has changed. She isn't the grandmother I encountered three years ago. She looks kinder, gentler, and completely alert.

"Thank you," she says, smiling. Then she walks past us to meet our mother, who is standing with Lucia by the opening we used to come through the woods earlier.

Mesmerized, I watch them hug and kiss each other. The scent of flowers is in the air again, and suddenly I feel it—*love*—it's everywhere around me. I smell it, strong as lavender, sweet as gardenias, and gentle as daisies.

I feel something touch my leg and I look down. Alexander is hiding behind me. His little hand is on the side of my thigh, and he is looking up at my sister.

"Mercy?" I call her attention to Alexander.

"I see him," she whispers.

When Mercy leans down, Alexander moves forward and slips into her arms. Tears start rolling down Mercy's face—huge, beautiful, crystal-clear tears that give voice to the soft sighing of her silent sobs.

I look up at the three women standing together at the edge of the woods and wonder why they are still there, why they haven't crossed over, like they should have done by now.

"Mercy," I whisper.

"What?" Mercy is crouched on one knee, holding Alexander, caressing his hair, holding his face between her hands, kissing his little hands.

"It's time," I whisper.

"Time?" she asks, looking up at me.

I point to our mother, who has left the edge of the woods and is now standing about ten yards away from us.

"What is it?" Mercy asks.

"Time to go," I whisper.

Mercy stands up. She is holding Alexander's hand. "Will we ever see you again?" she asks our mother.

"In time," my mother says, and her eyes mist over with unearthly tears that glimmer like celestial gems in the morning sunlight. "Years and years from now. But I will come back, to guide you then."

"I love you." The words come out all warbled, choked and suppressed by the loss and love that live in my heart.

"I love you too," our mother says. "Always."

"I go-go?" Alexander asks Mercy.

Mercy hugs him and cries. Her shoulders shake and she nods as she lets him go. "Yes," she says. "You have to go."

Then, because her emotions have the best of her, she calls after him, "I love you, baby! Mommy loves you!"

They go through the woods quietly, Lucia, Alexander, my mother, and her mother. They push branches and limbs aside and leave us standing there, listening to the silence of lost love that echoes in our lives.

CHAPTER THIRTY-SEVEN

Eagle Pass, Texas

August 2012

AFTER MERCY LET ALEXANDER GO, WE drove up to the postecito and called the police. They rushed over in their howling patrullas, looked down that well, and called to Manuel over and over again, trying to figure out if he was dead or just unconscious.

The commotion brought neighbors from all over the area. Some of them wanted to help, but the police told them to keep away. This was a live crime scene. They stayed as far back as they could, taking shade under the mesquites and huisaches while they watched the drama unfold. In the end, the rescue squad hoisted a young policeman down the stinky well, and he declared Manuel dead.

My father showed up just as they were pulling the old man's crumpled body out of the hole. To my surprise, my father wasn't alone. Daniel was with him. This was not the way I wanted to discuss my mother with him, but I was glad that he was there to witness when the nightmare was over.

I didn't tell Daniel about my echoes right away. I had to be sure we were really going somewhere, as a couple. And for that, he had to earn my trust all over again, which he has. But we have a good understanding now.

He knows that I have things I want to do, dreams I want to accomplish, before I settle down with anyone. For now, we're just having fun, going out, taking things slow on the dating bench, getting to know each other. It's nice that he's always there, supporting me, cheering me on, without pushing me into anything more.

All of that has led us to this moment, where I stand on the porch, giving my grandmother one last kiss before we go. Her eyes are misty, but she smiles and pushes me toward the steps gently, firmly.

At the bottom of the stairs, Daniel wraps his arm around my waist and asks, "Ready?"

I nod and swipe the moisture off my lashes.

"That's it," my father says, and he shoves another box into the back of Mercy's car, because this is happening. Mercy and I are following through on our plans—we're heading to Austin today. "Nothing else will fit. Whatever else you two want to take with you is gonna have to wait until I see you next week."

"You don't have to come right away," Mercy says. "I mean, that stuff in the closet can wait till you have time."

"It's not a problem," my father says, slamming the trunk lid down and giving a final push with the palm of his hand, to make sure it's completely shut. "That chambita in San Antonio puts me right down the road. I can be over there in an hour every day after work, if I want to."

Mercy puts her hand on his shoulder and says, "Please. Don't want to *too much.*"

My father looks shocked. "What is that supposed to mean?"

"It means they don't want us around all the time," Daniel says, tightening his arm around my waist. "I get it. You need your space."

"All the space!" Mercy says, leaning over to kiss my father on the cheek as she delivers the final blow. "We need *all the space.*"

"Some space," I correct her. "Seriously, though, Dad. Those things can wait."

"Can I have Friday-night dinners, at least?" my father asks Mercy. "I'm buying."

Mercy pretends to think about it. "Hmmm . . . How

about Wednesdays?" she asks, clinging to my father's neck and laughing out loud at the face he makes. "What? Fridays are for parties and sororities and . . ."

"Studying," I say. "She means studying."

I give Daniel one last peck on the cheek and he releases me.

"See you in a few weeks?" Daniel asks.

I don't answer right away, which makes Daniel blush. Then, because I've made him wait long enough, I laugh. "You'd better," I say, and I hug him again.

My father smiles and shakes his head. "Don't forget to text me when you get there," Dad says, reminding us that we have cell phones now. Because he doesn't want anything else to ever happen to us when we're out there, in the real world, without him. "Let me know you made it safe and sound, okay?"

"Come on!" Mercy slaps my behind as she runs around to the driver's side. "Let's go! I want to get there in time to catch that movie in the student center."

"She's going to be a full-time job," I tell my father when I give him one last hug.

"Yeah, well, you asked for it," Dad reminds me. "She wouldn't be going if it wasn't for you."

I look into my father's glistening eyes and I know he's proud of me—proud of us—but he's too choked up to say what's in his heart. He's always been that way.

I suspect he'll never change. Although if Mercy could make such big strides, I don't see why he couldn't.

"You're welcome," I say, and my father rubs a tear away with the knuckles of his right hand.

"Yeah," he says. "You did good, m'ija."

Mercy leans on the horn and hollers, "Come on, Grace! The world awaits!"

I kiss my father and Daniel one last time, and then I get in the car.

Mercy puts her hand on the gearshift. "Are you ready?" she asks.

"Yes," I say. "Yes, I am."

"Good," she says, putting the car into drive and rolling it out of the driveway carefully. "Aaaand—we're off."

We drive up to Brazos Street all the way to Main and head out of town. Mercy doesn't say anything until we are up on Highway 57. "Hey," she says, snapping her fingers in my face. "You doing okay?"

"Yes, yes," I say. "Why?"

"No reason," Mercy says. "You looked a little—pensativa."

"You're not worried, are you?" I ask her. "About me. About the things you're just beginning to experience?"

"A little bit," Mercy says, as we head up to Austin, where we will study psychology, because we've both decided we want to help others deal with the dark things in their lives. "Promise you'll tell me," she continues. "If it gets bad again, this gift—this don—we got from Mom."

"I will," I promise. "And you will too—you'll tell me if it happens to you again, right?"

"Yeah," she says. Then she takes my hand in hers and squeezes it tight. I lean over and kiss her cheek. I love my sister more than she will ever know. "Because I'm here, you know. To help. In any way I can. Always."

"I know," I say, flipping the visor down so I can check my mascara in the mirror.

In the hazy horizon, way back there behind us, I see and hear and feel an echo extending through time— the tower bell of the Sanctuario de Nuestra Señora de Guadalupe rises and lolls back and forth. Its toll is an ancient call for faith and communion. Between us, the International Bridge, a gray petrified caterpillar, extends itself across the length of the Rio Grande. In the morning light, it awakens and comes to life, undulating its body up and down gently against the skyline, each segment separating then reconnecting as we drive off, moving onward with our lives.

Acknowledgments

FIRST AND FOREMOST, I want to acknowledge my beloved family. To my husband, Jim, thank you for always being there, supporting me in this dream. You are my daily reminder that I am blessed, that I am loved. To my sons, James, Steven, and Jason, and to our extended family, Carelyn, Julie, Jeremy, Sara, Groot, and Bucky—you are the reason I get up in the mornings. Your love calls to me from across this country, it fills me with fortitude, and makes life worth living.

Next, I want to acknowledge the rest of my familia, my brothers, One and Albert, and my sisters (mis cinco hermanitas) Alicia, Virginia, Tina, Roxy, and Angie, because we are the Garcia clan, the warriors, the dreamers, the children of two very courageous people, Onesimo y Tomasa, our dearly departed parents, our most beloved.

I also want to acknowledge my professional family. To my friends at George Fox University, Gary Tandy, Melanie Mock, Bill Jolliff, Jessica Hughes, Brooks Lampe, Dana Robinson, Abigail Favale, and Joseph Claire, thank you for all your support and encouragement as I continue with this work that is so close to my heart.

Last, but not least, I want to acknowledge my agent and publisher. Andrea Cascardi, mil gracias—thank you so much for taking this project on and working so hard to see it published. You are my rock! And to my publisher, Stacy Whitman, thank you, thank you, thank you, for always believing in me and my stories. I am blessed to be part of the Tu Books/Lee and Low family. Thank you for always making my work shine, ladies! I owe you two so much!

You are all my heroes. Thank you for your kindness. Thank you for your compassion. Thank you for your love!

—Guadalupe

Author's Note

I STARTED WRITING *Echoes of Grace* in 2016, after hearing of a tragedy involving the accidental death of a two-year-old in our neighborhood. I wrote mostly at night, como lechuza, because Graciela's story came in long, wild spurts, building itself out from visions and fragments of poetry. There was so much of it that touched on important topics in our community, how poverty, abuse, and social stratification can cause familial and generational trauma, and how we are currently failing to address these important topics in our society.

As the story evolved, however, I started noticing other aspects creeping into the narrative. Family secrets, dark imagery, distorted memories, ghosts, and other otherworldly characters manifested themselves on the page, forcing me go beyond the personal, the known, down into the bowels of this world I was creating and look closely at what was really at its core. *What is this dark thing?* I kept asking myself as the second story in the dual timeline started to grow. Until finally, when I was done with the first draft, I realized that this was about gender-based violence and the most foul of crimes against women—femicide. Gender-based violence is a systemic violation of our most basic human rights that transcends borders, class, and ethnic backgrounds. It's a global issue affecting every community in every corner of the world.

For centuries, women along the border of the Rio Grande have been telling the story of the beautiful young woman who disobeyed her mother and went to the baile only to find herself dancing with the devil and dying for it. I think that old cautionary tale was to warn young women of the evils that are out there, waiting for them, if they were not careful.

But it's time to update that story. It's time to show that the problem is not with the young women who go to school or to work, like the hundreds of young women who are still losing their lives in Ciudad Juarez, or the hundreds of thousands of women who are the victims of gender-based crimes all over the United States every year. No, the problem is with the devil himself—the men who for centuries have abused, violated, and killed women all over the world simply because they can.

Although set in modern times, *Echoes of Grace* uses common elements present in gothic novels such as *Jane Eyre* and *Rebecca*, novels that I read as a young woman. However, because it's set in deep South Texas, the book draws its gothic undertones from the paranormal elements so prevalent in our border stories.

Like many gothic novel heroines, Grace lives in an old, run-down house. This gloomy home implies that there was once life and joy inside its walls, but that joy has been tragically lost. However, that is not the only ruined, decaying structure in Grace's life. As in *Rebecca*'s Manderley, Abuela Estela's house in Piedras Negras, the place Grace runs to when she wants to escape the disappointments of her youth, is a much darker, more atmospheric place than her father's forlorn house, especially at the end, when Grace returns to it with her sister and sees it for what it really is—a ruin. So much about these abandoned, decaying spaces speak to the neglect and abuse that plagues our underprivileged and marginalized communities, especially because social organizations, community outreach initiatives, and government programs which could provide support to people like Grace and her family are so often underfunded and understaffed.

Ghosts or the semblance of them are an important element in gothic novels. However, the apparitions that haunt Grace are more than specters, they are representative of the old-world belief systems that have oppressed women for centuries—concepts and ideals that reinforce the old, misguided axiom that women have much to lose as mothers and daughters when they attempt to empower themselves through education and progressive thinking. As a fallen victim of the circumstances stacked against his caregivers, Alexander, Grace's deceased nephew, represents the loss of innocence. He is trapped, lost in the house after his demise, much like Grace herself is trapped after the tragedy. And just as Alexander represents lost innocence, Grace is a mirror of the multitude of mujeres in our world whose lives have been derailed, suspended, even terminated because of the cycles of abuse, neglect, and gender-based crimes that plague our society.

By taking the terrifying, even grim elements of classic gothic works and using them within the context of a contemporary piece meant for young adults, I am hoping to inform the text in a way that sheds light on the dark, grotesque conflicts and struggles women continue to face, conflicts and struggles that, though important, we are often hesitant to talk about with our young people. But our young adults are the ones we need to enlighten. They are our next leaders, our future teachers and healers.

I hope this book moves us all into action. When we consider the prevalence of gender-based crimes, how so many of them could have been prevented, and especially how often they go unchecked, it's important for all of us to advocate for true gender-equality. We need to revisit, renew, and continue to improve laws to provide protection for *all women*, including immigrant and Native American women. It is only by shedding light on the dark, oppressive, sometimes horrifying corners of our world, where neglect, abuse, and femicide take root, that we can begin to talk about how to better educate and train authorities and first responders on the nuances of domestic and intimate partner abuse. I hope this book elicits conversations that bring about real change—powerful change—because we need to make this world a fair and safe place for all women, regardless of who they are or where they come from.

Resources

RAINN and the National Sexual Assault Hotline:
800-656-4673, rainn.org

Resources by state on violence against women, Office of
Women's Health (OWH), 1-800-994-9662,
womenshealth.gov/relationships-and-safety/get-help/
state-resources

The National Domestic Hotline, 1-800-799-SAFE (7233),
thehotline.org

Family Violence Prevention and Services Program
(FVPSA), 1-800-537-2238, benefits.gov/benefit/626

National Coalition Against Domestic Violence (NCADV),
1-303-839-1852, ncadv.org/resources

Casa de Esperanza, 1-800-799-7233, esperanzaunited.org